AFTER THE REUNION

Rebecca Bridges

TABLE OF CONTENT

Judy

I hope you enjoy
the trip to Georgetown.

Robert
Bridges

ACKNOWLEDGEMENTS

After the Reunion is not the first book I've written but it's the first to be published. The journey from idea to finished book, especially the first one, is long and arduous. Many thanks to my husband for his endurance while I took classes, attended critique group meetings and explored the publishing process.

Thanks to all the members of the Coastal Authors Network and Carolina Forest Authors Club. Your support, enthusiasm and critiques helped me complete this manuscript.

A special thank you to Mike Aldridge, retired DEA agent. He graciously shared his knowledge of DEA procedures with me. If there are any mistakes in this book about the DEA they are mine alone due to a misunderstanding.

Saving the best for last, thank you Betty Bolte, editor extraordinaire. You helped me make this book shine. I look forward to our next collaboration.

CHAPTER ONE

Trent Meyers chewed vigorously on the toothpick stuck between his teeth as thoughts of how the upcoming confrontation would play out. Lifting the miniature eye glass again, he gazed toward the brightly lit resort. In less than a minute he spotted his quarry arriving in style. A vintage Mercedes 450SL whipped into the slot reserved for registering guests.

"All right, let's get this party started," Trent muttered to himself spitting out the toothpick. Putting the scope in the saddlebags of his bike, he slipped on his leather driving gloves before kick-starting his machine, a black and chrome Harley Davidson with studded leather saddlebags. The beast gave a satisfying rumble and leapt forward as he exited through the back of the parking garage, before making a two block circle and parking in view of the front doors of the resort.

Sauntering into the luxurious vacation haven he felt out of place. Normally he inhabited a tent in the desert or the streets of a city. Here the marble floors, mahogany reception desk, and sea murals on the ceiling and walls emphasized his unpolished clothing and manners. Through glass doors at the back of the three-story-high lobby he spotted an Olympic-sized pool leading to the beach and ocean. His old classmates gaped at him as if he belonged in the *Ripley's Believe It Or Not* attraction.

"Well, I'll be damned. It's Trent. Trent Meyers." Beauregard Dillon Jackson IV walked over and slapped him on the back. "Hey, man, I thought you dropped off the face of the earth."

With a single nod of acknowledgement, Trent responded, "Beau. After ten years I didn't know if I'd recognize anyone." Not showing an eagerness to reconnect worked best in this situation. Playing down the importance of the meeting would keep things less suspicious later.

Beau still stood about five feet nine inches. His lack of stature had rankled him in high school. Trent could only imagine how he compensated now. A full head of coal black hair gave him a youthful appearance.

"Like before graduation. How come you didn't show for the big day?" Beau continued his queries. Now that the other alums knew who stood in their midst, they returned to their own conversations.

Trent refused to share his reasons for what he'd done. "I shipped out a couple days early. Uncle Sam had his own schedule."

Beau looked skeptical. "You joined the Army?"

"Couldn't wait to move on with my life." Events prompting his enlistment steeled his determination to complete this mission successfully.

"Looks like the army didn't agree with you." Beau pointed to Trent's face.

"It could have been better," Trent traced the scar that started at the corner of his right eye and traveled down his cheek three inches. "After ten years I'm done with all that now. Moved on to more pleasant pursuits." The memory of the IED explosion followed by screams of wounded soldiers and the silence from dead ones erupted in his mind.

Trent's attention wavered from Beau as Shelby Cornwell walked nearby. He smiled in approval of Shelby's great legs and other body parts. Beau would believe his interests had nothing to do with Beau's operation. Shelby's presence had become evident several days ago during his reconnoiter of the resort. She planned the reunion, which made sense because she worked at the resort. To avoid questions about his manifestation at the resort prior to the reunion, he stayed out of her line of sight. The plan required people to assume he arrived in the area yesterday.

The Shelby he knew from high school had worn her luscious brown hair pulled away from her face in one of those bands like women used in the gym. The current short and curly style suited her. Her turquoise eyes reminded him of the ocean. When she laughed, they sparkled like jewels.

Being an event planner at a resort didn't fit her high school personality. Her shyness and quiet ways must make her job more difficult. She blushed at his long perusal. Her girl-next-door looks appealed to him then and now. Back in high school his studies, work, and caring for his mother hadn't left time or money to date her.

Walking toward the group, she stopped between Trent and Beau. "So you're back in the area for good?" Shelby's question came out in a nervous squeak.

"Maybe." Trent shrugged. "I'm trying to decide." His full attention switched to Shelby. Let Beau think he didn't care about him.

"What will make you stay?"

Flirtation in her voice and the rush of red in her cheeks caused Trent to smile.

"A job, for one. We'll have to wait and see what else." His suggestive tone made Shelby's blush deepen.

"Excuse me. As you see, there are many more classmates arriving." She motioned toward the desk. "My job requires me to make sure registration goes without a hitch."

"Don't let us take you away from your duties." Beau bowed toward Shelby, then turned to Trent. "Let's grab a drink." He pointed to the hotel bar.

As they meandered into the bar, Beau asked, "That Harley of yours looks like a sweet ride. When you goin' let me take it out for a spin?"

"Never." Trent looked at Beau with wide eyes and pursed lips. "I'm the only one who rides the Grim Reaper."

"Grim Reaper?" Beau chuckled. "I forgot how anal bikers are about their machines."

The bar area sported lots of chrome and glass. The shiny surfaces reflected the outside sandy beach and waves. Upholstered chairs in shades of blue, green, and yellow dotted the room. Televisions broadcasting various sports channels hung from the ceiling so everyone had a view.

Football, golf, and other sports became the key topics. Like the old days, Beau's exploits topped everyone else's. Good. It couldn't be going better. He needed to keep Beau believing he had total control. Worming his way into the inner circle might be easy. This would be his first undercover job. The importance of his success not only impacted his career, but also the welfare of people in his home town. People he cared about.

The agency provided him with a mountain of information about Beau and his operation. "What have you been up to since graduation?" How much would Beau divulge?

"Beer and shots all around, barkeep." Beau turned back to Trent. "I graduated from MIT as planned. Or should I say, as my parents dictated? The change from mechanical engineering to chemical engineering came with their approval. Oh, the switch changed a four-year degree to five." Beau made it sound like he'd partied too much to make it in four. The dossier painted a different picture. Additional classes not in his major as well as revelry took up the extra time. Classes where he learned techniques helpful in drug manufacturing.

"Impressive. An MIT graduate. Am I supposed to bow as you walk by or doff my hat?" The snide remark would keep Beau talking.

Beau knocked back a swig of beer. "You can grovel at my feet, Bud. Family tradition and all that. Fourth generation to receive a degree from MIT. Seriously, the celebrating became old after the first two years. Then I studied hard. When I came back, I used the land from the family farm and built a pretty damn good business. I manufacture pesticides and fertilizers."

The acreage held a wealth of timber, the twenty-first century cash crop for the area. Development of more than pesticides and fertilizers happened at Beau's plant, which was why Trent had been recruited.

Trent leaned an elbow on the bar, "Not exactly the sexy job you talked about in high school. What happened to The Jackson Modeling Agency plan? You intended to have hundreds of leggy women offering themselves to you at your Manhattan office." With a shake of his head and a sly grin, he ribbed Beau about his foolish teenage idea of success.

"Oh, Lord, I hadn't thought about that in years." Slapping his forehead, Beau chuckled.

More classmates strode into the bar and joined their conversation. As the small town big shot Beau bought everyone's first drink. Trent expected it.

"You're not keeping up." Beau pointed to the still full glass of beer and shot.

"One of the other guys can have it. I'm sticking to soda."

"What? Go ahead, have some fun. How often do you attend a high school reunion?"

"Can't. I'm six months sober. I refuse to be controlled by alcohol." He didn't have a problem but keeping a clear head could mean the difference between staying alive and being killed.

"That sucks," Beau said. "I can't imagine not throwin' back a few with my buds."

"I still manage to have fun without it."

Losing interest with Trent, Beau turned to others at the bar.

Shelby watched them at the bar from her vantage point of the registration desk. Her eyes flicked back to him often. Initially she hadn't recognized him. Growing taller, heavier, and of course the scar changed him. Since she'd filled out from a skinny kid to a shapely woman, she suited him fine. Although somewhat shy, she wore her confidence like a cloak. Probably the same height as in high school, a few inches more than five feet, but the high heels made her seem taller. Her curly brown hair framed her face, giving her an angelic look.

Nodding and laughing at the conversations around him, Trent's real attention stayed with Shelby. The first day of their freshman year in high school flitted through his mind. Everyone had tried to stuff books, gym clothes, and lunch bags into their lockers. Shelby dropped a box of pencils and pens that scattered up and down the hallway. She scrambled to gather them while her face flamed with color. Helping her collect the errant objects while other kids laughed earned him her inaudible thanks.

Shelby and the other people handing out reunion registration packets began closing up for the evening. Before they finished, a long-legged blonde flew through the lobby and launched herself at Beau. "I'm sooooo glad to see you, dahlin'." The kiss she planted on Beau's cheek left a splash of red lipstick.

"Missy, we saw each other last week, *sugah*." Beau pecked her cheek then reached in his pocket for a handkerchief to wipe off the blood-like makeup. Beau's gaze, like his own and every other male's within the viewing area, lingered on the blonde's ample breasts. Difficult not to notice since they almost spilled out of the low-cut sun dress. Trent glanced up in time to see Shelby roll her eyes and then turn back to check in the stragglers.

A man followed in Missy's wake. "What's up?" Slapping Beau on the back, he placed a proprietary hand around Missy's waist, hauling her close.

Only after the man spoke did Trent recognize him. Lines around Jamie Strong's eyes and a reddish complexion spoke to frequent drug and alcohol consumption.

"Hey, Bud," Beau responded, "look who came back for the reunion." He pointed to the man next to him at the bar. "Trent."

"Trent?" Jamie squinted in his direction. "Hey, man, where've you been hidin' all these years? I don't know if I woulda recognized you on the street." Jamie's slurred words and out-of-focus gaze indicated Jamie's stoned state. An unfortunate side-effect to the business they conducted. Hiding his disgust took effort. Jamie appeared older than his twenty-eight years. His once dark brown hair had thinned and the remaining contained tufts of grey. Lines around his mouth and eyes aged him even more.

Disgust threatened to weaken Trent's attempt to be pleasant in spite of the importance for his plan to infiltrate their organization.

"The army. That's all over. I've been roamin' around these past few months. I saw the notice on Facebook about the reunion and decided Myrtle Beach might be a good place to hang. For now anyway. What you been up to?" The DEA's dossier pegged Jamie as Beau's right-hand man.

"Me and Missy got married." His intense glare indicated he dared anyone to deny it. When no one said a word, he continued. "And keeping Beau straight, same as in high school." Jamie puffed up like his efforts had created Beau's success. "You sign up for tomorrow's football game?"

"Wouldn't miss it." One of the planned activities of the reunion included the contest at a local park for the male alumni. No doubt the idea came from Jamie. He always enjoyed making a hit, usually a dirty one. Being the recipient of more than one of those hits during practice, Trent looked forward to putting him in his place.

"If you boys plan to talk sports I'll head up to the room and unpack." Missy didn't wait for a response from Jamie. She tossed her hair with a glance back as if to be sure they all watched while she strutted to the elevators. Trent enjoyed the view although her overblown sexiness didn't turn him on like Shelby's quiet confidence. Stopping at the hotel desk, Missy registered and picked up a key.

"How'd you get so lucky, Jamie? I thought Missy belonged to Beau?" Not that he cared, but Missy and Beau had dated all through high school. Beau, the quarterback. Missy, the head cheerleader. A small mystery to uncover on how Jamie and Missy ended up married.

"She didn't look twice at me until Four left for college." The nickname they'd given Beau as the fourth Beauregard Dillon Jackson drew him further back to high school memories. His reverie ended in time to hear the rest of Jamie's explanation. "He dumped her graduation night." Although Jamie's verbal shrug indicated no big deal, his body language screamed a different reality. Staring at his drink, Jamie's smile turned into a grim downturn of his mouth.

"Hey, if she loved me she'd have been here when I came back from MIT." Beau tossed back a shot of whiskey and followed it with a sip of beer. "She loves you, not me."

The comment sounded like an automatic response. One said so often he didn't even have to think about it. If the two men started arguing over Missy, they'd expect him to choose sides. That wouldn't be good. While he tried to come up with a change in subject, Shelby ambled up.

Fidgeting, she glanced between the three of them. "Sorry to interrupt. Could you help me move everyone into the Magnolia Room? It's almost six o'clock and we've scheduled the official reunion mixer there."

"I'm not sure everyone wants to navigate that far from the bar." Beau followed his statement with a laugh.

"Not to worry." Waving her hand, Shelby held up a couple of blue tickets. "It's where these will buy two drinks. They can be found in each registration packet. A bar is set up in the room." Shelby's hand shook and she didn't make much eye contact.

"In that case, no problem." Beau followed-up with an ear-splitting whistle. "Everyone, this way to some free drinks!" Like high school, they followed the leader.

CHAPTER TWO

The Georgetown ten year High School reunion provided the chance Shelby Cornwell needed to prove the events could be money-making projects for the Sea Wind. Her boss didn't believe her, but the receipts for this extended weekend would confirm it. The mere thirty miles between Georgetown and Myrtle Beach ensured the people who still lived in Georgetown could drive easily, and it made a more vacation-like destination for those who no longer resided there.

Shelby forced a smile on her face during registration and the mixer. Yoga lessons taught her how to put aside her natural shyness. The senior class hadn't been large, only two hundred and fifty-six graduated, but she knew several alums made it big. The top spot belonged to Beau. Of course, old family money gave him a head start.

Shelby flushed when he'd taken her hand and kissed it as if they were an eighteenth-century lord and lady. Maintaining visual contact with him had been difficult. Irritated when her timid nature returned, she forced herself to look Beau in the eye. Beau hadn't changed all that much since high school. His uncommon black eyes seemed to look right into your soul. She shivered.

Trent Meyers' arrival surprised everyone. He didn't look the same. Those biceps of his must have taken a lot of hours in the gym to build up. The way his T-shirt strained across his chest and arms, a six pack must be hidden beneath it. His scar had gone unnoticed by her until Beau drew attention to it. Trent would never be called good looking, but there was something about him. A presence. And what a body! Most women would be satisfied with that. She felt heat spreading up her neck. Since the incident during her sophomore year of college she hadn't experienced this strong a feeling at the mere sight of a man.

"Shelby, you've done a great job." One of the guests grabbed her and gave her a hug.

It brought her back to reality. She stiffened at being touched so intimately by a male she didn't recognize. She glanced at his name tag and gave him a weak smile in spite of her uneasiness, then chatted a moment.

Ever since her sophomore year at college she had searched the face of men she'd known to see if he might be the one.

Once she'd enlisted Beau's help in getting everyone into the Magnolia room, she felt the tension evaporate as she slipped into the role of professional event coordinator. Meandering through the crowd, she stopped at each table making sure everyone had what they needed. Trying not to be too obvious about her real objective—seeking out Trent—she headed toward his location. Trent sat visiting with Beau and a few others.

"Shelby." Beau stood up and gave her a kiss on the cheek. "Please join us. We are all impressed with what you've done so far. Can't wait to see what you have planned for tomorrow night's dinner."

The only available chair happened to be located between Beau and Trent so she sat and settled in. The contrast between her delight in seeing Trent and the unknown reason for her nervousness sitting next to Beau caused her pulse to race and sweat form on her upper lip.

Heat rose from her neck to her forehead. "Thank you, Beau. This is my reunion, too, so I wanted it to be perfect. Be sure to let me know if there is anything else I can do." She'd said that same thing so many times tonight it rolled off her tongue like ripples through water.

Their school colors of blue and white appeared in all the decorations. A photo booth located in a corner of the ballroom contained props, like caps and gowns, yearbooks, and football helmets. A person wearing their bulldog mascot costume wandered around the room for more picture options. The constant flashes going off meant a success.

A touch of Trent's hand caught her attention. "It's good to see you." His voice sounded like a deep rhythm-and-blues melody.

His calm, gentle demeanor drew Shelby like no one else. "When did you return?" she asked, a bit breathless.

"Yesterday. I arrived in time for the reunion." He smiled at her for the first time. The small dimple in his right check appeared and the flash of mischief lit up his eyes. The transformation caused Shelby to stare.

Taking a moment to appreciate his smile, she asked, "Are you staying at your old house in Georgetown?" If he planned to stay there perhaps she could see him when she visited her family.

"For now at least. How about you? Do you commute?"

"No, I moved to Myrtle Beach after I graduated from college." She spoke only to Trent, having little interest in Beau and the other people at the table.

"Ah. Stayed close but not too close?" Once again, he touched her hand, leaving a tingly feeling all over her body, not simply the one spot.

She shrugged. "Where else do you have such great beaches and wonderful weather?"

"I have been to a few fantastic places, but since you weren't there, they can't compete." A sexy grin spread across his face.

A snicker from some of the men at the table drew her attention. It sounded like a line he'd used more than once, so she called him on it. "Does that work for you?"

Trent's devilish smile did funny things to her insides. "Usually."

Shelby's stomach tightened in reaction to Trent's comment. Knowing her response was unreasonable, she decided to leave before saying something ridiculous. She stood up and addressed the entire table. "This is my cue to move on. I need to make sure everyone else is having a good time."

As she left she heard Beau say, "My man, Trent, you crashed and burned. Next time you need to eliminate the line."

The rumbling chuckle Trent emitted a few moments later made shivers run up her spine. Trouble had arrived and it was spelled T-r-e-n-t.

The other conversations in the room drew her attention. Most talked about what they'd done since high school. A lot of photos were being shared while oohs and aahs escaped as they pointed to the people posing in them.

The schedule called for the mixer to last until eight o'clock. The alums didn't start leaving until ten in spite of only appetizers to feed them. Drinks seemed to be more important. With an early breakfast the next day, the crowd broke up. Overall the evening had been a huge success. Most people consumed more alcohol than the two tickets included in the package. It should help gain her bosses approval of this new venture for the resort.

"It's late, go ahead and close up the bar," Shelby told the head bartender. Gathering the receipts she sauntered back to the office to tally them.

She carried the results next door to her boss. "Wanted to give you the totals for tonight's mixer."

He looked them over. "I admit I didn't expect much since the package included two drinks. This bottom line more than covered the appetizers. Your idea has some merit." He didn't smile.

Satisfied for the moment with his admission her plan made money on the first night, she returned to her desk. By the time the reunion ended he'd have to agree the resort should capitalize on this new endeavor.

Making her way to her suite she mentally patted herself on the back for her success. This accomplishment ensured her ability to compete with other event coordinators in the chain. The crazy hours she worked would be worth it. Since events happened at all times of the day and evening she sometimes started at six and others ran until midnight. This reunion had been created by her, so there wouldn't be a minute she wasn't involved. Her dream to transfer to a more exotic location drew ever closer.

Negotiating the suite as part of her salary came in handy on late nights like this one. Once inside she slipped off her shoes with a sigh. Fatigue enveloped her. With a small groan she recalled breakfast began at eight o'clock in the morning. In spite of it not being among her usual duties, no way would she miss the preparations of the meal. She'd be in the kitchen by seven to make sure all arrangements were perfect.

As she prepared for bed, Trent's face appeared in her mind. God, her hormones hummed. Before tonight she believed the accusations from the only two men she shared a relationship with were right. She had no feelings, a cold bitch. Now, with fuller understanding she agreed with comments other women made about getting hot and bothered when a hunk they desired walked by. A cool shower would help her sleep. She stripped and headed to the bathroom.

Her dreams that night starred Trent. Striding out of the ocean and then onto the beach toward her, he looked magnificent. Neither of them wore clothes. The water streamed down him in rivulets. The washboard abs she'd imagined weren't his only wondrous attribute. His dimple appeared as he smiled at her and the heat in his eyes set her afire. His hand reached toward her. Trying her best to grasp it, they never touched.

CHAPTER THREE

Driving back to Georgetown Trent enjoyed the rush of cool, salty air on his face. Until his return to South Carolina he hadn't realized how much he missed the smell of the ocean, the screech of the seagulls, and the feel of the offshore breeze. The drive also awarded him time to sort out his impressions and prepare to debrief the boss.

Trent spent ten years in the army as a military policeman and then graduated from the Charleston Police Academy. The Drug Enforcement Agency offered him this undercover assignment. His boss, the DEA Task Force Supervisor, worked with him for the last two weeks to prepare. The agency had never succeeded in infiltrating this drug operation. Beau hired men he knew from high school. Most were former football players. The DEA recruited Trent as soon as they found out he knew Beau. If the DEA had the facts right about the situation he wanted to be involved in the take-down. Some of his army buddies sought drugs to ease their nightmares and reminders of unsuccessful mission. Their lives ended too soon because of it. The pressure for success loomed large.

Focusing on the job at hand caused him trouble. His thoughts kept drifting to Shelby. An all-grown-up Shelby. Shaking his head, he put those images aside. At least for the moment. Tonight would be the only time his boss planned to meet him at his mom's house. Discussion of future locations for their clandestine meetings topped tonight's agenda. No doubt Jamie or Beau would have someone keep an eye on him once he became part of their organization. Or even before.

In his mind the place would always stay his mom's house. In reality, it belonged to him and his brother. Jason hadn't lived there since he landed a job in Ft. Jackson, the military base adjacent to Columbia, after graduating from college. The last Trent heard of his sibling he'd been doing well as a civil servant working with military budgets. The hurt he felt with their estrangement needed to be set aside for another time. Living here wouldn't make it easy. The single-wide trailer held lots of recollections, some good, some bad.

Years ago the temporary home satisfied his family's need until the real house would be built on the property. Then a drunk driver T-boned his dad's car. Age ten, his brother eight, Trent became the man of the house. The attack of memories crowded his mind. Putting a stop to all of them would be monumental.

Yesterday he officially had arrived, as far as the Georgetown residents knew. The house needed to be opened and stocked with groceries. He'd called to have the utilities turned on prior to his arrival. Unoccupied for over four years, it smelled musty and in need of repairs. Thank God Jason made arrangements for someone to hack down the weeds once a month and for a routine pest control service. Around here, it didn't take long for a place to become infested with something. He noticed a car pull in behind him as he passed the last paved road. Probably his boss. He grabbed the pistol strapped to his ankle as soon as he parked. No sense taking chances.

Moving to the corner of the house, Trent watched the car pull in the drive. With no street lights available and the car's dome light too faint, it made determining the identity of the man stepping out of the car impossible. The light he had left on in the house shown through the window, drawing every bug in the county.

A car door slammed shut followed quickly by slapping noises. "Get the damn door open so I can escape these little blood suckers."

"Sure thing, boss." Chuckling as he stowed the gun back in the holster, he tramped up the porch where Jim impatiently waited. Trent made a mental note to put in a motion sensing light over the carport. It would help keep people from sneaking up as well as draw the bugs away from the front door. No telling how long this assignment would last, so he might as well make a few updates on the place. Make it easier to sell later.

Jim, the designated senior agent on this sting operation, told him he'd been trying to put in an undercover agent for more than a year.

Jim stood well over six feet, slender, and in his mid-forties. Initially he'd been a small town police chief then switched to the DEA a few years ago. He'd no doubt seen a lot of operations like this. Trent felt comfortable with him as the lead.

"Want a beer?" Trent reached in the refrigerator. With thoughts of Shelby, the case, and his memories, he needed one.

"Sure. How'd it go?" Jim grabbed the offered beverage and then slumped onto the old couch in the living room. Trying to see the house through Jim's eyes, Trent acknowledged it had passed its prime, but the furnishings were in good repair and tidy. Old-fashioned curtains hung on the windows, and pictures of his younger self with his even younger brother dotted the walls. A wedding picture of his parents stood next to a lamp on the end table.

"Not bad." Trent took a big swig of beer. "I didn't receive a job offer tonight. No surprise there. However, I think I intrigued Beau. People usually hang on his every word. I didn't. He'll want to make sure I do."

Settling into the recliner across from the couch, Trent felt like his father's arms wrapped around him. The enjoyment of the simple comfort had been a long time coming. Jim's voice snatched him out of his reverie.

"I can't believe our luck finding someone like you. His crew is crazy loyal. Like a bunch of religious fanatics."

"Yeah. That's how it is around here. Their families have owed their living to the Jacksons for generations." Would his father think his actions disloyal?

"I'm an exception. Not for two generations, anyway. Mine and my parents'. Dad joined the army right after graduation and took Mom with him, returning here once he left the service. Then he taught at the high school. You know the rest."

"Yeah." Jim frowned, then changed the subject, "So who else showed up at the reunion?"

"Only Beau and Jamie." Jim's interests lay solely with Beau's crew. The other guys' absence puzzled Trent. "More might show up tomorrow. As part of the reunion, there's a pickup style football game at a park. Most of the fellows you suspect as members of the operation played on our high school team."

Discussing plans again, where and how they would stay in touch, filled the rest of the time. The DEA set up a special phone number for him. An agent would answer and pass on the coded message. Rules required daily check-in between noon and two. No direct contact with Jim except special circumstances. Discussion about the various other agents and dead drops completed the arrangements. A box under the flowers at his parents' grave served as one of the locations. If followed, no one would be surprised if he drove there on multiple occasions. The chest would be large enough so any items he might need from the DEA or he supplied the DEA could be left without fear of someone else finding it. They checked the GPS in his watch to make sure it functioned properly as a backup locator, and then ended the debriefing. Nothing would be left to chance.

"You need to work on securing this place." Jim glanced around, checking out the trailer. "It doesn't have a back door, so make some kind of escape route in case your cover gets blown and they come after you. Stay alert. Just because it's home doesn't mean it's safe."

After Jim left, Trent made a list of all the things he needed to buy to fix up the house to make sure no one could sneak up on him.

With the inventory complete, his mind drifted toward Shelby. He knew from the Facebook posts she arranged all the details for the reunion. As a resort employee she'd finagled great rates for them. The DEA scrutinized their whole class. Thank goodness she had nothing to do with Beau's drug operation. After this weekend, he wouldn't have a reason to be in contact with her. To his surprise, the realization stung. The clothes she'd worn today seemed like a uniform. A simple white shirt, a skirt, and blazer. Nothing sexy. However, thoughts of removing each item to reveal what lay beneath turned him on. Putting those pictures out of his head grew more difficult as he prepared for bed.

CHAPTER FOUR

Deciding a shower would help him relax, he shucked his clothes and step into the stall. The initial cold water helped. Then images of Shelby joining him in the tight space shot through his mind. His hands moving over her body and her hands on him. Turning the water to its coldest setting helped the heat in his body cool down. Stepping out of the shower that had become a torture chamber he toweled off quickly and headed for bed.

He laid on the mattress and prayed for sleep, which was a long time coming.

The next morning Trent arrived at the park where the male alums divided into two football teams. There were a couple of guys from the year ahead of them and a few who'd been sophomores and juniors. They needed the extra men to form two teams. Surprising no one, Beau selected the men who the agency identified as members of his drug operation.

"What do you mean you don't want to be on my team?" Beau's tone was belligerent.

"With you and Jamie on the same side, I figured the other team needed help." Trent smiled as he sauntered over to the other group.

In fact, he wanted the opportunity to give Jamie the pounding he deserved. Jamie always enjoyed hitting his opponents and had a reputation of dirty shots. Trent hadn't played football in high school after their sophomore year. Still, he'd had plenty of practice at pick-up games with his army buddies. He also knew the best way to prove his worth to Beau meant he needed to squash his second in command Jamie.

"Hey, Trent, you want to be the quarterback?" The question came from their former backup quarterback who organized the other team.

"Nah, I prefer to be a linebacker." Trent's smile widened at the idea of taking Jamie down.

"You sure got the muscles for it. Let's get started."

They barely had enough people for two teams. Each man had to play both offense and defense. No extras for substitutions. Lining up across from Jamie, a waft of fetid breath added to Trent's feeling of hostility. Did he sense Trent planned to take his place? Good. Trent wouldn't need to hold back.

"You should have stayed with us. There's no way you'll win with that bunch of wimps," Jamie taunted.

Jamie's smack talk hadn't changed. Nonstop before and during the game.

At first the men played it safe, trying to determine what worked and who had the skills to perform the various positions. Each side scored a touchdown. Trent noticed a slight nod from Beau to his team. The rhythm changed.

Beau's group went in for the kill. They put points on the board twice against Trent's crew and his guys incurred several injuries.

They took a short break in the game. Some of the wives and girlfriends sat in the bleachers. The injured men were patched up and received sympathy from their women. Trent took a seat next to Missy, Jamie's wife. Jamie and Beau stood apart from the crowd, whispering. They no doubt made plans for their next attack.

"Trent, you picked the wrong squad in this game." Missy swung one leg back and forth multiple times in beat with popping her chewing gum.

"Your husband told me the same thing. I suppose it depends on what you want as the result."

Missy frowned, stopped all motion, and then looked at Trent. "What do you mean? Winning is what everyone wants, right?"

He shrugged one shoulder. "Not always. The journey can be as important as winning. Spending time with friends. Stuff like that."

Missy's frown disappeared and her movements returned. "Oh, yeah, I suppose that's true. At least for some people." Her eyebrows rose and she tilted her head. "Of course, with Jamie, winning is the only important thing."

"Then I'm sorry for him. He needs to learn to appreciate and enjoy the ride with the people he's with."

Missy's smile faltered and her eyes lowered. "If only he would."

As he wondered what she meant, Beau called them all back to the field.

After a few more plays Trent planned to elbow Jamie in the nuts. Jamie had inflicted that injury on several others. Instead they became tangled up and Trent kicked him in the knee. The game stopped with a scream from Jamie.

"Holy Shit, Trent," Beau yelled, "didn't you know Jamie had a bad knee?"

"How would I know?" Trent hadn't known, but this might work out well for him. He had no remorse, but put on a show that he did.

"Missy, call the damn ambulance. I think Jamie's hurt bad," Beau instructed.

The game ended on that sour note. The ambulance arrived and took Jamie away. Missy followed in their silver Jag.

"Honest, Beau, I didn't do it on purpose." It took a lot for Trent to make those words come out of his mouth. Jamie deserved the injury and more.

"Yeah, I know. Sorry I yelled at you." Beau smiled what Trent considered his sneaky smile. He knew something was about to happen. "I forgot you haven't been around for years. Jamie blew out his knee in a college game. The other guys know about it and give him some space."

"I guess I'll have to send him some flowers or something." Trent continued his act of remorse.

"Hell no. He'd be more pissed about that than the fact you wrecked his knee. A dozen cigars would be more appreciated."

"Right." Trent allowed himself to smile. "I can do that." Beau slapped him on the back, and they walked toward their vehicles.

The players headed to a local sports bar for lunch. While they ate, drank and relived all their high school football games Trent recognized one of the men as Shelby's brother, Mike. He must be involved in the drug operation. If he took down the ring Shelby would be crushed.

About an hour later Trent noticed Beau answered his phone and took it outside. When he returned, Beau headed right to him.

"Jamie's going to need surgery on his knee. He'll be out of commission for a few weeks." Was Trent imagining it or did the look Beau give him indicate he wanted something from him?

"Man, I hate that." Trent hoped with Jamie out of the picture he'd have a better chance to infiltrate Beau's operation. "Looks like I'll need to do more than buy him a dozen cigars."

"You owe me more than Jamie." Beau's expression grew serious.

"You? Why?" Trent gave Beau his best puzzled expression.

"With Jamie out for who knows how long, I'm down a man in my operation. You need to make it up to me."

Leave it to Beau to make Jamie's injury all about him.

"Sure, Beau. You know I'll help out, but I don't know a damn thing about pesticides or fertilizers." Trent shook his head and shrugged his shoulders.

"Don't have to. Jamie helped me with security, not the chemical stuff."

"Security? Well, sure. I used to be an MP. I can walk around the plant at night to make sure no one breaks in. Is that what you need?" Trent wanted to be sure Beau didn't think he knew about the other work going on in the plant.

Beau grinned. "It's exactly what I need. Meet me at the plant Monday at one o'clock. We'll work out the details."

Beau told the rest of the group about Jamie's surgery. Trent didn't think anyone seemed too concerned. As he kept an eye on Beau, he noticed Beau drew one of his men aside to have what looked like a serious discussion. Trent took a drink of his beer and positioned himself to appear to be in a discussion with some of the men when in fact he watched Beau. He motioned toward Trent during the discussion. He bet Beau told the man to check him out. Good. Beau wouldn't hire him unless he did a background search. The DEA had fixed it so he'd pass anything Beau's men could find. When Beau walked away the man pulled out an iPhone. Trent had to smile. He was right.

CHAPTER FIVE

While the men played football and ate lunch somewhere off site, Shelby had arranged a fashion show with a light lunch for the women. A few of the ladies went with the men to watch, but most preferred to indulge in the services of the resort after breakfast. Shelby swelled with pride when she discovered Beau's mother asked to be included for the show. Her boss told her fashion shows were outdated. No one would attend. When she informed him of Mrs. Jackson's interest, his attitude changed.

"Shelby, if you convince Mrs. Jackson to have some kind of family reunion or party here at the resort it would be a big coup."

Making a good impression with Mrs. Jackson at the fashion show would pave the way for future events. "I'll see what I can do."

Lunch went well. The chef's chicken salad with pecans and grapes was a hit with the ladies. The fresh banana bread disappeared moments after the servers set the baskets on the tables.

The fashion show started out fine. Then one of the models protested the products made of leather. Stunned at the tirade about cruelty to animals, it took Shelby a moment before she called security.

A flurry of activity ensued with the guard taking the protesting woman to the room setup as a dressing room for the models. Shelby, the owner of the fashion line, and one other hotel employee managed to remove the garments from the model. The entire time she shouted her stance against killing animals for their hides. Shelby had no idea how much of the noise spread to the ballroom.

After the woman put on her own clothing, the guard removed her from the premises. Shelby and the owner of the shop providing the clothes set about resuming the show. The models who followed the protester on the runway had pitched in and wandered through the crowd explaining their garments during the lull. They assured Shelby little noise had drifted to the room.

The show continued with a more excited atmosphere. The interruption energized the crowd instead of subduing it. Shelby glanced in the direction of Mrs. Jackson to see her reaction. The woman chatted with another lady so Shelby couldn't judge her response.

When the show ended and the women started to leave, Shelby's boss arrived and motioned her to the kitchen.

"What the hell happened earlier?"

"Sorry, sir. One of the models started protesting…"

"Never mind. I heard. Why didn't you keep it from happening?"

"How could I?"

Her boss shook an admonishing finger at her. "It's your job to know and keep it from happening."

"But, sir—"

Making shooing motions, the man cut her off before she could say more.

"Get back to the women. If Mrs. Jackson files a complaint it could be your job." He stormed out of the room.

She glared at his back then returned to the ballroom remembering to smile as she entered. Some of the women approached her. "I enjoyed the lunch so much. And the fashion show. Good heavens. We'll be talking about it for months. Did the police arrest that woman?"

"Um, no. We provided an escort out of the hotel."

After hearing more comments Shelby realized most of the women saw the protest as a form of entertainment. She held her breath as Mrs. Jackson approach.

"Shelby, dear, I wanted to congratulate you."

Her eyebrows rose. "Thank you, Mrs. Jackson."

"The food tasted delicious. I haven't seen a local fashion show in years. The way you handled that woman. Job well done. It's good to know you can overcome a difficult situation quickly. I'm sure you would have been discreet had the woman allowed it."

"Thank you. I appreciate your comment."

"Heaven knows when our family parties together we have some kind of incident or another. Of course, never anything about animals and their hides."

"Of course not." Shelby had no idea how else to respond to her comment. She felt relief run through her, knowing her boss wouldn't fire her.

Once the ladies left, she made sure the staff knew to open the room divider after their cleanup to reuse the ballroom for the night's dinner dance. The other half of the room had already been set up so they only had to add a few more tables, chairs, and the dance floor.

Shelby prepared a plate of food and made her way outside to a table where she ate lunch and reviewed the events of the day. The more she considered her boss's unreasonable expectations on how to prevent the outburst, the angrier she became. She'd start looking for another place to work.

After her lunch, she checked the ballroom and discovered the DJ setting up his equipment. Shelby looked at her watch and figured she had plenty of time to shower and change before returning to welcome her former classmates. Tonight's event would be the largest one of the weekend. Some graduates opted to attend only this single affair.

Back in her room, Shelby took off the flats she'd worn all day and propped her feet up for a few minutes. "Salute." She toasted herself with a bottle of water. "You survived the first half of the weekend."

After her shower, she fixed her hair and makeup, then stood in her sexy lingerie and took her dress out of the closet. Conjuring a picture of Trent and her dancing the night away, she slipped it over her head, the coolness of silk caressing her body as it settled in place. It had been years since she'd even wanted to dress like this. She'd bought the gown after her best friend coerced her. Surprisingly, the zipper slid up with ease. She'd lost a few pounds since the purchase. Must have been all the running up and down the hallway. Facing the mirror, a stranger looked back. No, not a stranger, but the girl she'd been before. Before the ugly night that shattered her world.

Memories from that time flooded back to Shelby. She'd left the college library late and walked toward her car when someone grabbed her from behind and put their gloved hand over her mouth. She could almost feel the pain again as her attacker hit her on the head. She didn't remember anything else until she woke up in the hospital bruised and aching. The looks from the nurses and the pains emanating from her vagina made her realize she'd been raped. Everyone told her what a blessing she'd been unconscious during the event. She hadn't felt blessed. Humiliated and degraded topped the list.

Always a shy person, she turned even more inward after the attack. The school gave her passing grades that semester in spite of her nonattendance. As a commuter, she'd been living with her parents. She hadn't left their house for three months once released from the hospital. One of the female ministers from her church caught her on the back porch. Until then she'd refused to see anyone. The minister's kindness and gentle ways finally drew Shelby back into the world of the living.

The physical scars healed. Her emotional ones became bearable. Somehow she'd never felt whole. Like a missing piece of her floated out there somewhere. Statistics said her attacker knew her. Every time she saw a man she'd known back then she searched his face. Not understanding exactly what to look for didn't stop her. She would know if he was the one.

No. She wouldn't think about that time. Not now, not ever again. Tonight she would be the confident woman she promised she would become. Had become. She forced her mind to think of happy things. Again, Trent's face appeared. Calm washed over her. Since Trent had been in the military and nowhere near the area during the attack, she felt confident he hadn't been responsible.

She and Trent hadn't dated in high school. Actually, she hadn't dated anyone due to her shyness. She'd been certain he planned to ask her to the senior prom and had been devastated when he didn't. Years later she'd realized his mother's fight with cancer kept him home. Perhaps now would be their time.

Making her way to the ballroom, she approved of the way the staff had transformed it. Once again the Georgetown High School colors of blue and white inspired the decorations. Their class slogan, United We Stand, hung from a banner, the centerpieces contained miniature bulldog-shaped balloons along with blue and white flowers. She'd kept the photo booth set up since there had been so many comments. Everything looked exactly as she'd instructed.

People started arriving and she switched to hostess mode. Keeping an eye on the door, she watched for Trent. She hadn't anticipated her feelings of unease as so many men she'd once known appeared. Trent arrived late, and she almost missed seeing him. She noticed the way he scanned the room. His gaze hesitated when he saw her, then moved to her left for a moment and back to her.

Trent ambled her way. The closer he came, the less aware she became of anyone or anything else. She knew the turquoise dress she wore hugged her curves and saw approval in his eyes. The front didn't show a lot of cleavage, but the back dipped down past her waist. The straps contained shiny stones the color of the dress. As he approached, she turned toward him. More of the stones were sewn into the fabric between her breasts. She grinned mischievously when he stared at her breasts before making an effort to move his gaze up to look into hers. *Damn.* Her mouth parted as she started to say something, but stopped without a word escaping. She wanted him to grab her and pull her against his hard body, but knew it wouldn't happen. Not right now.

"Hello, gorgeous." She didn't recognize his voice. It came out low and gravelly.

"Hi, um, did you just arrive?" Her voice sounded an octave higher than usual. She wet her parched lips with her tongue.

His eyes narrowed as he followed it.

"Yeah. Do you have room at your table for one more?"

"Sure. Right next to me." She motioned to two vacant chairs and started to pull one out.

He intervened and pulled it out so she could sit down. Then he slipped into the other one. He kept a hand on the back of her chair. His thumb caressed her back. Did he hear her sigh? This is how she'd imagined their prom night would have been so many years ago. Only he'd never asked her.

"It's a bit warm in here." Although it only felt that way after Trent walked in. "You might want to take off your leather jacket before you start to sweat." Shelby's eyes darted everywhere except at him. She caught a glimpse of his grin and hoped she wasn't making a fool of herself.

"I have a feeling I might be sweating whether I keep the jacket on or not." He shrugged out of it and hung it over the back of his chair without standing. His eyes never left her.

"Excuse me. One of the staff is motioning to me. I need to see what they need."

Beau, as the president of their class, started speaking into a microphone at the end of the room. Shelby had a podium set up by the DJ's equipment for that purpose. Once he managed to quiet everyone, he said, "I'm not going to make a speech right now." A few cheers went up. "I'll save that until after we eat." Now moaning started. "It's time for Billy to say a prayer before we dig in. Those of you who stayed in the area already know he became a preacher man. Go on, man."

He took over the microphone, introduced himself, and then gave the invocation. Immediately following amen the staff started distributing the meals. Before their table was served Shelby re-joined the group. She felt calmer after performing her duties and providing instructions to her staff.

"Glad you made it back to eat. Looks like you could use a little fuel." Trent stood up and helped her back into her chair.

"Are you saying I'm skinny?" She grinned, keeping the comment light.

"I don't think a man in this room would say that." Trent reassured her and the other men at the table murmured their agreement. "It's the fact you are running around making sure everything is set up correctly, you need some food to keep up the pace."

She swelled a bit with pride.

"So what did your staff need?"

"With a dinner this big there is always something. This time the chef said the sauce he'd prepared should be served in a separate mini ramekin instead of poured directly on the chicken. The fact we didn't have any didn't deter his decision." She gave him a wry grin.

"So you managed to fix it?"

"What he really needed was a reminder from someone of his genius and to gush over his superb meal."

"Which you did."

"Of course. Now all is right with his world. Until the next time."

The food arrived and they all started eating and chatting. Making small talk with the other women felt easier than with the men. Being surrounded by so many former classmates must be causing her to return to her shy ways from high school.

"So, man, how did you wind up with a scar on your cheek? Car accident or did some lady take a knife to ya'?" Bubba joked with Trent. The woman on Bubba's right, his wife, jabbed him with her elbow. In high school Bubba had been handsome with sandy blond hair, soft brown eyes, and a boyish grin. Now his hairline receded, the brown eyes looked cold, and a gold tooth made his grin less than pleasant. His wife had graduated a year after them. She'd been a cute, petite brunette with an infectious laugh. Shelby had yet to hear her laugh tonight.

Although curious about the scar, she couldn't imagine asking such a personal question in a group setting. Still, Bubba had always been a bit crude.

"Army. Afghanistan. You should see the other guy." The way Trent replied with short staccato-like words made it clear he didn't want to discuss it further.

A simple "Oh" came from the man then a change in subject. Shelby was pleased when no one pursued the topic of the war in Iraq or Afghanistan, because she wanted this to be a fun and happy evening.

Bubba's wife took over the conversation, probably trying to keep Bubba from asking any further embarrassing questions.

Turning to the obviously pregnant lady at the table, she asked, "When is your baby due?"

"Before Christmas. I'm hoping early December but the doctor assures me it will be closer to Christmas."

"Do you know if you're having a girl or a boy?"

"A boy. We're thrilled."

Her husband, sitting next to her, smiled. "I'll have him out tossing around a football before he's two."

The mom-to-be gave him an indulgent smile.

Once dinner plates were swept away, Billy the preacher returned to the podium and talked about their wonderful high school days. Shelby had a much different memory. Her extreme shyness had led to a lot of teasing and hurtful comments.

Shelby took over the MC duties to dole out prizes.

"How about our president of Spanish club and his senorita? I think they've been married longest. Has anyone else been married over ten years?" As they walked up to take possession of their gift, Shelby continued. "I remember the Monday you two showed up at school sporting matching wedding bands. One week before graduation. Congratulations." Everyone applauded the couple.

"I don't know who's traveled the furthest. Let's start with who is more than one state away." The questions continued until a winner was determined. "You came all the way back here from Nevada for the reunion?" After his nod, she asked, "So what do you do in Las Vegas?"

"I'm a black jack dealer," he said as he accepted the prize.

"Sounds like an interesting job. I bet you have some good stories to tell."

"Now let's figure out who has the most children. Anyone have more than three?"

After one hand flew up and then acquiring the details, Shelby returned to the mic. "Having one child followed by triplets two years later must be more than a full time job. Congratulations and good luck." Shelby concluded the prize portion of the program.

Different people took over the podium to made announcements and acknowledgements. Updates about what people did following high school would have interested Shelby more if she didn't have Trent sitting next to her. She kept thinking of Trent wrapping her in his arms. Once the music started she planned to ask him to dance if he didn't ask her first.

"Those speeches droned on forever," Shelby whispered to Trent and he rolled his eyes in agreement. At that moment, the music started.

"Let's head out to the dance floor. Somebody needs to be first." Trent didn't waste any time taking Shelby by the hand and winding through the tables to reach their destination. Once they arrived, a few others joined them. Beau arrived with a former cheerleader. Missy glared at him the entire song.

"See, I knew we'd start a trend."

As they gyrated their way through a couple of songs popular from the year of their graduation, they waved to and chatted with other people on the dance floor. One of Trent's old friends whispered loud enough for Shelby to hear him say, "I saw you talking to Beau earlier. Since you've recently returned you need to know he's changed. Best to steer clear of him."

Trent gave him a nod and made a point of moving further away.

"I wonder what he meant?"

Trent shrugged. "Probably jealous of his success. Money changes people."

Shelby tilted her head and gave Trent a puzzled look. "But Beau's always had money."

"True. But now he's in charge. It doesn't belong to his family. It's his."

When a slow dance started, Shelby forgot about the cryptic message as Trent took her in his arms. His right hand splayed across her back, warming her.

Shelby sighed. Being held in Trent's arms felt even better than she dreamed. Breathing in his scent of soap and some cologne reminding her of woodlands made her want to bury her face in his neck. He held her close, but not too close. Far enough away to make her breasts brush back and forth across those hard pecs, causing her nipples to harden. Her backless dress gave him access to a lot of bare skin. His right hand started out slightly above her waist, but now it wandered lower. She couldn't help but take in a quick breath when his gentle touch dipped even lower to caress the skin just inside the material of her dress.

Trent's touch felt better than she'd ever imagined. For at least a year after the incident in college she flinched even at the suggestion of a man planning to touch her. Her reaction gradually changed, but she still stiffened at initial contact. Perhaps her knowledge that Trent had been far away and couldn't have been her attacker made the difference. Or the fact she'd had a crush on him in high school, a lifetime before college.

"I'm hoping you sighed with contentment and not annoyance." Trent moved them toward the edge of the dance floor.

"Definitely not annoyance." Shelby was surprised her voice sounded so breathless.

"Good." Trent bent his head so his mouth almost touched her ear. "Would you like to leave the dance and be alone with me?"

CHAPTER SIX

Surprised, Shelby stopped and Trent stepped on her foot.

"Oh, I'm so sorry, Shelby." Trent grabbed her around the waist to help her off the dance floor.

"No, it was my fault. I stopped too quickly." Shelby limped along with Trent's assistance.

Trent led her back to their seats. All the other people from their table had made their way to the dance floor. "Here, let me take a look at your foot." Trent tried to grab it.

"There's no need." She swatted his hand away. "It's fine." She didn't look any more convinced than he was.

"You limped as we left the dance floor."

"It only hurt for a moment. It's fine."

Remembering why she'd stopped so suddenly, he apologized. "I'm sorry if my question upset you." Trent reached out to caress her cheek.

"It didn't upset me at all." Shelby leaned into his hand. "It was a surprise. That's all."

"A surprise? I hope a good one." Trent dropped his hand.

"Yes, of course." Shelby lowered her eyes and he noticed a flush creep up her neck then proceed higher.

"Then do you want to leave here or stay a while?" Trent asked in a whisper.

"My, um, work," she stammered. "I can't leave right now. I have to be here in case there are any problems. When all the guests are gone I'll have to be sure the staff cleans up. So I'll be stuck here for a few more hours."

"Of course, I should have realized. In that case would you do me the honor of dancing all the slow dances with me?"

"I'd like to. A lot. Yes." The smile she gave Trent made him hope he still had a chance.

While they sat at the table to allow her foot to rest, Trent noticed Beau and his crowd continued to knock back shots. The volume of their foul language increased.

"Would you like me to call security?" He motioned toward the group.

She frowned indicating her concern. "I want everyone to have a good time, but if one group turns rowdy the others will leave and ruin everything."

"Let me see if I can maneuver them somewhere else." Trent didn't want to leave Shelby's side. However, it reminded him of the real reason he'd attended the reunion. His undercover assignment. Perhaps he could capitalize on the opportunity to insinuate himself into their group.

He made his way to their table. "Hey, Beau, you guys seem to be having all the fun." Trent slapped Beau on the back. Hard. Hard enough to stop Beau in mid-sentence.

"Trent, buddy. You deserted us. I can understand why. Shy little Miss Shelby is looking mighty good tonight." Beau rocked his chair back and ogled Shelby.

The hair on the back of Trent's neck stood up, but he squelched the desire to hit Beau in the face for the offensive way he spoke. Trent realized he needed to keep Beau's attention away from Shelby. Perhaps he should keep his distance from her as well.

He ignored the comment. "I think you fellas had something other than a few drinks to be in such a good mood. You wouldn't want to share, would you?" Most of the people at the table looked stoned rather than drunk.

"Share? Do you plan to share Miss Shelby too?" Beau gave Trent a greedy look and appeared much more sober than Trent believed Beau to be.

"She's not mine to share. Says she has to stay here and work. Think it's time to take the party somewhere else?" Trent hoped he spoke quietly enough to keep Shelby from hearing his comments. He didn't want to hurt her feelings. He hoped to have a shot with her, but with his assignment and Beau's interest the timing wasn't right.

"I have a suite upstairs. Let's go on up and see what kind of fun we can conjure up." Beau motioned to his group and they started gathering up their stuff to move on.

Trent wanted to return to Shelby. However, if he left with no explanation it would keep Beau from seeing further proof of his interest. That might be important to keep Shelby safe.

Once they arrived at Beau's suite, the crew set about their duties. One guy left to gather up some ice, another stepped behind the bar to set up drinks, and a third started making some lines of cocaine on the coffee table. The suite had a main living room complete with bar and stools, a raised dining table that sat eight, and two seating areas each with a couch and two side chairs. An interior door, he assumed, led to the bedroom. A balcony ran the length of the living and dining room as well as the bedroom, complete with a view of the ocean. Someone must have opened a window because he could hear the waves crashing whenever the noise level subsided.

As the new guy, Trent didn't have a designated assignment, so he bellied up to the bar. "I'll take a club soda."

The man looked at him. "That's it?"

Trent glared at him and repeated, "Club soda."

With a shrug, the other man filled a glass. Trent stood around making a mental note of the names of the men. His job proved easier since they all wore name tags. He believed they were part of Beau's drug crew. He noted the bag of pills next to the cocaine on the coffee table. He struggled to not to show his disgust. Trent tried to chat with the various men in the room, but they seemed reluctant to say much and glanced at Beau. He assumed they didn't know how much they could say to him.

Missy, Jamie's wife, snuggled up to Beau on the couch as if she belonged there instead of at the side of her husband's hospital bed.

"Missy, when will Jamie be released from the hospital?" His comment would not be well received, but he needed to know how things stood before he made a mistake. If Jamie didn't know about this alliance, it could become an issue between Beau and Jamie. Either way, he needed to understand.

He slumped in a chair next to the couch where Missy and Beau snuggled. The rest of the men and their women lounged, drank, snorted coke, and made out. They all talked in loud voices and each couple groped one another, not caring what anyone else saw or did. One pair had sex behind the bar. No one else thought it remarkable.

"Not sure. Maybe Monday or Tuesday. He'll call." Missy shrugged and dismissed any more talk about Jamie by leaning over and giving Beau a kiss that would make a weaker man blush. She ran her hand up and down his leg, leaving no doubt as to her desire.

Did she really love Beau? Want his approval? Why did she stay married to Jamie? In high school she'd been crazy about Beau but acted like a nice girl. He never would have dreamed she'd do this. How had she lost her way?

When they came up for air, Beau grinned at Missy. "Why don't you take a hit and then head into the bedroom. I'll join you in a few minutes. Trent and I need to talk."

To snort a line Missy stood up then bent over the table, putting her face close to the coke and her backside to Beau. Once finished, she wobbled out of the room on her red stilettos. Her blouse was so low and fit so tight it remained a miracle that her breasts hadn't popped out for the crowd to view.

"She's a great piece of ass, but don't let Jamie know I'm tappin' that. Right?" Beau grinned an evil looking smile. He looked more like a wolf than a man.

Trent held up his hands. "Not my business. I keep what I see and hear to myself."

"Good. That's the way I like my employees. Closed mouthed. You've passed two of the requirements. We'll see Monday how things go. It could turn into a permanent job."

"If Jamie's security, I don't know what I'd do for you once he's back on his feet." Trent shrugged as if he didn't care one way or the other.

"Jamie's head of the department. There's more than one man on the team. I'm always looking for qualified candidates."

"You must have a big plant if you need more than one guy. Don't you have cameras and stuff? Or dogs. I know we used dogs when I was an MP. They hear better than humans and cost a lot less."

"Yeah, it's big and I have cameras. Nothing like having a man you can count on. I can count on you, Trent, right?"

"Sure. We've known each other since we were kids. A buddy you've played football with is like a brother. Maybe even better than a brother, at least better than the one I have." Loyalty remained key with Beau.

"Exactly. I knew you'd understand. I'm going to say bye for now. If I don't see you at breakfast, be sure to come by at one o'clock on Monday like we discussed." Beau rose from the couch and stuck out his hand for Trent to shake. It was evident what Beau had on his mind. His erection pushed against his pants. "I have some business to take care of, if you know what I mean." He grinned and motioned with his head toward the bedroom. "Stay here and enjoy the goodies." He indicated the cocaine and bags of pills littering the coffee table.

"Thanks. Don't mind if I do. Enjoy yourself." Trent hid his repulsion as he pretended to look over the options on the table.

"I'm sure I will. I'm sure I will." Beau muttered as he strutted toward the bedroom.

Trent picked up a couple pills from the table then wandered to the bar to fix a drink. He pretended to down the tablets before making his way back to his chair. Some of the men eyed him and only a fool would think they wouldn't report to Beau in the morning. He made a show of consuming liquor although he only drank club soda. Flirting with the women pissed off their men and gave him a good excuse to leave.

"Looks like all the women are taken here, so I'll find my own." Trent spoke loud enough to draw the attention of his fellow alums as he marched out of the suite.

Trent made his way back to the ballroom to see if he had a chance of one more dance with Shelby. He probably shouldn't but Beau and his men weren't here to see them together. As he approached, he noticed a steady stream of people coming out the door. He heard music so at least the DJ continued to play.

"Ah, I see you made it back." Shelby greeted him as he walked to the table next to the dance floor where she sat. She didn't look mad but he heard a bit of frost in her tone. Only a dozen or so people remained in the room. The way he'd left earlier, he didn't know what kind of reception he'd get.

"Needed to pick up my jacket. Looks like the party is winding down, any chance of one more dance?" Trent tried not to sound like a beggar.

"I planned to tell the DJ two more dances and call it quits. I'll make sure he makes one of them a slow dance." Shelby gave him a small smile as she walked toward the DJ. Her gait gave away the pain she must feel. Damn, he'd really hurt her when he stepped on her foot.

As Shelby walked back, Trent asked, "I messed up your foot, didn't I?" The DJ started up a lively tune and a few of the stragglers made their way to the dance floor.

"I confess it does hurt a bit, but I'm at fault. I'm certain a little ice tonight will fix it right up. It's already much better."

"Good enough for another spin around the floor?"

"I wouldn't miss it." The DJ announced the last dance of the night. They heard a few groans of disappointment.

Trent swept Shelby into his arms. In spite of the dozen or so couples, they existed in a cocoon no one else could see or penetrate. A few short minutes later the music stopped. And the moment evaporated. He snapped back to reality.

"I have an early morning and need to put some ice on my foot." Shelby's voice held a contrite note.

"At least I can walk you to your car. Or do you have a room here? I insist you lean on me." Trent put one arm around her waist and almost lifted her off her feet.

"I won't turn down the offer. Yes, I have a room." Shelby replied with a smile.

As they walked toward the elevators Shelby provided a few last minute instructions to her staff. More than one gave her a sly smile as they noticed Trent and his hold on her.

"You plan to be at breakfast tomorrow, right?" Shelby asked as they approached her room.

"Sure do. I heard rumors of a big spread." Trent grinned down at her.

"Yes, there will be. It starts at eight, so I'll be there about seven-thirty." Trent noticed the vein in her neck pulsing rapidly. He hoped she wouldn't hyperventilate.

"That's pretty early considering how late it is right now."

They moved slowly. Trent did so because of her foot but it gave him the extra bonus of more time with her.

"I know, but I have to make sure everything is perfect."

Trent chuckled. "I'm sure everything you do is perfect."

Blushing, Shelby replied, "I try." They paused at her door and she pulled her key card from her purse. Trent took it from her and opened the door then continued inside with her.

"This is a lot nicer than the room I have." Trent looked around the suite and assisted her to the couch, then pushed the coffee table close to her and placed a pillow on it. The suite consisted of two areas, one a bedroom and the other a living room. Only an archway separated the two. Beyond the bedroom he noticed a door ajar that appeared to be the bathroom. The art work looked more personal than a normal hotel room.

She propped her foot on the pillow. "It's my house," Shelby explained.

"You live here?" Trent looked at her, astonished.

"Part of my salary. The commute can't be beat," she said with a shrug.

"How do you relax? You're always at work." Trent looked around and saw personal items such as a picture of her family and extra end tables and lamps.

"Relaxing is overrated."

"Where's the ice machine? I'll fill a bucket for you." Trent followed Shelby's directions and returned a few minutes later.

He found Shelby had taken off her shoe and replaced her foot on the pillow. She held a pillow on her lap and picked at a loose thread.

"Are you sure you don't want me to take you to an emergency room? It could be broken." Trent inspected the purple-colored foot. He wrapped the plastic bag full of ice in a towel and placed it on her foot. Her indrawn breath made him glance at her face.

"It must hurt," he said with a grimace.

"Some. The cold of the ice took my breath away. I'm sure it'll be fine by morning." Color drained from her face.

She hugged the pillow to her chest. Trent didn't understand what happened but something had. Her eyes showed fear. Of him. Why?

"Go on. I'll be fine. See you in the morning." Shelby made shooing motions with her hands.

Why the sudden change in attitude? He wanted to stay and ask questions. However, she seemed too irritated. He mumbled a goodbye and left.

He contemplated her change of attitude. She reacted as if he'd somehow threatened her. Did she think he planned to force her to have sex? Maybe she realized she didn't really know him. He hated to think she feared him.

As he meandered to his own room Trent sorted through his feelings for Shelby. Holding her in his arms during the slow dances reminded him how long it had been since he'd bedded a woman. At the time, he had planned to take her to his room and make love to her. He still wanted her. However, Beau's comments about Shelby and the way he treated Missy made him realize how selfish it sounded. Beau's attitude toward women made him question his own. Shelby didn't seem like the kind of woman who would settle for one night or even a week. She'd demand forever.

Did he desire Shelby because of his feelings for her in high school? Or because of the woman she'd become? Did he even know who she was? She sure as hell felt good and looked great, but did he want more than one night of sex?

Right now his undercover operation took priority. Would he endanger Shelby if he continued to see her after the reunion? How would his boss, Jim, view a relationship?

CHAPTER SEVEN

The evening had been like the prom she'd never attended. Even better. They weren't teenagers with their first crush. She felt the connection between them growing strong. When Trent asked her to leave the dance the rush of desire nearly made her heart stop. Then she'd ruined everything by standing still as Trent kept moving.

Being brought back to reality when he stepped on her foot hurt more emotionally than physically. When he took off with Beau and his crew she'd been certain she wouldn't see him again that evening. She should have known his chivalrous ways would insist he return. He had been such a gentleman and solicitous of her injury.

Shelby hoped she covered her nervousness once they'd entered her suite. Being alone with a man in such a small space didn't happen often. She'd made sure of it. This time she didn't know if her nerves were caused by old hurts or the possibility of new experiences.

She didn't know if her foot would be okay, but she didn't want Trent to feel any worse than he already did. After fifteen minutes of ice, she prepared for bed. First, she checked her cell phone. She missed a message from her mother. Knowing her mother to be a night owl, she called in spite of the late hour.

"Hi, Mom, it's not too late for a call, is it?"

"No, dear, you know it isn't. I want to hear about the reunion. This was the night of the big dinner and dance, right?"

"Yes. The party went off without incident. Beau Jackson, the president of our class, was his usual charming self. He performed the duties of emcee to perfection." Her mother would want that tidbit of information since everything the Jacksons did would be news in Georgetown. Her mother would also want to make sure the men at the reunion hadn't triggered a setback.

"I never doubted he would. Did you have anyone arrive who you haven't seen since graduation?" Her mother had always been involved with her friends and classmates.

"Actually, we did. One of them was Trent Meyers. Do you remember him?"

"Of course, I do. His family had so many tragedies. First his father died when Trent was a boy. Then he joined the army the minute he turned eighteen. Not many young men would do that to support a younger brother and dying mother." Her mother's voice broke before she continued. "Magnolia Meyers was such a sweet woman. She died way too young. I'm sorry. I didn't mean to bring up unhappy memories. How is Trent? Is he still in the army?"

Shelby hadn't realized Trent joined the army to support his mother and brother.

"No, he isn't. He left recently and is figuring out what to do next. You called his mother Magnolia just now. Before you always called her Maggie."

"She insisted on the nickname. Said Magnolia was too old-fashioned. Now that you mention it, I do recall someone saying his old house was occupied again. People suspected Jason had returned."

"No, it's Trent. He told us he spent time in Iraq and Afghanistan. He has a scar on his cheek so he must have been wounded."

"Oh, dear, what a shame. I remember him as such a handsome young man." Her mother made a *tsking* noise.

"He's still handsome, no doubt about that. And tall. My goodness, I don't remember him being over six feet back in high school." Shelby had difficulty not gushing about him.

"Then I don't know if I'd recognize him."

"I didn't. Back to the discussion of the reunion. I think everything is going well. Oh, wait, one bad thing happened." Shelby hesitated but knew her mother wanted all the details. "Jamie Strong broke his kneecap during the football game. He's in the hospital. I think he had a previous knee injury and this made things worse."

"Oh, dear, I hadn't heard. I'll be sure to call his mother tomorrow."

Shelby stifled a yawn as a smile formed on her lips. Her mother enjoyed being the one to have new information to share. In a small town like Georgetown, it didn't take long for news to spread.

"I need to head to bed, so I'll say good night."

After talking about Trent, she knew his mother had died of cancer during the time she recovered from her rape. Shelby hadn't left the house, not even to attend the funeral even though she'd been sad for Trent and his brother. His brother had graduated from high school only a few weeks prior to their mother's death. Trent's mom had struggled to stay alive long enough for Jason to reach eighteen and graduate. Once he did, she gave in to the cancer. Tears threatened to roll down thinking of their sorrow.

Knowing Trent stayed at the resort for the one night, she considered calling him. No, she looked at her watch and realized how late it was. Too late for a phone call. She'd have to wait until tomorrow. There would be plenty of time to talk. He'd come back to Georgetown, and they could see each other whenever they chose. She planned to see him. Now she had to convince him to want to see her. She grinned; she'd made a lot of progress to that end this evening.

CHAPTER EIGHT

As Trent drove to Beau's plant on Monday afternoon he felt calm and confident. He wanted to take down this drug operation, and everyone connected to it. His unique qualifications made him the one man who could succeed. And he would.

The plant was located on the property Beau's family had owned for generations. His parent's house sat close to the entrance of the land and the plant at the furthest distance from the house. It also happened to be adjacent to the river. As he maneuvered to park near the largest building he noted a small structure adjacent and a medium size one behind. He saw Beau coming out of the back one.

"So, you ready to start work?" Beau said in greeting as Trent swung his leg over his bike.

"Don't I need to fill out some paperwork or something?" Trent asked, shaking hands with Beau.

"We'll do that eventually. I want to show you around the place. Introduce you to the boys. You knew most of them in school, but we've all changed. Some more than others." Beau slapped Trent on the back and ushered him into the building toward some kind of locker room.

"Man, the smell is strong outside, but inside it almost takes your breath away." Trent commented before they started the tour. The combination of chemicals had an acrid smell worse than burnt wood, gasoline, bleach and ammonia rolled into one.

"Yeah, it does. Not much we can do about it except keep the ventilation fans running at top speed. Here, put this on." Beau handed Trent a respirator and ear plugs. Trent trailed after Beau as he pointed out people manning the two lines, one for pesticides and one for fertilizer with a cinder-block wall separating them. The ceilings stood twenty-feet high. The roar of the ventilation fans made communication almost impossible. All the employees had on respirators for the toxic fumes and ear plugs for the noise.

The tour included introductions to Beau's crew. Because of the required safety equipment, hand signals and name tags on people and stations were displayed. Most employees had titles consisting of "overseer" to this or that. Only a couple did any real work. Their real jobs no doubt were performed elsewhere.

"This a twenty-four-hour operation?" Trent asked when they returned to the soundproofed main lobby so they could carry on a conversation without shouting.

"No. We run two shifts. They overlap so one shift is seven to four and the other is three to midnight. I want you here when the place is empty. Arrive here around eleven-thirty to make sure everyone exits the plant then close it up and stay until thirty minutes after the first shift starts."

"I noticed you have a bunch of cameras. That's not good enough?" Trent had counted thirty-seven inside. He'd have to wait and see how many were outside.

"We have a lot of chemicals in here. They can be volatile. I want someone on site in case there is an attempted break in or if a fire starts. Being this far away from a fire station the whole place could go up before someone watching a tape saw something or a smoke alarm went off." Beau's assertions almost sounded sincere.

Trent gave his best alarmed look. "Volatile? Like they can blow up?"

"Given the right situation. Yeah, they can," Beau shrugged as if he didn't really care in spite of his words. "We do our best to make sure it doesn't happen."

"If some of that stuff gets on me, will it eat my skin off or something?" Trent looked toward the entrance into the main part of the plant with concern.

"If you follow the rules, you'll be fine. Don't stick your arm or any other naked skin in the chemicals and you'll have no problems."

"Can't imagine why I'd want to do something like that." Trent shook his head.

"Exactly. Now, two things I demand." Beau pointed a finger at Trent and jabbed him a couple of times. "You have to stay awake the whole shift, and make sure you change up your routine. Walk the perimeter as well as inside the plant." He waited for Trent's agreement.

Trent gave him a short nod. "I noticed you have a loading dock in front and out back. How come you have two locations?"

"Different chemicals. They don't mix well. I like to keep them separate." Beau tried to sound nonchalant, but Trent knew he'd hit on something key. All he had to do was figure out the real reason for the two docks. It probably had something to do with his drug operation. He planned to look into it when left alone.

"What about the building out back?" Trent had been aware Beau didn't mention it earlier. "Do I check on that one too?"

"Nah. It's the office area. We keep records there and stuff. And some research and development. Nothing volatile. There will be people coming and going at all hours. You know these scientist type guys. They like to work weird hours. Something to do with a creative mind. Or so they tell me. It has its own security set up. My boys love technology. They're always trying out some new software to make things safer for the lines and more secure. This building is your concern." Beau waved his arm as if the office area was insignificant. That only aroused Trent's suspicion.

"It has a loading dock too," Trent pointed out.

"Part of it used to be the plant, but we needed more space and built this building leaving that one for the offices," Beau responded.

The questions annoyed Beau so Trent tried to come up with a compliment. "If you've had to expand already, then business must be doing well."

Beau puffed out his chest. "Best decision I've ever made."

"Is this what Jamie did for you?" Knowing full well it wasn't, Trent wanted to see how Beau would respond.

"No. He's head of security. I moved some of the guys around and this is where I need you right now. Who knows? If you do good work, I'll see about getting you one of the jobs with better hours," the magnanimous Beau responded. At least Trent interpreted it that way.

"Hey, I'm not complaining. Asking a simple question. Is this only good until Jamie comes back? Again, wondering if I need to keep looking for a job." Trent bent his head and shuffled his feet to make Beau think he was humble.

"If you fit in, then I'll make it permanent. If not, you're free to head out after Jamie comes back." Beau slapped his back and grinned.

Trent shrugged and looked Beau in the eye. "Thanks, man. Don't know why I won't fit in."

"Now, let's head over to the security office and fill out that paperwork. We need to fit you out with some firepower too." They walked to the small building beside the plant.

"Damn, Beau. You expecting some terrorists?" Trent asked when they walked into the room housing the weapons. He considered his selection between an Uzi and an HK MP5, both 9mm automatic weapons.

"We have some serious chemicals in here. I don't want you to lose the battle if somebody decides they want to take off with some."

"You don't think you're going a little overboard? I mean, you even have night vision goggles, binoculars, and flash grenades. There are enough weapons to outfit a small army." Trent allowed his surprise and awe to show.

Beau's eyes narrowed. "This is a dangerous business. I plan to win if something goes down. You have used these before, right? When you served in the army."

Trent gave him a wink. "I can't say they were standard issue, but yeah, I've some experience." Let Beau think he participated in a non-sanctioned event.

"I figured. So which do you like best?"

"If I'm going semi-automatic, I like the MP5 best, but for full auto, the Uzi can't be beat." Trent made sure to clear the chamber when he picked up each in turn.

Beau shrugged. "Hell, take one of each. Then you don't have to choose."

"Hey, man, that's great. Is there someplace around here I can practice. It's been a while."

"Sure. I have a spot set up out in the woods. Grab some mags and we'll see who has the best aim." Beau picked up an Uzi and some ammo then headed out of the building.

.

CHAPTER NINE

Shelby hadn't heard from Trent since the reunion. He didn't have her phone number but he could have called the resort. Instead of waiting, she took the step of showing up at his door without an invitation or calling ahead. Screwing up her courage, she drove the final few yards to his house, parked the car, and took a deep breath.

"Okay. You can do this. You're not some shy little teenager anymore."

Shelby knocked on Trent's door with her left hand as she balanced a pie in her right. A basket of other food sat at her feet. His Harley parked in the carport confirmed his presence. After her second knock, she heard a thud and some grumbling. When Trent flung open the door her mouth watered at the sight of his bare chest and jeans buttoned but not zipped. His hair stuck up like he'd slept on his right side. His stubble appeared to be growing into a beard.

"What?" Trent snarled then his eyes focused on her. "Oh, Shelby. Sorry. I didn't expect anyone. Uh, come on in." He stepped back so she could enter.

"Sorry. I figured noon would be a good time to stop by. I see you must have been asleep." She picked up the basket and handed him the pie, then made her way into the house.

"Yeah, I was." Trent set the pie on the kitchen table then picked up a shirt from the couch and shrugged into it. "I work nights now."

"I'm so sorry. I didn't know. I hadn't heard from you, so I stopped by with lunch." Shelby knew her face burned. Her timing sucked. What else could go wrong?

"I snagged a job at Beau's plant the day after the reunion. My shift ends at seven-thirty in the morning. It's been a couple of weeks and I'm still adjusting. Sorry. I didn't mean to snap at you." Trent took the basket from her and placed it on the table. "This is nice of you to bring lunch. What kind of pie did you bring?"

"Blackberry." Shelby hoped the offering would appease him. "I recall it as a favorite of yours."

"Blackberry?" Trent looked at her with a smile that made her knees weak. "Hell, yes, it is. I didn't think I could eat right now, but if it's blackberry pie I know I can manage a slice."

Trent headed down the hallway. "Give me a minute to become a little more presentable. Fix yourself something and you can cut me a slice of that pie." His crooked grin calmed her nerves.

She heard the shower running and pictures of a naked Trent formed in her mind and had her pulse racing.

Looking through the cabinets, she found plates and some plastic containers with lids. To keep busy, even if her attention drifted away from her task, Shelby fixed a plate for herself. She put the rest of the ham, potato salad, and squash casserole in the refrigerator so Trent could eat later. A worn, plastic tablecloth with a yellow daisy pattern covered the table. She figured his mother had chosen it years ago.

She cut a huge piece of pie, setting it on a dinner sized plate, and placed it on the table across from her food. After looking in every drawer, she finally found silverware in the last one. With only beer in the refrigerator, Shelby added two glasses of water to their place setting. Even if Trent wanted beer, he probably wouldn't like it with blackberry pie. Shelby looked to see if Trent had some tea bags and sugar. He did, so she made sweet tea while waiting for him.

By the time she'd fixed the tea Trent walked back into the kitchen with wet hair and clothes that weren't rumpled. She didn't know which version she preferred.

"Sorry for my manners earlier. I'm not known for my sunny personality when I'm half asleep."

"It's my fault. I would have called, but didn't know your number. This is one of my days off, and when I visited Mom and Dad I decided to stop by. Of course, being a proper southern lady, I couldn't invite myself over unless I brought food. So here I am. With food." Shelby hated the fact she rambled. Trent must think she was an idiot.

Trent had already taken a bite of pie while she talked. "Anytime you want to bring a blackberry pie is fine with me. Even if it's in the middle of the night." He took another giant bite and chewed slowly with a look of rapture on his face. Once he swallowed, he grinned at her before popping another bite into his mouth.

To keep from babbling, Shelby refrained from further comment. Instead, she started eating. When Trent finished the slice of pie, she asked, "Do you want another piece?"

"I better not. Don't think I'm going to let you go home with the rest of that blackberry pie. It stays right here."

Shelby grinned and relaxed a little. "Of course. I made it for you."

Trent took his dishes to the sink. "So today is your day off? Do you always have Tuesdays off?"

She nodded. "And Wednesdays. I have to work the weekends since it is our busiest time. People checking in and out and lots of parties on Fridays and Saturdays." Shelby finished her lunch and took her dirty items to the counter where Trent loaded the dishwasher.

"Have a seat and I'll join you when I finish this."

Shelby wandered into the living room and sat on the couch. "The living room is exactly as I remember." The open floor plan made it easy to converse in spite of the fact they occupied separate rooms. "Those pictures of you and Jason are hanging in the same spot. Our mothers worked together making these curtains and some for our house."

"When did you visit here?" Trent joined her. Sitting in the recliner he pushed back, reminding her of his father when he'd done the same thing.

Frowning, she thought a moment. "I think it was a birthday party for your mom. My mom decorated cakes back then, and she brought one over for the party. I came with her. Before your Dad, um…" She couldn't bring herself to say *died.*

Trent's expression changed. "Oh, it must have been her fortieth birthday. Dad ordered the cake. It looked like a basket full of flowers, right?"

Shelby didn't have to think about it. "I'm sure you're right. Mom loved to make that one. She enjoyed making all the flowers. She made every one a different color."

"That brings back some great memories. Before Dad's accident and Mom became ill." The smile on Trent's face indicated they'd been good times, but his eyes told the story about the bad ones.

"What about Jason? When's he planning to visit? I'd love to see him again."

Trent's expression changed, his mouth thinned and his eyes clouded. "We aren't close anymore. I haven't told him I'm living here."

"What? How is that possible? You two used to be so tight." Shelby realized how harsh her words sounded the second they escaped her mouth. Trent's expression took on a look of defiance.

"Stuff happens. We drifted apart. I'll call eventually. When I'm settled." He shrugged as if it didn't matter, but she knew better. Their rift hurt him. Shelby sensed he had no intention of reaching out to Jason and wondered what happened to set them so far apart.

"I guess I better be going." She rose from the couch as a knock on the door sounded. If she hadn't been looking directly at Trent, she might not have noticed how his expression changed and his hand shot down the side of the recliner.

Trent remained seated. "Who is it?" he asked in a hard voice she'd never heard him use. It sounded more like a bark than a question.

"Ted Harper. Your neighbor," a gravelly voice replied from the other side of the door.

Trent stood and walked to the door, opening it. "Mr. Harper." He sounded like himself again. "Nice to see you. Sorry I haven't come around for a visit before now. Come on in." He stuck out his hand for Mr. Harper to shake.

As the elder Mr. Harper entered, he said, "It is you. I wondered whether you or Jason had moved back."

"This is my lucky day. Two visitors. You remember Shelby Cornwell?" Trent motioned to Shelby as they all sat down.

"Sure do. How are you, girl? You look more like your Momma every day." Ted Harper went to the same church as Shelby's parents and grandparents.

"I'll take that as a compliment, Mr. Harper." She received the comment often from people who'd known her mother since childhood.

"What brings you here today, Mr. Harper?" Trent inquired.

"It's that camera of yours." He waved toward the other side of the road.

"What camera?" Trent looked at a loss as to what Mr. Harper was talking about.

"The one out in the woods. The kind that takes pictures when animals walk by. It's on my property. Now, don't think it matters to me," Mr. Harper assured him. "You can set up as many of 'em as you want. If you're trying to figure out where the deer trails are so you can shoot one, then we need to talk. The season started a while back, but nobody's been on my land." Mr. Harper shook his head. "You got the damn thing pointed this way instead of toward the woods."

"Oh, right," Trent responded, but Shelby didn't think he had known about it before now. "I, uh, set it up to find out what's getting into my garbage can. Not sure if it's some raccoons or a coyote. That's why I set it up pointing this direction."

Why did Trent lie about it? What other lies had he told?

"Garbage can? Well now, how come you don't know how to secure one so as not to have those problems?" Mr. Harper looked surprised. "Could be either one. Don't know why a coyote'd be out here. You don't have a small dog do you?" A puzzled expression came over Mr. Harper's face.

The question caused a frown on Trent's. "Dog? No, why do you ask?"

"Coyotes go for dog food if you leave it outside and they'll make a meal out'a small dog. People have to keep them inside at night." He shook his head again at the idea.

"I'll remember that if I acquire one. Thanks, Mr. Harper." Trent's face relaxed and his lips quirked a bit.

"If you want to bag a deer this season come talk to me. I'll let you set up a stand on my land. The damn things keep gettin' into my corn. Make sure you don't go shootin' toward my house." Mr. Harper pointed a finger at Trent.

"I'll keep it in mind, Mr. Harper." Trent grinned at the comment. "Thanks for dropping by." Trent stood up when Mr. Harper rose from the couch.

"I need to head out too." Shelby rose with the men. "Mom and Dad will wonder why I've been gone so long."

"Shelby, thanks for bringing the blackberry pie. I'll be sure to bring your dishes back to you." Trent sounded distant again to Shelby. Like he had something else on his mind. She didn't know for sure if she'd be welcome if she came back. Now all her doubts showered down on her again. The visit hadn't gone as well as she'd hoped.

Shelby considered Trent's demeanor as she drove to her parent's house. Initially Trent had been grouchy, but no doubt due to being awakened. That she understood. Then he warmed up as they ate and talked. Things took a turn for the worse when she mentioned Jason, then it went further downhill after Mr. Harper's arrival. What about the camera thing? She didn't believe he'd known about it so why lie to Mr. Harper? And who would install a camera across from Trent's house? It didn't make sense to her. As she pulled into the drive, she stopped thinking about it. She'd wait until after the visit with her folks.

"Sweetheart, come in here and let me hug your neck," her mother called from the kitchen door after she barely set foot out of her car.

"Momma." Shelby gave her mother a hug and peck on her cheek. "Where's Daddy?"

"Went down to the hardware store for something. He'll be back in a minute. Sit down and tell me more about the reunion. I've heard a few things from my friends but I figure you'd know all the behind-the-scene stuff."

"I can't imagine what you'd want to know. We had a routine crisis in the kitchen. I've told you about how our chef has crazy requests when there's a big event. Did you hear Mrs. Jackson came to the fashion show and lunch?"

"No, I didn't. She's such a smart dresser I'd be interested to know which outfits she liked."

"Sorry, she didn't share that information with me. However, she did approve of the way I handled a small disturbance."

"The model who ranted about the cruelty to animals?"

"I see you already know about it." Shelby sat at the kitchen table.

"It's the biggest topic in town." Her mom fixed them each a glass of sweet tea then joined Shelby at the table.

"Well, Mrs. Jackson told me I did a quick and efficient job of removing her."

"Of course, you did. Why would she doubt you?"

"My boss became more upset than anyone else."

"That man. I hope you find a job with a better boss."

"Trust me, I'm looking. Thank goodness Mrs. Jackson explained the great job I did or he might have fired me."

"Fired you?" Her father's voice boomed from the doorway while he walked in the house.

Shelby turned to acknowledge her father. "Don't worry, Daddy. He didn't follow through with the threat."

Shelby changed the subject before her father became riled. "Mrs. Jackson called me a couple of days ago and we've planned a meeting to discuss the possibility of a family reunion at the resort."

"Really? I hadn't heard about it."

"It's not finalized so don't tell the world about it yet. If they have one, they plan to hold it Christmas Eve."

"How perfect for you. I know it is a slow time of year at the resort."

"Exactly. Although if she changes it to the day after Christmas, it could pose a problem for ordering supplies."

"I'm sure you'll figure it all out."

Shelby wondered how to ensure fresh food without imposing on the kitchen staff's Christmas. Deciding to think about it later she enjoyed a lengthy conversation with her parents. In a flash, the time arrived when she made her way to her car waving and saying goodbye to them.

While Shelby drove back to Myrtle Beach she went over her visit with Trent. She couldn't help thinking about the mixed signals he gave her. Sometimes he stayed distant, other times he drew closer as if wanting their relationship to go further. Or was she projecting? She wished she could discuss her feelings with someone else. Maybe she needed to visit Amy.

Since she had tomorrow off, she called and set up a lunch date with Amy English, the minister who'd brought her out of despair after the rape. It had been too long since they'd talked. Amy became her best friend during that time and remained so. She was seven years older than Shelby. Her olive skin, dark hair and eyes gave her an exotic look. Most people thought she was Native American when she had an Italian background.

Arriving at the West End Diner the next day they said hello, then placed their food orders. Amy watched Shelby twirl her straw in her glass.

"So what's bothering you, Shelby?" Amy reached over and stilled her hand.

She shrugged and looked directly at Amy. "Am I so obvious?" Her hands dropped to her lap, and she picked at her dress.

"Not to people who don't know you. I like to think I know you well enough to see when you're struggling with a dilemma."

"Dilemma?" She sighed. "Leave it to you to head straight to the point. Yes, I suppose I do have one."

"So spill it," Amy encouraged.

"You remember I set up a high school reunion a few weeks ago?"

"Yes. It's been the big topic in town." Amy thanked the waitress with a nod as she put their food on the table.

"One of the guys in my class left a few days before graduation, and no one had seen or heard from him until the day of the reunion."

Amy raised her eyebrows. "Just one?"

"No. There were more, but only one I'm interested in," Shelby admitted.

"Interested? I think this is a first for you." Amy's voice changed from flippant to serious in a second. Amy understood the difficulty Shelby had lowering her personal wall of protection to allow anyone close.

Shelby blushed. "Yes, interested. I had a crush on him years ago, and after meeting him again at the reunion, I thought there might something between us."

"Are you sure it isn't a simple case of yearning from a time when you were both innocent?"

"No, I'm not sure," Shelby admitted. "Let me explain what's happened."

As Shelby told her about the reunion weekend and her follow-up visit, Amy's expression changed from pleased and hopeful to worried.

"Why the frown?" Shelby asked.

"As you know, I counsel a lot of people in Georgetown. I can't discuss their conversations."

"I realize that, but what does it have to do with me and Trent?"

Amy put her fork down. "I'm not sure. You mentioned he works at Beau's fertilizer plant?"

"Yeah. You know how Beau's plant brought a lot of prosperity back to Georgetown. Now they have more than tourism and the paper mill to keep people employed. I think Beau gave him a job because of their high school connection. He's done it for a lot of his old buddies."

"I can't really explain right now. Let me think about this and call you. I don't want to speak out of turn. In the meantime, could you avoid him? I promise I'll tell you more later."

Shelby's silverware clattered onto the table. "Amy, you're scaring me. Why do I have to avoid him?"

"I don't want to scare you. Give me a few days and I'll see what I can dig up." Amy patted Shelby's hand.

"Dig up?" Her eyebrows shot up. At Amy's calm stare, Shelby relented. "Of course. I've complete faith in you."

Satisfied at Shelby's acquiescence, Amy said, "Now, let's change the subject. What have you been doing besides scheduling reunions?"

Shelby tried to continue their conversation on other topics, but her mind kept drifting back to Amy's comments about Trent. Or was it more about Beau's plant? Or the people who worked there? Her ideas went around in circles. Once she sat in her car heading back to the resort, she couldn't remember whether she'd said a proper goodbye to Amy or not.

What significance did the camera Mr. Harper found have? Why had Trent lied about it? Also, the way Trent shoved his hand down the recliner when Mr. Harper knocked on the door, what had he tried to grab? She didn't understand, but she would follow Amy's advice and avoid Trent for a while. It would be easy since she still didn't have a phone number for him.

CHAPTER TEN

Trent knew Beau would keep track of him, but he had no idea the man had put a camera outside the house. Beau or one of his men must have installed it when he'd been at work. Anyone who stopped by would be seen. He had to admit it made sense. Good thing he kept in contact with the task force via the secure phone. He'd created his escape route behind the house, out of sight. Unless a second camera lurked back there. He'd better check it out.

The fact Shelby had shown up would be captured by the camera. He'd have to make sure she never came back. He didn't know what might happen if Beau recognized her importance to him. As a dangerous drug dealer, Beau would take notice of anything or anyone he thought could be a weakness to his enemy. Or friend. Trent would never forgive himself if something happened to Shelby. Or his brother, Jason. Thinking of his brother made him nervous. He'd better convince Shelby not to contact him. He also didn't want Beau to know about Jason, a definite weak spot for him. If he did his job right the people he cared about would never be in danger because this would be over before Beau knew about the task force. Still, he couldn't take the chance.

After dealing with surveillance near his house he had to switch gears as he sorted through the information for his DEA contact. His initial task had instructed him to draw up a diagram showing the positions of all cameras at Beau's plant. Later that day, he spoke to his contact.

"You received the list with all the specifics about the equipment, right?" He'd sent everything more than a week ago. It'd taken a couple of weeks to gather the intel. He didn't want anyone to be suspicious if they noticed him taking notes. Beau would no doubt have someone review the security tapes showing his activity during his shift.

"Yeah, we found it. Good work. It took a while to determine where we can set up our surveillance equipment without being detected. We'll leave it for you at the dead drop in the Georgetown cemetery. It'll have a map with the exact spot to set it up."

"If we hadn't figured before now the main plant is a blind then the location of all the electronics would have pointed it out. No way can the main building watch all parts of the other two buildings."

"You might want to mention to Beau that you can't see activity from the other two buildings when you watch the footage. Then he'll know you are aware. Otherwise, he might think you are either too dumb or you're a cop."

Trent nodded in spite of the fact he spoke into a phone and the other man couldn't see him. "Good point. I don't want him to become suspicious."

"Exactly. You could end up dead."

"I'm sure my hours and everything else are a test. They may also be taking this time to dig deeper into my background." He'd worried about the phony story the DEA had set up. "You sure your guys have everything covered?"

"Don't worry. We've have our best men on it," the disembodied voice assured him. "Make sure you know all the details in case they question you about it."

"It's the first thing I memorized. Beau let it slip his guys have some mad technology skills. They clone phones and hack government databases and other stuff."

The voice on the other end sounded testy. "We know, we know. Calm down. We have it covered. That's why we gave you this encrypted phone. It would be best to keep it at your house to ensure no one from his crew sees it. If they spot it, they'll know you're law enforcement since no one else has this kind."

"Sorry. I understood this deal would wrap up in a few weeks." Trent started pacing around the house while they talked.

"You're an optimist. These things can take months, sometimes years, before everything comes together. Hang in there. You're doing a great job."

"Years?" His comment stopped Trent cold. When he accepted the job, he'd known it would take more than a few days. But he'd never imagined it could take years. What the hell had he signed up for?

"You've already gathered more intelligence than anyone else has managed. This could be the shortest undercover operation in history."

Trent started pacing, and breathing, again. "That'd be great."

"Keep your watch on at all times. The built in GPS allows us to track it so we know where you are."

He hung up the phone and tried to think of other matters. He'd never go to sleep going over the conversation in his head. Images of Shelby came to mind. Images which kept sneaking in at times they shouldn't. She hadn't come back after her first visit. Had he scared her away? For her best interest, they should remain apart. However, he wanted to see her again without Beau or his guys knowing about it.

He considered several ways to finagle an undetected visit, until he finally settled on one that would permit him to fall asleep with her image foremost in his mind.

CHAPTER ELEVEN

Shelby frowned at the knock on her door. She wasn't expecting anyone, so assumed it was work related as she jerked the door open. "Oh, uh, it's you."

Trent stood with his hands full, a smile on his face, and a glint in his eyes.

"I guess I'm not who you expected. Hopefully, it's not a bad thing."

"Oh, no. I mean, I didn't expect anyone, but when the knock came I thought one of the staff had come up to ask me to do something. It's my day off."

"Exactly. It's why I'm here. I wanted to give you back your dishes. Sorry it took so long."

"Where are my manners? Come in. Have a seat." Shelby stepped back, allowing him entrance. She scanned the room to make sure there weren't any clothes laying about. "Set them on the counter. I'll put them away later."

"I hope you don't have plans for the day." Trent placed the dishes on the miniature counter top and then sat down on the loveseat. The last time he'd been there he'd noticed the two burner stove and small refrigerator. Until now, he hadn't noticed the small oven.

"Nothing special. The usual errands. Why?" Shelby settled into the chair across from him.

"I hoped you would go with me. I planned to take the Grim Reaper on a trip up to Calabash for lunch. The temperature is cooling down, the sun is out, and it should be a nice ride."

Shelby couldn't tell if she saw hope in his eyes or her desire mirrored there. Either way, how could she say no? "I'd love to go."

"What about your errands? Do you need to do something before we head out?"

"They can wait until tomorrow."

"You need to grab a warm jacket. The extra wind on the drive will make it chilly." He looked down at the sandals on her feet. "And shoes. Do you have some with closed toes? Maybe some kind of boots?"

She grinned. "Of course I have boots. I suppose gloves would also be in order?" She turned to her closet and rummaged in the back to find everything.

"Absolutely."

As she changed from sandals to boots, she asked, "Why Calabash?"

"The drive is pretty nice and I remember going to a little restaurant there with my folks and Jason. It's more about the drive than the food."

"No telling if the place is still open, but there are lots of options. I doubt many have closed yet for the season."

"I hadn't even considered that." Trent shrugged.

"I'm ready. Do you have an extra helmet?" They made their way to the parking lot.

"Of course, I wouldn't think of asking you to ride with me without one."

"This is my first time on a Harley," Shelby admitted.

"Really?" Trent looked at her with surprise. "With the number of bike weeks they have here, that's hard to believe."

"I'm usually too busy at work during the rallies to take time off for a ride." Shelby handed her purse to Trent so he could stow it in one of the saddle bags, then put the helmet on he offered her.

"I'll climb on first and you climb on behind me." Trent mounted the beast and kick started it. The engine's throaty rumble provided a background to his instructions. "When I lean in, you lean in the same direction. During the ride, if you need to stop or tell me anything, tug on my right arm and I'll stop. Otherwise, the only time I'll be able to hear you is when we stop at a light."

"Got it." Shelby wiped her hands on her pants before slipping on the gloves.

She climbed on the back of the growling monster and wrapped her arms around Trent's middle. Um. She hadn't considered this advantage. His stomach felt as hard as a tree trunk, yet warm as her favorite afghan. As she snuggled closer she became aware of the heat between her legs. Oh, lord. What had she gotten herself into?

The ride along the coast felt fabulous and looked spectacular. The smell of the ocean with its tangy, salty scent mixed with Trent's cologne was her idea of heaven. On the left mostly pine trees stood but a few scattered oak and maples exploded with color while the sandy shore and ocean waves lapped on the right. The sun shone on the water making the ocean look like a blanket of shiny diamonds. Shelby couldn't think of anything other than the man trapped between her legs.

When Trent had asked her to ride with him, she had a moment of doubt. Her promise to Amy to avoid Trent for a while until she found out more about him made Shelby squirm. Or did Amy's inquiry have more to do with the plant where Trent worked? Either way, she promised. Well, technically she *had* waited a while. More than ten days. She hadn't heard from Amy. Amy always fulfilled her promises. With some guilt, she decided to call Amy tomorrow. Today she would enjoy every minute with Trent.

Trent reined in the Grim Reaper once they entered Calabash. He stopped in the parking lot of a restaurant, one that looked closed for years.

"Is this the one you remember?"

"Yeah, it's the one. Guess I'm a few years too late." Trent sounded so defeated Shelby had to do something.

"There's a note on the door. Let me run up and see what it says." Shelby hopped off the bike and realized her legs were stiff from staying in the same position for over an hour. It felt good to stretch.

When she returned, Shelby smiled as she said, "They moved a couple blocks down." She pointed in the direction they needed to go. "It may not be the same building, but the people who own it still have the restaurant." She climbed back on the bike.

Trent eased out of the lot and down the street to pull up at the new location. He removed his helmet and then ran his fingers through his hair. "I'm glad you stopped to read the note. I've been thinking about their she-crab soup. I don't remember having better."

Shelby laughed. "Well, they have to be pretty spectacular to compete with some from Myrtle Beach."

"Agreed. Let's see if I remember it correctly." Trent fished out Shelby's purse from the saddle bag and they both stopped at the restrooms before being seated for lunch.

Shelby couldn't believe the mess her hair looked after being smashed under the helmet. No wonder women who rode on bikes wore their hair in pony tails. It would be the only way to control your hair and not have a bad case of helmet-hair when you took off the helmet. She combed and fluffed it. It would have to do.

Perusing the menu, Shelby realized she was starving. "I think I'm starting with the clam chowder, then a flounder sandwich and sweet potato fries."

"Man, I haven't eaten those kind of fries in years. They are fantastic. I'm still going with the she-crab soup. I'll have the grouper basket, it comes with hushpuppies as well as the fries."

After placing their orders, they looked around the building.

"Is this anything like the old place?" Shelby asked.

The windows steamed due to the warmth inside versus the cold exterior. The clank of silverware on dishes along with the murmurs of people chatting gave a homey feel to the restaurant. Plastic tablecloths displayed a variety of colors that evoked sea life and beach goers. Shelby grinned when she recognized music by the Beach Boys her grandmother enjoyed hearing.

"Actually, it is. Looking at these old pictures, they must have been shot in the '50s and '60s with people fresh from offshore fishing alongside whatever they caught. I remember seeing these types of photos in the old place and the scenes with tourists at the beach."

"What makes you think they're tourists? They could be locals," Shelby suggested.

"Nah, look at what they're wearing. Bermuda shorts and Hawaiian shirts that haven't faded. See the shiny new stuff they brought with them like beach chairs with metal frames. Locals would have rusty and used items. It doesn't take long for a beach umbrella to fade and tear, not with the sea breezes around here."

"True. Now that you mention it, we have to replace umbrellas every couple of years at the resort. They start out a nice hunter green and by the second year they're the color of celery."

Their orders arrived. She watched Trent take a spoonful of soup. "So does it taste as good as you remember?"

"Heaven, it tastes like heaven." Trent closed his eyes and savored every bite.

Shelby watched his mouth as he took each spoonful. His tongue darted in and out to capture each errant morsel. Spellbound by his tongue, her soup grew cold as her face warmed along with the V between her thighs. Her hormones hummed with expectation.

"Hey, aren't you going to eat your soup?" Trent indicated Shelby's still full bowl.

"Of course," she murmured and took a mouthful to cover her embarrassment.

Recovering from her momentary fascination, Shelby chatted about unimportant things. Once finished with their meal, they wandered around the shops nearby the restaurant. They contained beach-themed items such as decorative bottles of sand, beach towels, swim suits, and tons of T-shirts.

"I hate to say it, but I'm getting tired. I need to head back home so I can catch a few Zs before my next shift," Trent admitted as a yawn escaped. "Sorry." He covered his mouth and then grinned, shaking his head as if to stay awake.

"I didn't realize you had to work again tonight. We could have done this another time when you had a day off."

Trent shrugged. "Our schedules are conflicting right now, so I don't think there is a good day for both of us."

"Then we better start back." Shelby turned and strolled toward the motorcycle.

The sun stayed out on the trip back and the vistas appeared as magnificent as the earlier ones. This would go down in her book as one of her favorite days of all time.

When they arrived at the resort, Shelby showed Trent where to park. "Why don't you come up to my place and I'll make you some coffee. It might help you stay awake. I'd give you a thermos, but I know you can't drink and ride a bike at the same time."

"Sounds like a great idea. I could use a cup after the big meal we ate."

They took the elevator up to her floor and went into Shelby's suite. She shrugged out of her jacket and dropped it on the bed, and then walked to the coffee pot and poured in the water. "This is one of those single serving type machines. Pick out which kind you want and it'll be ready in a jiffy."

"I need to buy one of these." Trent selected a K-cup. "I'm using Mom's old Mr. Coffee. It works, but this is much cooler." Trent looked over the machine as she fixed the brew.

"I love the options. And how quick it works." She finished his cup and made some hot chocolate for herself. They sat down together on the loveseat.

"Hmm, this is good. I hate I have to end our day so quickly."

"I understand. I haven't had so much fun on my day off in a long time. I enjoyed my first bike ride. Or maybe the driver made it better." Shelby shocked herself by saying her thoughts out loud.

Trent set his mug down and turned to look at Shelby. "I have to admit, I have never enjoyed an outing more. I know it had more to do with my passenger than the location."

He took Shelby's mug from her and set it down next to his. He placed a hand on each side of her face. His thumbs brushed away her hot chocolate mustache. He leaned forward and pressed his lips to hers. Initially a gentle pressure, his hands moved to her neck and the pressure of his lips increased. Shelby sighed and he took the moment to slip his tongue into her mouth. He tasted of coffee. Her hands wrapped around him and pulled him closer. She didn't know how long the kiss lasted, but it ended too soon.

Trent pulled away. "I'm sorry, Shelby. I didn't mean to kiss you." He stood and paced toward the door. Then turned and looked at her with an expression she didn't understand.

"I'm not sorry. We both enjoyed it." Making a small shrug, she indicated no big deal in spite of her real feelings.

"Exactly. I enjoyed it too much." Trent came back and sat down next to her. "I think we need to slow down."

"Slow down? We've hardly seen each other." Shelby couldn't help her instant reply.

"I care for you, Shelby. Maybe too much. I want to make sure this is real. Whatever it is. Not something we remember from our past." He took both of her hands in his.

Shelby let out the sigh she'd been holding. "You're right. I had a crush on you in high school. Maybe I'm playing out something I wanted back then. Not something we have now." Her face grew warm.

"You had a crush on me?" Trent's eyebrows almost disappeared into his hairline. "What a coincidence."

"What? You too?" Shelby knew her jaw dropped at Trent's admission.

"I wanted to ask you to the prom, but well, I couldn't afford it," Trent admitted as color formed on his cheeks.

"Oh, Trent." Her heart melted at his embarrassment. "You can't know what it means to me that you wanted to. I didn't know then what difficulties you had with your mom. I mean, later, when she um, passed away, I realized what you must have gone through." He loved his mother. It was apparent to anyone who ever saw them together.

"It's not something I like to think about. Let's change to a happy subject."

"Of course. So, when can we meet again?" What could be happier than future plans together?

"With our conflicting schedules, I have no idea. Why don't you write down your schedule and let me figure something out, and I'll call you." Trent stood up to go.

"Give me your number so I can reach you." Shelby picked up her phone to enter his digits.

"Uh, well, I work such crazy hours it might be better if I call you. OK? Include your number with the schedule. I left my phone in the saddlebag."

"Oh, sure. Yes, that will work. I'll wait until I hear from you." Shelby grabbed a paper and pen and then wrote down her number and schedule. She handed him the paper with a smirk. "Don't lose it."

Taking the piece of paper, Trent walked to the door, opened it, and then looked back with a smile. "Until later." The door closed with a whisper.

CHAPTER TWELVE

Amy would be furious she'd seen Trent. She called and when Amy didn't answer, Shelby left a message, glad for the reprieve.

Once her shift ended for the day, Shelby made a quick change of clothes when she returned to her suite and tidied up before adding water to the coffee brewer. She picked out her favorite blend, and had just pressed brew when she heard a knock on her door.

"What a great surprise, Amy. I expected a call not an in-person visit." Looking closer she felt a moment of apprehension at Amy's obvious distress and her furtive glance down the corridor before she stepped inside, shut the door, and then turned the deadbolt with a swift click.

"What's with the act of paranoia? Or do you plan to kill me?" Shelby meant it as a smart-aleck comment, but was taken aback at Amy's intense glare.

"This is nothing to joke about." Amy shook her finger at Shelby. "I could be in trouble, and I didn't want to bring it to you."

"Trouble? What kind of trouble could you be in?"

"I told you I wanted to look into Beau's plant. I'd heard rumors." Amy slipped out of her jacket, hat, and glasses, and then collapsed on the love seat. "Let me catch my breath, have a cup of coffee, and I'll explain what I know." Amy snapped her fingers and pulled out a white paper bag from her coat and handed it to Shelby. "I brought brownies. I hope they aren't crushed."

Shelby took the brownies and put them on a plate. They were actually big chunks and lots of crumbs. Deciding it would be easier to eat with a fork, she put out two paper plates, napkins, and forks. She fixed Amy's coffee, then sat down opposite her. "Spill it. You have my undivided attention."

Giving an appreciative sigh of contentment after a sip, Amy waited to talk until she'd taken a bite of brownie. "I've heard rumors. You know how small towns are."

"Right. And?"

"I'm beginning to think there is something else going on besides the manufacture of pesticides and fertilizers."

"What else do they say he makes?" Shelby frowned.

"Drugs." Amy spat the word out like a sour grape.

"Drugs? What kind of drugs?" Shelby felt her eyes grow wide while the cup she held stopped before it arrived at her mouth and then traveled back to her lap.

"The illegal kind." Amy said in staccato. "I don't know. Meth maybe." She shrugged in a helpless manner.

"No way. I mean, no way would Trent be mixed up with meth." Shelby set her cup on the table a bit too hard. The contents sloshed over the rim.

Amy placed her hand on Shelby's arm, and asked quietly, "Are you sure? You haven't seen him in ten years. He could have changed."

"No." Shelby ripped her arm away from Amy. "No, I won't believe it."

"I know there's more than one building. He might work in the one with the legitimate stuff. I've been trying to figure it out. How could they be doing both legal and illegal manufacturing? There's more than one building, that's how." Amy answered her own question. "Some of the people work in the legitimate one, some in the other."

"Now I understand why you looked so nervous when you arrived. You didn't want to tell me Trent might be involved. Have you told the police?"

"Since he's the first man you've been really interested in, I didn't want you to become hysterical. In answer to your question about contacting the police, no, not yet. I don't have any proof."

"It's what the police are supposed to figure out. Once you tell them about your suspicions." Shelby became more animated at the idea.

Amy pursed her lips. "Maybe in some circumstances. Not these."

"Why not? What's different?"

"Beau's family, the Jacksons, they make it different. You know they've been here for generations. And lots of people are loyal to them. How do I know if the police would believe me?" Amy asked.

"You have to try," Shelby insisted.

Amy shook her head. "I agree I need help. I can't figure out what agency to go to with this. You know the current chief of police is Beau's best friend's dad."

"Right. I'd forgotten." Amy's meaning became clear. "I see what you mean. Going with local law enforcement might be useless. Trent being involved doesn't make sense. He's only been back in town a few weeks. Would Beau trust him to be in on this business?"

Amy's frown deepened. "I've been wondering the same thing. Maybe he isn't right now," she admitted with a shrug. "You said he's a night security guard, right?"

Shelby stood up to walk around a bit. "Yeah. He says the only thing difficult about the work is staying awake."

Amy nodded her understanding. "This is why I needed to talk to someone else. None of it is making sense. The more I think about it, the more confused I get. What about the FBI?"

Shelby had her eyes closed and stood motionless. "What about them?"

"If I can't go to the local police, what if I contact the FBI?" Amy's frustration evident in her voice.

Shelby opened her eyes and sat down. "Good idea, but wouldn't the DEA be better?"

"Oh, you're right. Then maybe we should call them."

"I don't know, Amy." Shelby put her elbow on her knee and then her chin on her palm. "I'm not sure they would accept all this conjecture stuff. I have to agree it points that way, but only because of the people we know. As you mentioned, we don't have any proof, or at least some kind of solid evidence of drugs."

Amy threw her arms up in resignation. "I guess I need to keep digging."

"No." Shelby slapped her hand on the coffee table for emphasis. "This can be really dangerous. If you ask the wrong people the wrong thing, you could be in serious trouble." The idea of Amy putting herself in harm's way made Shelby mad. Mad at the people who dealt the drugs in her hometown. Mad at Beau for putting them in this position. Mad because Amy might be in danger trying to help.

"But now I know, I can't sit back and let it continue."

The pain on Amy's face made Shelby scared. Amy had always been the strong one. To see her in pain made things even more real to Shelby.

Shelby searched her face. "If something happens to you, I don't know what I'd do." Her voice sounded so small she wondered if Amy could hear. "Promise me you won't do anything until I have time to think about this." She could see her plea meant something to Amy.

"What do you have to think about?"

"Another way to find out more information. A way for you not to be hurt."

"So I'm supposed to let you end up hurt instead?"

"I haven't been the one stirring up trouble."

"I didn't stir up trouble."

"Maybe not, but you could have alerted someone. That's why you snuck in here tonight, right?"

"Okay, okay. I'll wait. Not more than one day."

"Good. I'll call by tomorrow evening. I'll think about what you said and maybe make some calls on my own."

Shelby's confidence surged when she thought of the perfect person.

"All right, all ready," Amy said. "Only one day. Then I'll start making calls unless you have something to share."

They each sat back, munching on the brownies and sipping coffee. Both absorbed with their own thoughts.

Eventually, Amy placed her cup on the table. "Now we've hashed it out, I need to head back to Georgetown."

"I never did tell you why I called." After everything Amy found out, Shelby hated to give her friend more unpleasant news. "Trent came by on Tuesday and I spent the day with him."

"What? You promised you'd wait."

"I know, I know. I didn't plan it. He showed up at my door without calling. After everything you told me tonight, I understand why you wanted to check him out. I'm sorry I upset you, but I had such a good time with him. It makes believing he's involved even more difficult."

"He might not be right now but he could. You need to be careful."

"I will. I'm so glad you shared everything you found out with me. We'll come up with something."

"We have to." Amy shrugged into her jacket as she stepped to the door. "Be careful what you say and who you ask."

Shelby stood at the door watching Amy's figure disappear down the hall, and then checked her watch. Ten o'clock. Too late to drive to Georgetown? This was too important to wait. She grabbed her jacket and rushed to her car.

She dialed her phone as she approached the house.

"What is it, honey? Is something wrong? You rarely call this late."

"Hi, Mom. I'm sorry to worry you, but I have some important questions for you. I'm pulling up to the house right now."

"You're here? Good heavens this sounds serious. Are you all right?"

As she pulled in the drive, her mother waited for her on the front porch. Shelby parked and rushed up the steps to give her a hug. Once they entered the house, they took seats in the cozy kitchen.

"I've been talking with Amy. She said there are rumors about a drug ring in Georgetown. Do you know anything about it?"

The look on her mother's face made Shelby more nervous.

Tina sighed and responded without looking at Shelby. "Yes, I have heard the rumors. Why are you asking? It doesn't concern us."

"Mother, drugs are everyone's concern. I can't believe you said that." Could this be the same woman who raised her? She never expected such a comment from her mother. She and her brother had been raised believing everyone should support the community to make it safe and beneficial to all.

"There have been rumors for years. Why the sudden interest?" Now her mother searched Shelby's face for something. Insight?

"Because someone I know might be involved. Or become involved. And I want to stop him if it's not too late." Could she manage not to tell her mother Trent's name?

"Someone? Who is this someone?" Her mother wouldn't make this easy.

Until now Shelby had successfully kept the knowledge of her involvement with Trent away from her mother. She knew how much her mother hoped she would someday have a normal relationship. Until she knew for certain a connection existed, she didn't want to introduce either of her parents to a boyfriend. Any boyfriend. At this point, she didn't know if she could qualify Trent as such.

She would try to use his name without labeling him a boyfriend. "Trent Meyers. You remember I told you he came to the reunion?" Shelby suspected the name would invoke sympathy due to his mother's untimely death. "I mentioned he decided to stay once he came back for the reunion. At least for a while."

Her mother's surprise appeared genuine. "How could he be involved with the drugs if he just arrived back in town?"

"Exactly. That's why I'm asking." Put out by her mother's non-answer she laid out her remaining cards. "I've heard Beau's plant is at the heart of the drug operation. Trent started working there a few weeks ago. So, are you going to answer my question?"

"Oh. Oh dear. Now Shelby. I've heard rumors, but I don't know anything for sure."

"Tell me what you've heard." Shelby recognized her mother's sidestepping comment and would have none of it. "It could be important."

"Yes." She sighed and then went on. "I've heard Beau's plant is where they make the drugs. A lot of the kids who graduated with you are said to be involved." Her mother's agitation made Shelby realize she disclosed the information reluctantly.

"Kids? We're not kids anymore, Mom. Is that why you didn't want to say anything? Because of me? Because some of the people involved are my friends?" Shelby had to make her talk.

"I knew you weren't involved." Her mother patted Shelby's hand. "I didn't want to say because of their mothers. Those *kids* have moms. Moms I've known for years. Don't you think it's tearing them apart?"

"Oh. I had no idea." Shelby finally understood her mother's hesitancy to respond. "I'm so sorry. Who do you know?"

"I promised I'd never say. And I wouldn't. Except, Trent must be important to you."

Shelby had no recourse, but to be honest. "Yes, he is, Mom."

"Are you, are you involved with him?" Her mother spoke in a whisper.

"No. Not right now. I'd like to be. Can you understand? I want a relationship and need to make sure he's okay."

"I think I can." After a lengthy pause, her mother continued. "All right, I'll tell you what I know."

Shelby's mother told her of the heartache her best friend had endured for years. The knowledge her son had a hand in making and selling drugs. Drugs that destroyed lives. She had few facts, but the one she did have confirmed Amy's suspicions. Beau and his plant occupied the heart of the operation. Without asking, she knew her mother would not repeat the information to any law enforcement. Besides, she didn't have any proof. Only the word of another mother.

Now what could she do? She could tell Amy without naming names. However, they still had no evidence to take to the authorities. And she didn't know if or how much Trent was involved.

CHAPTER THIRTEEN

Trent watched the monitor in the security office as Jamie limped from his car to the entrance of the building. He had no idea how this confrontation would end. He hadn't seen Jamie since the day of the football game. Would he be fired? Trent didn't think Beau would allow it unless his cover hadn't held. He guessed he'd find out in a matter of minutes.

Trent placed the Uzi and the MP5 within reach. Just in case. He met Jamie at the office door. "Hey man, good to see you walking about. You know I didn't have any idea about your bad knee." He knew better than to look ashamed. Wild animals attack the weak.

Jamie sat down in the visitor's chair. "I know. I know. Beau kept telling me. Thanks for the cigars. Of course, I couldn't smoke one until I left the hospital and rehab."

Was rehab for the leg or his drug addiction? No matter. "That sucks. So what brings you to the office at this hour, boss?" Trent figured his acknowledgement of Jamie's position would ease some of the tension.

"I've heard about the good work you've done. You pointed out some of the camera blind spots."

Trent propped his hip on the desk. "I don't know why someone hadn't figured it out before. We can't look at all the entrances to the other buildings. A few more cameras will fix it with no problem. I'd be happy to install them if you want."

Jamie waved his hand in dismissal. "That won't be necessary. I'll have some of the maintenance guys take care of it. Would you like to move off the night shift?"

"Hell, yeah, I would." Trent couldn't help the surprise that must have shown on his face.

"Fine then." Jamie frowned in spite of his positive words. "Finish out the week and you can start the day shift on Wednesday. You'll have Mondays and Tuesdays off."

Trent stuck out his hand to shake Jamie's. "Thanks, man. I figured I'd be on this shift for a year or so. No hard feelings?"

Jamie looked at Trent's hand, but didn't take it. "Beau insisted. If it'd been up to me you would have. Don't think I won't pay you back if I get the chance." Jamie glared at him.

Putting his hand in his pocket, Trent said, "Then I guess I'll need to keep on my toes." He'd need to be vigilant around Jamie. No telling what the man would do.

Jamie limped back to his car and drove to the other building.

The next hurdle would be for Beau to ask him to participate with the drugs. He didn't know what might be asked of him. Could be transportation or sales, probably not manufacturing. How they made the shit he had no idea. He'd perform whatever task requested in order to close down this operation. He didn't know how much or exactly what kind of drugs they manufactured, but he suspected a boat load. It would be a privilege to shut it down.

His mind drifted back to Shelby. Dull didn't begin to explain how working the night shift felt. It took a lot of effort to not think of Shelby. Not being able to spend much time with her was torture. Remembering the time they drove to Calabash on the Grim Reaper made him smile. With his new shift they would both have Tuesdays off. Shelby would be happy about it, too. He needed to check whether Beau's camera still recorded his movements. If it did, he couldn't allow Shelby to visit him. They'd have to meet somewhere or he'd go to her. He didn't need Beau to find out about their relationship. The DEA wouldn't be happy either. They warned him to not become involved while undercover. It would be a distraction.

When he left work, he called her from the Thomas Cafe. Most days he ate breakfast at the café in downtown Georgetown, which had stood there longer than he'd been alive. Luckily, they still had a pay phone. Using it would keep Beau's guys from knowing about the call.

"Shelby, I've great news. I'm going to be on the day shift by next week."

"Trent, how wonderful." Her voice didn't sound as excited as he'd hoped. "It's good to hear your voice."

"You might like to know I'll have Mondays and Tuesdays off, so we'll be able to see each other more often." He felt sure this would elicit an enthusiastic response.

"Great news." This time he heard more joy in her voice. "Did you have something in mind for this Tuesday?"

"As a matter of fact, I do. Now that the weather is getting cool, I plan to buy an old pickup." As much as he loved the Grim Reaper, when the weather turned cold he preferred an enclosed vehicle.

Shelby chuckled. "I can't say I blame you for wanting a warmer ride. Not to mention dryer."

"Exactly," Trent said with enthusiasm. "I can handle the cold, but not the wet combined with it. It's not as fun to ride in the cold rain as it is on a sunny day."

"I can only imagine." She hesitated a moment before she continued sarcastically, "So you're asking a girl if she wants to go shopping?"

"I didn't think you'd be able to turn me down. Remember, we're only shopping for a truck. No shoe stores." Trent enjoyed the easy banter between them.

"What? Wait a minute. How did you know I love shoe stores?"

Her mock surprise made him chuckle. "You're female, right? How about I pick you up at nine, we stop for breakfast, then check out the car lots."

"Perfect. I'll be ready." Trent could hear the smile in her voice even over the phone.

Trent needed a vehicle he could use in the event he had a requirement to tail someone. The Grim Reaper stood out too easily and the noise he made didn't allow stealth. It also allowed him an excuse to spend the day with Shelby.

CHAPTER FOURTEEN

Shelby called Amy with her update. "That's right, Mom confirmed your suspicions, but we still don't have any proof. The last thing I want is to have some cop question my mother."

"I understand. Besides anything she says is hearsay. I also came across more news. I heard there is a big drug shipment once a month. I'm not clear where they send the drugs, but it's by boat, not car or plane."

"Did they say when the next one is due to go out?"

"Usually on a night with no moon. That's Tuesday night." Amy shuffled paper in the background.

Shelby chewed her lip. "Should we call the DEA?"

"I'd like to confirm it first." Amy's voice grew firm. "Are you willing to go with me?"

"Go? Go where?" Shelby didn't like the sound of this.

"Where do you think?" Amy sounded put-out at her question. "We need to see for ourselves if it's true. Then we call the DEA as it's going down. They can't ask for more proof than eyewitness testimony."

"If Beau catches us, what do you think he'll do?"

"We won't be found out. One of the perks of being a member of my crazy family is hunting experience. I have a canoe, weapons, and night vision gear, and I know how to use them."

Shelby didn't know who Amy was trying to convince, herself or Shelby.

"That's hunting. Not spying."

"Same skills. Besides, you know I teach a self-defense class. You took it. As long as you wear dark clothes and keep your mouth shut they won't spot us."

Shelby continued to hesitate. "That was a few years ago. If we wait to notify the DEA until after we see them, won't it be too late for them to respond? I mean, I don't think they have a local office. There may not be anyone close enough to arrive before Beau and his guys are done."

"You do have a point. If they don't show and call the local cops it could be a problem if they're in on it." Amy paused. "Maybe we'll just observe then notify the DEA so they can be ready the next time."

Shelby gave a sigh of relief. "That sounds like a better plan. We can give eyewitness testimony."

"Right. As long as we know for sure what's in the shipment."

"You're saying we need to watch them move the drugs *and* open a container to make sure of the content? I don't know, Amy. It seems risky."

"Shelby, you know this is the only way. We need proof and this is our chance."

Shelby took a deep breath before replying. "You're right, Amy. If we don't do it, no one else will." She hoped they wouldn't regret their decision.

CHAPTER FIFTEEN

The days dragged by until Tuesday morning arrived cold and cloudy with spurts of misty rain. Great. What a day for car shopping. She didn't want to consider what the night would bring when she and Amy staked out the plant.

Promptly at nine o'clock a knock sounded at her door. She had her coat, gloves, and purse ready when she opened the door to a man she could only assume was Trent. Laughing at his appearance, she asked, "Do you want to leave some of your gear here and take my car?"

"Hell, yes." Trent's reply sounded a bit muffled as he unwound the scarf from around his head, peeled off his coat, a short jacket, and two sweaters. He put the coat back on. "Much better. I can walk with my arms at my side instead of stuck out like some kid in a snowsuit."

Shelby couldn't help it when a giggle escaped before her reply. "You did remind me a little of the kid in the movie *A Christmas Story*."

"Trust me, I needed the extra layers to stay warm. I appreciate the offer to take your car. Do I need some kind of pass to leave my bike in the staff parking area? It's safe, right?"

"I notified security. This time of year there is plenty of space. You parked in the covered area, didn't you?" At his nod, Shelby continued. "There are security cameras everywhere."

"Of course there are."

They exited the room and made their way to her car. Unlocking the doors to her Ford Fiesta, Shelby slipped into the driver's seat as Trent squeezed into the passenger seat. She noticed he moved the seat back all the way before squeezing in.

She put her seatbelt on and glanced at Trent while he did the same. "It looks like I don't have to worry about you asking to borrow my car." She couldn't help the grin that appeared on her lips.

"No offense, but now I understand how a sardine feels." Trent chuckled at his own joke.

"At least it will keep us dry during the search."

After breakfast they went to several dealerships, used car lots, and even checked out a couple online ads. At the end of each visit, Trent pulled out a tablet and entered statistics on a spreadsheet.

"I have enough information but I want to review it all before making a final decision." Trent perused the data. "How about we have some lunch while I look it all over?"

"It's about time you asked. I'm starved." Shelby drove to her favorite restaurant at Broadway at the Beach.

"No wonder, you only ordered milk and a piece of toast for breakfast," Trent teased.

"I plan ahead. I wanted to have a shrimp po' boy for lunch," Shelby replied.

"I have to admit it does sound good."

They walked along in companionable silence to the restaurant. After they sat down, they placed their order and then Trent pulled out his spreadsheet and made notes. "I've made a decision."

Before he could share his announcement, their lunch arrived.

"Hallelujah." Shelby bit into her sandwich.

As they ate Trent explained which truck he decided to buy and which location they'd need to return to.

Once finished, Shelby drove Trent back to the second dealership they'd visited, where he haggled the price for a Ford F150 extended cab pickup. Shelby knew nothing about pickups, but she liked the shade of blue.

"I'll meet you back at the resort." Trent climbed into the cab of his truck.

Now if he needed to tail anyone he'd have something unassuming. Besides, you never knew when you'd need to haul something.

CHAPTER SIXTEEN

"Now that you have the pickup, how do you plan to drive it and your bike back to your place?" Shelby asked as they strolled into the resort.

"I've been thinking how to accomplish it." Trent punched the button on the elevator. "Would there be a problem if I leave the Grim Reaper here in the employee lot for a few days?"

"I'll make sure it's not a problem," Shelby said as they stood in the elevator.

"Thanks. I'll have someone drive me over in the pickup and I'll drive the bike back to my house."

After they removed their coats and hats, Trent settled on the couch as Shelby walked to the coffee machine. "More coffee?"

"I think I've had enough today. What else do you have?" Trent looked over toward Shelby.

Searching through the K-cup selections, she said, "I have a variety of teas. Or would you rather have a gin and tonic? It's the only liquor I have on hand."

"Now that sounds like a winner." Trent smacked his hand on his leg. "I could go for a gin and tonic."

Shelby prepared it and handed him a glass.

Trent took a sip. "Ah, perfect."

Shelby took a sip from her own glass and sat down next to Trent. "Hmm. Yes, it is."

Trent draped an arm across Shelby's shoulders and pulled her close. "It's not the only thing that's perfect. He took a few more sips and then nuzzled her neck.

Shelby enjoyed the closeness and turned to give him better access. "When do you have to head back to Georgetown?" Her voice sounded husky to her own ears.

"Not for hours." He set his glass on the table and reached for hers, placing it next to his.

He gathered her in his arms and pressed his lips to hers. She opened her mouth to his probing tongue. He tasted of gin and his special flavor. A jolt of pleasure raced through her body, centering in the area between her legs. Shelby placed her hands on his chest and caressed him. Her fingers grazed his nipples, eliciting a moan of desire from Trent.

He ended the kiss and placed his hands on either side of her face as he allowed the distance to grow between them. Her hands stilled on his chest. The rapid beat of his heart pulsed against her palm.

"Shelby, in spite of the fact we met more than ten years ago we don't really *know* each other. Not the people we've become. I don't want to rush you into anything you'll regret."

He'd given her an out. "You're right, Trent. We've both become different people. And I like the one sitting next to me. A lot. I think we need to know each other better before going to the next step."

She saw the disappointment in his eyes for only a second. "Right. I think you're right." Trent gathered her close again and she closed her eyes.

Taking a deep breath, she drew in his scent. She moved her hands down his hard chest and around to his back, giving him a hug. They both sighed at the same time and leaned back.

"I think it's time for me to leave." Trent watched her with a turned down mouth and sad eyes.

"Yes, it's a good idea. Before you go, I wondered if you have Thanksgiving Day off from work? I know it's not your usual day off, but if you can I'd like you to have dinner with my family and me. My mother and yours were friends. Mom knows you're in town and will be upset if she thinks you're spending the holiday alone."

Trent's eyebrows rose and his eyes sparkled. "Thanksgiving? I hadn't even thought about it. I'll have to ask. Are you sure it's okay with your folks?"

"Naturally it is. They love to have people over for the holiday. It'll be a way to get to know each other. And my brother Mike and his girlfriend will be there. Do you remember him? He's a year younger than Jason."

"Sure, I remember him. He joined us for the reunion football game."

"He did? I didn't realize that."

"We needed an extra body. He'd been on the team when the other guys were seniors."

"True. Speaking of brothers, I know you don't want to contact yours, but if you change your mind, be sure to invite him too." She wanted so much for Trent to reconnect. Family was important. The only family he had was Jason. "Let me know what you find out about getting time off." Shelby stood up and retrieved Trent's coat.

"You're right. I don't want to talk about Jason." Trent paused before continuing. "What time do you usually have dinner? I have no idea how a holiday schedule works and I may only have a couple of hours."

Shelby knew better than to push the issue about Jason. "Normally we eat at two o'clock, but we can eat after your shift is over depending on when it is."

"I don't suppose you'll have blackberry pie?"

Laughing, Shelby swatted him. "I'll see what we can come up with. Not satisfied with the usual pumpkin?"

"I won't turn it down."

"Trent, I enjoyed the day." Her feelings grew and not from youthful fantasy, but current day experience. "I hope we have more like this one."

"So do I." He paused with a smile. "I better head out."

Trent gently took her face in his hands and gave her the sweetest, feather light kiss she'd ever experienced. Her heart melted and heat spread throughout her body. He looked in her eyes as if he searched for an answer. She hoped he found the right one.

Abruptly, he let her go and put his hand on the door knob. "I'll call," he said in a husky voice as he pulled the door open and exited in a flash.

Shelby stood for a few moments contemplating her reaction to Trent. More specifically the way she had not looked at him like so many other men. She didn't search his face wondering if he'd been the one. Even men she didn't know prior to the rape came under her scrutiny. Not Trent. Somehow she understood his inability to harm her or any other woman that way.

As she washed up the glasses Shelby daydreamed about what might be. Trent's observation about their initial attraction being their past acquaintance seemed correct. Now she felt a growing knowledge of this new Trent. And she liked her discoveries. No way could he be involved with the drugs from Beau's plant. Beau's plant! Oh, my God. She'd almost forgotten about her meeting with Amy. Taking a quick look at her watch, her momentary panic subsided.

Good thing Trent left when he did. She'd have time to eat a bite, change, and drive to Georgetown. Amy would be waiting for her at nine o'clock. They had no idea what time Beau and his men would make the transfer, but figured it wouldn't be until late at night. Amy wanted to find a spot where they could watch the warehouse and not be seen.

Shelby made herself a sandwich and ate while she looked over her clothes. She needed to wear black or some dark color. Picking out a black, long-sleeved turtleneck sweater and pair of plain dark jeans satisfied the requirement. Fortunately, her heavy coat and gloves were black. She rummaged around to find a navy knit cap she used to cover her hair. It would be cold out there so she pulled on two pairs of socks and located a second pair of gloves.

On the way to Georgetown, Shelby stopped at Walmart to pick up some hand warmers. Amy would need some, too, so she bought a dozen. The instructions said they would stay warm for ten hours or more. They shouldn't be out that long, but they would need some for their feet and hands and maybe their backsides. Good thing she had back pockets in her jeans.

"Are you as nervous as I am?" Shelby asked Amy when she stepped inside her house.

"Yes, I am," Amy admitted. After a pause, she continued. "I drove out to the warehouse yesterday."

Startled, Shelby stared at her for a moment. "What? I didn't think you wanted any contact."

"I needed to check out the road leading to the place," she explained. "It would have looked more suspicious if I'd turned around after I found a good spot so I went on to the warehouse."

"What excuse did you give to be there?" Shelby frowned hoping Amy hadn't given them away.

"Donations. I asked to see the manager. Thank goodness Beau wasn't there. I'm not sure I could have pulled it off talking to him. So I spoke to one of his men and asked if they would sponsor a church baseball team. Believe it or not, it is something we've talked about at the church."

"I'd have had a heart attack." Shelby sighed with relief. "No way could I have done that without giving myself away." She waved her hands in a slashing motion.

Amy shrugged her shoulders. "It wasn't easy. And he said he'd talk to Beau, but figured he'd agree to it."

"Hopefully, the ruse worked. Did you find a place where we can park and not be seen?"

"Yeah. I did. It's a straight shot once you're off the main road. We'll need to kill the lights before we turn. It's an open meadow for about a mile. I'm sure they'll have a lookout who would spot us in a second if we keep the lights on."

"We'll take my car," Shelby insisted. "Yours is white and will be too noticeable."

"I agree. Let's take out the bulbs or somehow turn off the dome light so it doesn't come on when we open the door." Amy had obviously been thinking ahead, too.

"Right. Anything else?" When Amy shook her head, Shelby took a deep breath. "Okay, here we go."

Shelby felt grateful for no street lights. With little traffic on the road, they drove past the corner on their first time by. After turning around, they waited until another car headed the same way. They followed and switched off their lights before making the turn onto the road they needed. Slowing to a crawl to make sure they stayed on the pavement, Amy pointed out the opening in the trees. Shelby backed into the cover of forest. Pulling out a dark blanket, she draped it over the front of the car.

"What's with the blanket?" Amy whispered as they closed the car doors with a click.

"If someone drives by, I don't want their lights to shine off the grill."

"Ah, I hadn't thought about that," Amy conceded.

"Trust me, the last thing I want to do is get caught. I hope we've considered everything."

Amy changed the subject. "We'll have to walk more than a mile through the woods to be close enough."

"These pen lights should keep us from bumping into a tree and not give away our presence." Shelby turned hers on, making sure to point it down.

"At least not to humans," Amy agreed.

"Thanks for the visual," Shelby grumbled. "Now I'll be jumping at every snap of a twig thinking a coyote is sneaking up on us."

Amy snickered. "They might be better than a skunk."

"Oh, lord. Don't start."

"Yeah, we need to keep quiet from now on." Amy's comment sobered them both.

The overgrowth and brambles made the trek unpleasant and noisy. At least, it sounded like a gunshot to Shelby every time one of them stepped on a branch. Each time it happened, they paused, waiting for a shout, but nothing happened. It took them more than an hour to arrive at a spot where they could watch the warehouses. At least two hundred yards of clearing stood between the woods and the warehouses. Settling down on a convenient log, they took turns looking through the night vision goggles. Shelby knew some of Amy's family members were survivalists. Knowing her skills would keep them safe and be able to procure the right equipment made this crazy idea not so crazy.

Neither of them remembered to bring a thermos, so all Shelby could think about was the Keurig back at her suite and how good a cup of coffee or hot chocolate would taste. After a couple of hours, she realized if they had brought something to drink, then the resulting need to relieve herself would have been even worse. Occasionally, they had to stand and flex their legs to keep the cold from stiffening their joints. Thank God she'd bought the hand warmers.

They only saw the night guard outside. He came in and out of the larger building, and walked around a couple of times each hour making sure no intruders skulked about. Fortunately, he never meandered into the woods. Cars sat in the parking lot of the other building, and they saw people through the windows, but couldn't make out what they did. With nothing else to do, they wrote down the license plate numbers of the cars they could see. About four in the morning, Amy nudged Shelby and indicated they should return to the car. Shelby agreed and they did their best to retrace their route. They overshot the car by at least a hundred yards and had to make their way back.

Once settled in the car, Amy spoke first. "What a waste of time. Good thing we didn't call the DEA. They would never have believed a thing we said."

"You're right. Now what do we do?"

"I have no idea. Let's go to my place and talk about it."

Each lost in their own thoughts, they remained silent until they collapsed on the couch in Amy's house.

"I'm not sure I can feel my nose. I think it's frozen," Amy said in a muffled voice since her gloved hand covered the lower half of her face.

"I knew that darn heater in the car was on the blink. All I want is something to drink. What do you have?" Shelby sat on the couch with her coat and gloves still on.

"I can make coffee, but I don't want it to keep us awake."

"No decaf?"

"Nope." Amy pulled off her boots and slipped on some fuzzy house shoes, and then padded to the kitchen. "Aside from water, I don't have much to offer. Oh, wait a minute. Here's some herbal tea."

"Perfect." Shelby purred with approval.

While waiting for the tea to brew, they both removed their coats and gloves. However, once ready, they clutched the mugs for the extra heat and sat on the couch with their feet beneath them.

"I can't believe we dealt with all that and have nothing more to give the DEA."

"So where do we go from here?" Shelby took another sip of tea.

"Doing this every night until we hit on the right one is nonproductive."

Amy said what Shelby had been thinking. "I concur. Being cold, wet, and miserable isn't how I want to spend my nights. I don't know how police on a stakeout do it. Somehow we need to find out when the next shipment is scheduled."

"There are still a few more people I haven't asked," Amy insisted.

"No, I don't want you poking around asking more questions." Shelby felt responsible for Amy since she only pursued the information for her. "Someone could become suspicious and it could end wrong. I'll do the asking. The only one I've talked to is my mom and she won't say anything. I have to figure out who to ask." Her brow knitted as she concentrated.

"There is someone," Amy commented in almost a whisper. "It could be a big risk."

Shelby looked over at Amy. "Who?"

"Missy Strong." Amy looked at Shelby then glanced quickly away.

"Jamie's wife?" Shelby asked, a bit puzzled.

Amy raised both brows. "And Beau's girlfriend."

"Hmm. I noticed them being a bit more than *friends* at the reunion." Shelby considered what she'd witnessed for a few minutes. "You're right, it would be a big risk. What makes you think she'd talk?"

Amy shrugged. "She looks and sounds unhappy." Looking down at her mug, she continued. "Maybe it only takes someone to show her a way out of her situation."

"I don't plan to ask how you know that. Right now I'm too tired to think straight." Shelby remained silent for a while before continuing. "I think we both need some sleep."

"Thank goodness my first appointment isn't until ten o'clock." Amy stood up and then took Shelby's mug as well as her own to the kitchen.

"Sorry we had to do this when you have to work tomorrow. Or should I say later today." Having stayed overnight with Amy previously she knew where the extra blankets and other linens were located to make up the couch. She set about fixing her bed for few hours sleep.

"Write me a note if you make a decision before you head back home," Amy insisted. "Otherwise call or text me."

"Right." Now she had to determine a way to approach Missy. What would the consequences be if Missy reported her conversation to Beau or Jamie? Drug dealers killed informants.

CHAPTER SEVENTEEN

On Monday Trent went to the local hardware store for supplies to add on to the carport. When he'd parked his truck he realized the Grim Reaper would have to be covered with a tarp until he expanded it. With limited daylight this time of year, he'd need to use his days off to work on it.

As he gathered items at the store, he once again wondered if it would be a good idea to go to Shelby's parents' house for Thanksgiving. He wanted to. It had been a long time since he sat at a family dinner. Images popped into his head of past holiday dinners with his family. It made him smile remembering the laughter and comradery. Then reality crept up on him. What if word got back to Beau? That required some serious consideration. He could always tell Shelby he had to work. His appearance might put not only Shelby in danger, but her whole family. He'd never let that happen.

Beau had started trusting him. First, the camera disappeared, then the change in his work hours. He hoped the next step would involve actual contact with the drugs. There would be a test of some kind. For his loyalty. Beau hadn't evaded capture for this long without making sure his men stood by him.

After he offloaded his haul, he figured he better retrieve his bike before he started. He went to Mr. Harper's house and knocked on the door. "'Afternoon, sir, would you do me a favor?"

"Did you finally decide to hunt a deer this season?" The hope in his voice touched Trent.

Although he hadn't given it a second thought, he said, "Yes sir, if your offer is still good."

"Of course it is, boy. Come on in and let's talk about it." The old man settled into his chair and pointed to the couch for Trent to sit.

"I'm off work next Monday, will that work for you?" Trent wanted to settle this before approaching him for the real reason of his visit.

"Monday'll be fine. Don't suppose you'd share some of the meat with me if'n you bag one?" The hope in his cloudy eyes shown through.

Now Trent realized the reason Mr. Harper had asked. He had cataracts and couldn't see well enough to shoot one himself, but he wanted the venison.

"I'm glad you asked. I don't think my old freezer would hold it all. It would be a help to me if you took some. Do you like venison steaks or sausage or both?"

"Whatever you're willing to share. Let me take you out to one of my old tree stands." The old gentleman stood up and shrugged into a coat. "Don't know if it's fallen down or still there. Great location. It never failed me."

He led the way with Trent keeping an eye on him in case he tripped on the overgrowth.

"This looks like a fine spot all right." Trent climbed up the tree while making note of some things he would need to correct before the shooting trip. "Yep, looks like the stand is still intact. This'll be terrific."

"Good, good. Now you know the way, I'll make sure the people in the area know when you'll be here and tell them to stay clear. Don't want any accidents."

"Agreed. That would be unpleasant for everyone."

After they returned to his house, Mr. Harper's breathing became wheezing gasps. "Can I get you anything? A glass of water?"

"Just need to set a minute. That's all. Not used to traipsin' around the woods anymore."

In spite of his cataracts, Trent figured he could still see well enough to drive the pickup. Not much traffic this time of year, plenty of daylight, and the old guy knew the area, so he should be fine. "I have another favor to ask, if you're up to it."

The smile on the old man's face showed his elation at being asked for help. "Course I am. Course I am. What can I do?"

"You might have noticed I bought a new pickup truck," Trent said.

"I saw it when you drove up. Nice vehicle." He gave Trent a puzzled look. "Thought you had a motorcycle."

"Yes, sir, I do. That's why I need a favor. I bought the truck in Myrtle Beach and couldn't drive both of 'em. I hoped you'd take a ride into Myrtle Beach with me so I can return with my bike and you drive the pickup back here."

"No problem at all." Mr. Harper smiled as if Trent had told him he planned to give him a million bucks. "When did you want to go?"

"If you aren't too busy could we go now?"

Mr. Harper stood up and shrugged back into his coat. "Now's as good a time as any." He waved Trent to the front door. "Let's go."

Chuckling to himself, Trent made his way out to the pickup and climbed in. "Thanks, Mr. Harper. I appreciate you taking the time."

"What are neighbors for?" His excitement was palpable just to have company and do something useful.

They chatted about football all the way to Myrtle Beach. As they pulled into the resort where Shelby worked, Mr. Harper squinted his eyes to read the sign. "This here the place the Cornwell girl works?"

Surprised Mr. Harper would know, he replied, "Sure is. She let me park the bike here out of the weather until I could come back for it."

"Her folks go to my church. They said something a while back when she started. She's a good girl. Too bad about the trouble she had some years back." Mr. Harper frowned as if remembering an unpleasant memory. He paused. "Course she seems fine now. Glad you two are gettin' along."

Trent had no idea about any trouble. What had happened to Shelby? Shaking his head, he gave Mr. Harper the keys and watched as he climbed into the truck. "Do you want to follow me out or do you know the way?"

"Hell, boy, I'm not senile. I been makin' this drive longer than you've been alive."

Trent tried his best not to laugh. "Sorry. I know you have, sir. Leave it at your place and I'll walk over to pick it up when I make it home. I'm going to drop in and see Shelby to let her know I've stopped by for it."

Mr. Harper waved and took off without a backward glance.

Trent walked to the front desk and asked for Shelby.

Coming from the office in the back, her smile looked like sunshine. "I didn't expect to see you today."

"Mr. Harper agreed to come with me so I could pick up the bike. Do you have time for a cup of coffee or are you busy."

"I can't leave the area but we can talk a few minutes," she replied. "How's the day shift going?"

"The job?" At her nod he continued. "Not as boring as the night shift. Can't complain. I also wanted to let you know I'm accepting your offer to come for Thanksgiving dinner. I'll bring some wine."

He didn't think Shelby's smile could grow any wider or brighter, but he was wrong. She almost exploded with her reply. "Great. I'm so happy. Is two o'clock a good time?"

"Yes. Beau rearranges holiday schedules so everyone is allowed a three-hour break. I have one to four. So it works out perfect." Trent knew his grin mirrored hers. He hadn't meant to agree. If Beau found out it wouldn't be good, but how could he disappoint her? Or himself?

"I guess I better let you go back to work. There's work waiting for me at the house."

"Time for some cleaning?"

Trent liked to think she made the comment because she didn't want him to go yet.

"More than that. I'm expanding the carport. It's too small for both vehicles."

They said goodbye and Trent walked back to the Grim Reaper smiling. Talk of Thanksgiving brought happy memories to mind with his mother and brother. She insisted both her sons remember good times when they thought of her or their father. No negativity. That had been her mantra. His mom would have loved Shelby. The cryptic remark Mr. Harper said about Shelby's trouble came to mind. Next time he saw Mr. Harper he'd ask for more details.

Thinking of Shelby reminded him of the intimate moments they'd shared last week. In the back of his mind, he knew if he had a taste of her he wouldn't be satisfied until she surrendered completely. He also understood Shelby wasn't ready. Something in her eyes told him. And he wanted her to want him as he stood now, not the boy he'd been ten years ago. He needed to remind himself now and again why they had to slow down.

A few days later Mr. Harper joined Trent for dinner. "Well, boy, I have to admit you make a good pork chop." Mr. Harper praised Trent as he polished off the last bite. "I remember your Mama as a right fine cook. Must'a learned from her."

"Yes, sir. Can't say I can do anything fancy like those chefs on TV, but I can manage some basic meals."

Mr. Harper wiped his mouth on the paper napkin. "Got to, when you're a bachelor, or you'll spend all your money eatin' out."

"Some of the places I've lived didn't have the luxury of restaurants and I don't like ham sandwiches every day." Trent cleared the table.

Mr. Harper pushed his chair back and took some of the dishes to the kitchen sink. "I'd like to repay your hospitality. My daughter's coming here for Thanksgiving and going to make a big meal. Why don't you join us?"

"That is kind of you, sir, but I've already made plans." Trent smiled, thinking about the upcoming holiday.

Mr. Harper's eyebrows shot up. "I bet you'll be havin' dinner with the Cornwell girl and her family."

"I will. I've asked her to make me a blackberry pie." He turned and looked at the old man. "Do you think she can find some blackberries this time of year?"

"Now days you can buy most stuff any time of year." He waved his hand in dismissal. "And there's always frozen berries. Me, I like pecan pie. Hmm-um. I can taste it right now." The old man sat down on the couch.

"I wouldn't turn it down if it's all they've got," Trent agreed.

Trent finished up in the kitchen. "You mentioned last time we talked about Shelby that she'd had some trouble a few years ago. What did you mean?" He watched for Mr. Harper's reaction.

"It's not for me to say. You'll need to ask her." He shot Trent a cautious look and mumbled something he didn't hear.

"Not drugs or alcohol or something like that?" Trent hated to push the old man, but he'd been worried Shelby had somehow been caught up in the drugs Beau created.

"Nah, nothin' like that. No, it was, well, not somethin' civilized people talk about. Now I'm not saying any more on the matter."

Shortly after his statement, he said goodbye and strode back to his place with a flashlight strong enough to light up half the front yard.

Trent considered his comment saying civilized people didn't talk about it. Had she been in an abusive relationship? It made him want to throttle the guy without even knowing him. Mr. Harper had it right. He'd have to ask Shelby. Decision made, he sat down to watch football and erase the images from his mind before going to bed.

The night before the scheduled hunt Trent felt some excitement for the upcoming event. Last week he'd bought his hunting license. He'd dug out some hunting gear from the closet in his old bedroom. The pants stopped a couple of inches short, but it didn't matter since he wore wool socks that came almost to his knees and old army boots. The jacket had been his Dad's, big enough to wear a sweatshirt and flannel shirt beneath it. A ski mask, orange hat, gloves, and his rifle completed the get-up. He had a pack with the other items he'd need like a tarp and knife. Setting the alarm for four in the morning he hit the sack early. After the alarm sounded, he padded to the kitchen to make coffee he'd put in a thermos. In no time at all, he stood ready for action.

The hunt took several hours, but he did manage to bring down a buck. Returning to his truck with one hundred pounds of meat slung across his shoulders turned out to be the most difficult part.

Trent went in the house to clean up before taking the deer to a processing house. There would be plenty of meat for Mr. Harper, himself, and Shelby's family. He had decided earlier if he managed to shoot a deer he'd share it with her family at Thanksgiving. It would take too long for one person to consume such a large amount of meat.

As he drove his buck toward town, his mind turned toward Thanksgiving and visions of Shelby. He tried not to think of her all the time, but it became more difficult the longer he knew her. He'd started to dream of the future. One with Shelby in it and one without her. The one without her held no joy. No happiness. After his mother died, he never considered being happy again. Then time went by and he'd grown satisfied with his life. He'd had moments of happiness, like the day he watched his brother, Jason, receive his degree from the University of South Carolina, and the day he'd been accepted into the Charleston Police Academy. Then he'd reconnected with Shelby. That's when he knew true happiness.

He spent the rest of his time off completing the carport expansion. He had no idea how long this undercover assignment would last but he'd have cover for his vehicles. If he and Jason agreed to sell the place, the addition would increase the value a little.

A few days later Trent picked up the venison. There were steaks, sausage, roasts, and ground patties. He borrowed a couple of coolers from Mr. Harper to add to the one he had. Once loaded he drove straight to Mr. Harper's house. The moment he pulled in the driveway Mr. Harper walked out the front door. He had a smile from ear to ear.

"Howdy, boy. I can't wait to eat some of the venison." Mr. Harper rubbed his hands together. "I been thinking about making a pot of stew since you called. Let me give you a hand with it." Mr. Harper had the tailgate of the truck down before Trent shut off the engine.

Trent chuckled at his enthusiasm. "Hang on a minute. Don't hurt your back trying to lift the cooler by yourself."

"Look at that. You must a bagged a monster if all those coolers are full."

"Pretty close to it. I hope you have lots of room in your freezer."

"Hell, about all I have in there are some frozen dinners."

"Well, let's see how much we can put in it." Trent lifted one of the coolers to the ground and used the built-in wheels to roll it into the house. After Trent filled the freezer about half full, he said, "There. It should be enough for the winter."

Mr. Harper watched in awe while Trent placed pack after pack in his small freezer. "I didn't expect you to share all this with me. I don't know if I can take this without giving you some money."

Trent made slashing motions with his hand. "I won't hear of it. I'm happy you let me hunt on your property. Some people make a lot of money for leasing their land." He knew he had to point that out so Mr. Harper wouldn't feel obligated.

Mr. Harper nodded. "Well, now, that is true, but then what are neighbors for?"

"Exactly. I'm sharing the same as you." They shook hands. "I need to put the rest of this in the freezer. Make sure your daughter fixes the roast for you."

"She will. I know she will. Thanks and see you later." Mr. Harper waved as Trent backed out of the drive.

Trent thought of the times his mother cooked venison for their family. Since he'd been back in Georgetown memories kept flooding his mind. He tried to hold on to the good ones and let go of the sad ones. He liked the idea of making new memories with Shelby. Concentrating on that thought he drove back home.

CHAPTER EIGHTEEN

"I'm so glad you invited Trent and Amy to join us today." Her mom placed the celery and onions they'd chopped the day before in a skillet. "I don't remember if I told you Mike invited two of his friends as well as Joyce. We'll have a total of nine today. I love having my chicks and their friends all gathered for Thanksgiving."

Shelby laughed. "Yes, Mom, you've mentioned it at least a dozen times in the past week." She prepared the ham and slid it into the oven. "It's a good thing we have extra people. With all this food, they better be prepared to take some of it home."

Tina waved her hand holding a spatula. "That's part of the fun of Thanksgiving, all the leftovers. I stocked up on some plastic containers so everyone can take some home."

"Then we should be having the best Thanksgiving ever."

"What is your father doing out there?" Tina craned her neck to look onto the screened porch where Greg should have been.

Shelby shrugged as she worked on the deviled eggs. "I think he's in the garage cleaning off the folding chairs."

Tina frowned. "We have plenty of chairs for the dining room table, so we won't need folding chairs."

"He said the men would sit outside on the porch to watch football after dinner." Shelby's dad didn't need much of an excuse to show off his outdoor man cave complete with a fifty-inch television mounted to the house exterior.

"Oh, well, I doubt they'll be out there long. Once the sun sets it becomes a little too chilly."

Shelby reveled at being in her parents' home. The kitchen needed an update, the appliances were white and well used, but their looks didn't matter as long as they worked. She enjoyed the smell of onions sautéing in the skillet. The aromas, along with the slam of the screened door as people came and went, all evoked the feeling of family and happiness.

Placing each finished egg on the dish designed specifically for them, Shelby sprinkled some paprika on top of each yellow center. "I guess they'll come in and take over the living room."

"They usually do, they usually do."

Amy arrived about twelve.

"Come in here and give me a hug." Shelby's dad gathered Amy in his arms for a big squeeze while Shelby rescued the sweet potato casserole she carried. "Let me have your coat and I'll hang it in the hall closet." Shelby's dad helped Amy divest herself of the garment.

Tina fluttered in to give Amy a quick hug. "Hello, dear, have a seat. Thank you for bringing the casserole. Shelby, put it in the warming oven."

"Of course, Mom. Why don't you have a seat and take a break. I can finish up in the kitchen."

"I will in a minute. Chat with Amy for a while, then we'll switch places."

Amy sat on the well-worn flowered couch and picked up a piece of stuffed celery sitting on a decorative plate among other crudités set on the coffee table. "How much food do you expect us to eat before dinner?" She perused the other snacks occupying every flat surface in the living room. The coffee table didn't have an inch of space left.

"You know mother, she has to prepare enough food for an army. I hope you plan to take your share home. It will be an insult if you don't." Shelby sat across from Amy in one of the two recliners, both well-worn with arm covers hiding the recently developed small holes. Maybe she'd surprise her parents for Christmas by arranging for the chairs to be recovered.

"I'm well versed in the requirements of a guest to a southern mama's dinner. I can't say I'm unhappy about it. I only had to make one dish and then have enough leftovers for the rest of the week."

"Don't be so cocky. Your casserole should feed more than twenty and we only have nine arriving for dinner."

"Exactly. It's that leftover thing."

Shelby's brother, Mike, and his girlfriend, Joyce, arrived next. They'd brought a cooler full of ice, another full of beer, and two pecan pies.

"Hey, we need some help out here." Mike's shouted request drifted inside as he unloaded the car.

Shelby helped with the pies and her dad carted one of the coolers to the porch.

Tina hugged the new arrivals. "Joyce, dear, we're so glad you joined us. How's your family?"

"They're doing great. We'll have to leave by five-thirty so we can go to their house for dessert."

"Oh, my, you aren't going to taste your own pecan pie?"

"I made two more to take to their house. You know Mike. He wouldn't let me bring one here and not eat any."

Tina chuckled. "That's sounds like Mike all right."

At that moment, the final three men arrived. Mike's friends arrived in one truck, and Trent pulled in behind them in his. Shelby had been so busy she hadn't had time to be nervous. All of a sudden, she felt overwhelmed with anxiety. Would her parents and brother like the man Trent had become? Why wouldn't they? He was a good man.

Shelby walked out the door to greet him. "Trent, you're just in time. Thank you for coming."

"You told me to bring wine, but I went hunting a few days ago so I brought a venison roast and some steaks, too. Maybe your family will enjoy them another day."

"How thoughtful." Shelby turned to find her mother right behind her. "Mother, did you hear? Trent brought us some venison."

"Yes, sweetheart, I did. And thank you, Trent. That is very considerate."

After Trent turned over the meat to Shelby, he reached back in his pickup and pulled out the bouquet of flowers. "You might enjoy these too, ma'am."

"How sweet. These will look wonderful on the dining room table." Tina glanced over her shoulder. "You need to call me Mom or Tina. All of Shelby and Mike's friends call me Mom."

Trent and Shelby followed her into the house. "Mama would turn over in her grave if I called you Tina. How about I call you Ms. Tina?"

Tina laid the flowers on the table and turned to Trent, giving him a pat on the cheek. "That will be delightful. I knew your mama taught you right."

Tina took down a vase and Trent and Shelby walked to the living room to greet the other people. Before they made it into the room, Shelby teased in a whisper, "Suck up."

"I know how important a Southern mama is to the family. If she's on my side, I'm home free," Trent whispered back with a mischievous grin on his face. He grabbed Shelby's hand and kissed it.

Shelby stuck out her tongue at him before putting on a serious face as they faced the crowd in the living room. "I think you know most everyone, but it's been a while." Shelby introduced Trent to the group, and the men shook hands. To her surprise, Mike held Trent's hand a moment longer than needed, and stared at him a few seconds with a frown on his face. She shot Mike a questioning look he ignored.

Shelby's mother entered the room. "I think we're ready. Let's move to the dining room. Greg, you can pour the wine. Mike, find out if people want water, sweet tea, or something else in addition to the wine."

They all assembled in the dining room and sorted out their drinks.

Greg said, "Amy, would you do us the honor of saying the blessing?"

The scrumptious meal took about an hour to consume. Leaving at least half the food on the table, they groaned as they stood up. "Men, I have a television set up on the porch to watch football. Let's help clear the table and adjourn there."

"Ms. Tina, I can't remember the last time I had a meal like that. Must have been the last time my mother put one together. Thank you for inviting me." Trent took a couple of the casserole dishes to the kitchen.

"It's my pleasure. I have fond memories of your mother. So tragic she died so young." Tina dabbed her eyes with a napkin. "We're so glad you joined us. Don't forget to take your share of the leftovers before you leave."

"Thank you, Ms. Tina. I'll be happy to." He hesitated a moment. "I don't suppose I can wrangle a piece of pie to go with the leftovers?"

Tina chuckled a bit. "Of course, you can. Shelby insisted she make a blackberry pie special for you. I'm guessing it's the kind you want."

The huge smile on his face made Shelby glad she prepared it. "Yes, ma'am! Thank you."

CHAPTER NINETEEN

"The Panthers are playing the Cowboys. They're still in the first quarter," Greg said as they settled in for the game.

"Hey, man, we need to talk," Mike whispered, then punched Trent on the arm and motioned to a spot near Trent's truck.

Trent followed him. "What'cha want?"

"I'm telling you I don't like the fact you're seeing my sister." Mike fisted both hands and held them stiff at his side.

Trent hadn't expected a confrontation. "Why is that?" He used the least offensive tone he could muster.

Mike replied in almost a growl. "I know where you work and I know what they make there."

Uh-oh. Trent hadn't counted on this. He'd need to play dumb. He adopted a puzzled look. "They make pesticides and fertilizers. What's wrong with that?"

"You can't be that dumb," Mike said as he continued to glare. "You know what I'm talking about. The stuff they make in the other building."

Trent shrugged his shoulders. "I have no idea what you're talking about. I understand the other building is for research and development. I've never been in there. What do you think they make there?" If he didn't ask, Mike would be even more suspicious.

Mike's voice calmed a bit. "Maybe you don't know." He stared hard at Trent. "You haven't been back in town long. Maybe Beau hasn't pulled you in yet. If that's the case, then the best thing you can do is quit. Find a job somewhere else."

Trent drew his eyebrows together before he replied. "Since they shut down the steel mill recently, it's easier said than done. I'm grateful to have a job and I don't intend to lose it."

"Then you need to stop seeing Shelby." Mike raised his right hand in a threatening manner. "She's had enough problems in her life. The last thing she needs is to hook up with some loser working at *that* plant."

Trent stood his ground and responded through gritted teeth. "Seeing each other is between Shelby and me. You don't have a say. And what do you mean, she's had enough problems?"

Mike paled at the question. "Never mind. If I hear you've upset her or she's become involved in the shit going on there, then you'll have to answer to me."

Trent tried to smooth things over. "I'm glad you have your sister's best interest at heart. The last thing I plan to do is upset her." He kept up the ruse that he knew nothing about the drugs. "I still don't know what you're talking about, but I can assure you I won't involve her in anything that could hurt her." Trent hoped he said the truth.

Mike glared at Trent before heading back to the football game as Tina walked into the yard. "Trent, there you are. I know it's about time you have to leave so I packed up your leftovers. And the pie." She handed them over. "Put them in your truck so you don't forget them."

Trent turned his back on the men and then smiled at Tina. "Thank you, Ms. Tina." He took the containers from her and strode to his truck, placing the items on the passenger floorboard.

"Don't you leave without saying goodbye." Shelby hurried to his side by his truck.

"I wouldn't dream of it. Wanted to ensure the safety of my meals for the next week." He laughed as he pointed to the stack of containers. "How much food does your mom think I'm going to eat?"

Trent grabbed Shelby's hand and they walked back into the house. "I need to head back to work, but I wanted to say goodbye and thank you again for the fantastic dinner. Not to mention all the leftovers. I promise I won't let them go to waste."

"Thank you for the venison. We'll enjoy that soon. I'm glad you joined us. Next time you'll have to bring your brother. We'd like to see him, too." Tina gave Trent a hug and a peck on the cheek.

Trent paused a moment before he replied. "I'll see what I can do." It would be nice, but there were too many other things going on to consider his brother right now.

As Trent and Shelby walked outside, Shelby whispered, "Sorry. I hope you aren't upset with Mom. I haven't said anything about your brother."

"It's okay. Maybe next year we'll have things sorted out." Trent smiled, squeezed her hand, and then gave her a peck on the cheek.

Once they stood next to the men watching football, Trent waited until a play finished before interrupting. He placed an arm on Greg's shoulder to gain his attention. "Thank you for having me for Thanksgiving."

Greg stood up and shook his hand. "Glad you could make it. Come back again. And if you want to bring more venison we'll be happy to take it."

Shelby sputtered at her father's lame joke. "Daaadddy."

Greg waved a hand at his daughter. "Don't get huffy, sweetheart, Trent knows I'm teasing."

Trent grinned at the byplay. "Yes, sir, I'll keep it in mind."

Shelby tugged on Trent's hand and they walked to his truck. "Thanks for coming."

"Thanks for inviting me. I can't remember when I've had a meal like that. And all these leftovers. Goodness, I'll be spoiled." He opened the truck door. It screened most of their bodies from the others. He gathered Shelby into his arms.

"I know you have to head back to work so I won't hold you up." Shelby looked directly into his eyes with what looked like yearning.

Trent bent down and pressed his lips to hers. He slipped his tongue into her mouth. His hands moved to right below her breasts and his thumbs grazed across her nipples. The quick response of his staff made him stop. Now would not be a good time. He disengaged his tongue and mouth from hers with reluctance. He placed his forehead against hers. "I don't suppose you have Saturday or Sunday night off, do you?"

"I'm happy to say my shift ends at six on Sunday," Shelby said, a bit breathless. "Did you have something in mind?"

"A real date would be nice." Trent pulled away to see her eyes.

Shelby's nose crinkled when she smiled. "As opposed to what other kind of date?"

Trent grinned. "It's occurred to me we haven't really been on a regular date. Like dinner and a movie."

"The time we went to Calabash didn't count as a date?" Shelby's eyes grew big.

Trent shook his head. "Not a regular one. So how about it? Can I pick you up at seven?"

"Yes, you can." Shelby stepped back. "You better leave or you'll be late."

The fact she still had her hands in his told him she felt as reluctant as he. "You're right. Thanks again, Shelby." This time he gave her a light kiss before climbing into the cab of his truck. He waved as he backed out of the drive and took off down the street.

He thought about the confrontation with Mike. He knew Mike didn't work at the plant. He'd checked. Was he one of the distributors? That would explain his knowledge. If the take-down included Mike, Shelby might hate him when Mike ended up in jail. There had to be a way to keep

Mike out of trouble. Perhaps he could turn State's evidence against the others.

Trent stopped by his house and dropped off most the leftover containers. Once at work he put the slice of pie in the break room refrigerator. He put a post-it-note with his name on it to ensure no one would abscond with it before he had a chance to eat it.

With the plant closed and only the security and maintenance people working, he had plenty of time to reflect on the day. The comment Mike and Mr. Harper made about Shelby and the trouble she'd had a few years ago concerned him. His initial determination had been an abusive relationship since Mr. Harper assured him it didn't have to do with drugs. If it had been abuse it would explain Mike's behavior, but what about Greg? Wouldn't he have reacted in a similar manner? Maybe she had a baby. If so, what happened to the child? She didn't strike him as the type to give the child up for adoption. He needed to ask her on Saturday. His plan made, he went back to work.

The next day the plant opened, but only a skeleton crew worked. Most took the extra day off. Trent didn't normally see Beau inside the building, but he noticed him walking to each station in the plant. He usually spotted his car in the lot by the other building, where he spent most of his time. Per his assignment, he recorded Beau's schedule, which seemed pretty random.

Beau walked up to Trent and motioned him to follow. He led the way to the break room. They took off their masks to talk. "Glad to see you settling into the routine."

"Yes, I am. I'm grateful to you for the job and switching me to the day shift." The best way to stay on

Beau's good side was to make everything about him and his generosity.

"Glad to have someone with your experience working here."

Trent nodded and waited for Beau to continue. Uneasy and excited, something important seemed imminent.

Beau grinned with what Trent described as his evil grin. "I hear you had Thanksgiving with Shelby and her family."

Trent never dreamed he'd hear Beau say that. How had he found out? He managed to reply without changing expression. "Yeah, great food. I missed home cooking, especially southern cooking, while I served in the army."

"You seem to be pretty cozy with Shelby these days." Beau's eyes gleamed with speculation.

"Nah, her mom made her ask me over, along with some buddies of Mike's. She probably knows I don't have any place to go. Ms. Tina and my mom were friends back in the day." He had to downplay his interest in Shelby. The affair Beau had with Missy might indicate Beau liked taking women away from other men.

"At least you got a good meal out of it." Beau didn't look convinced.

"Exactly." Trent switched the conversation away from Shelby. "So how about your day? Did you and your parents have dinner or did you go somewhere else?"

"Momma always makes a big deal out of Thanksgiving and Christmas dinner. She had a house full of people over. Fortunately for all of us, she only prepared the cranberry salad. Pearl made everything else."

"Pearl still working for your folks?"

"Yes, thank goodness. I'd never eat a decent meal there if we had to depend on Momma."

"I should stop by and visit her sometime. She brought over food and stayed with my mother there toward the end." Trent had to pause a moment before he choked up, remembering those days. "She still live in that old house down by the water?"

"Yep. Still there. Couldn't blast her out with a stick of dynamite."

The trivial conversation ended abruptly when Beau became serious. "I'm hoping you'll join me and some of the guys for a special project."

This is it. "What kind of project?"

"I'll fill you in Friday."

"Secret, huh? Who else will be going?"

"Some of the guys from the plant."

Trent shrugged. "I guess. Tell me where and when." He hoped his reply sounded nonchalant. He didn't want to look too eager.

"Next Friday night. We'll meet at the other building at eleven at night."

"What in the world are we going to do at that hour? Wrong time for a hunting party."

"It's a special project we do now and again. You won't have to arrive for work until noon on Saturday. Jamie will rearrange the work schedules."

"Now I'm curious. Count me in."

"See you next week." Beau turned and left the building.

All the waiting and planning was about to pay off. Trent allowed a smile to spread across his face. Wait until he called this in to the task force.

CHAPTER TWENTY

Shelby thought back on her discussion with Amy when she managed to find Shelby alone on Thanksgiving.

Once Amy pushed Shelby to admit she'd grown attached to Trent she acquiesced. She insisted he had nothing to do with the drugs.

Amy pushed Shelby to find out more for the DEA. She'd been trying. She called Missy several times and left messages. Still no return calls. This morning she'd tried again. Perhaps she needed to show up on Missy's doorstep.

When Amy reminded her to be careful with her heart, she couldn't promise anything. If Trent turns out to be on the wrong side in this she didn't know what she'd do.

Shelby pushed the thoughts away as she looked forward to her date with Trent. Her feelings for him grew each time they met. She struggled with the decision to tell him about her rape. It hadn't gone well with the one other man she'd confided in. However, Trent seemed different. Would he blame her for it? Would his feelings change toward her? If the timing seemed right, she'd tell him. If he didn't call after her revelation, then better to find out now rather than later.

After her shift finished, Shelby made her way to her suite where she set to the task of picking out an outfit to wear. After only a few minutes she looked at all the clothes on her bed. She'd pulled almost everything out of her closet one item at a time. Deciding what to wear on this date with Trent had her spinning in circles. Dinner and a movie. What kind of restaurant? He hadn't mentioned where so should she be casual or dressy?

Remembering Trent at the reunion she realized he didn't have much in the way of dressy clothes, so she'd go a bit more casual. Movie theaters always felt cold. With all that in mind, she selected a light wool skirt with a glen plaid design in brown and green, a matching green mock turtleneck sweater, and a gold and green scarf with a gold scarf pin. She looked over her outfit and then added some green tights and brown boots.

It took much longer to return everything to the closet. Frustrated, she looked at the clock for the tenth time making sure she wouldn't be late. She didn't want Trent to arrive before she picked up her place and changed her clothes. Living in a hotel suite did have its downfalls. With no door between the living room and bedroom area, she had to keep it tidy if she didn't want visitors to see her mess.

Rushing, she managed to have everything complete except her hair when a knock sounded at her door.

"Come in." She jerked open the door. "I'm not quite ready. Have a seat. Make yourself a drink if you want." She turned to make her way to the bathroom when Trent took her arm to stop her.

"Hold on a minute. What about a hello kiss?" He grinned at her surprised look, then gathered her in his arms and pressed a kiss on her lips.

Whoa. That was all she could manage to think. Shelby put her arms around him as she melted against him.

Trent released her, which caused her to stumble. "Steady there, Shelby. It's just a hello kiss. Finish up and we'll head out for dinner." He gave her such a mischievous grin she figured he must be up to something.

Shaking her head to clear her mind, she found her voice. "You forgot to tell me which restaurant. I hope I'm dressed all right."

"You're always perfect. You look wonderful. Get a move on. If we're late to dinner we might miss the first part of the movie."

"You're the one who started this." She smirked at him then turned to head back to the bathroom.

"And I'll be the one to finish it … later." Trent's husky voice set her nerves to tingling.

She stopped for a minute. "No fair."

"Exactly." His voice implied more exquisite torture to come.

Shelby managed to make it to the bathroom to finish fixing her hair. Distracted, it took twice as long.

"There. I'm ready." Shelby walked back into the room.

Trent sat on the couch with his coat unbuttoned. He wore black jeans, black boots, a grey shirt, and black tie beneath his leather coat. She loved how the clothes fit his personality. Nothing flashy or stuffy. Comfortable, yet stylish. He'd worn the same outfit to the reunion. Impressed he dressed in his best clothes for their date, she acknowledged to herself her correct choice of ensemble.

"Great. I'll help you with your coat." Trent rose and took her coat off the hall tree near the door.

As he held her coat Shelby slipped into it and appreciated the extra moment he took to hold her close before opening the door.

"How about the Sea Captain's House for dinner?" They strode down the hallway.

"Ah, that's one of my favorites. I haven't been there in while."

"You can't beat the view in the daylight. Since it's already dark, we'll have to settle for the sound of the ocean waves."

"If there is any white water we should be able to see it as well."

"Then I hope there is some."

Arriving at the restaurant, Trent put their names on the list. Only a ten minute wait for a window seat. "I don't mind the tourist season, but I have to admit it is nice not to have to hang around for an hour for a table."

"Absolutely. Since they don't take reservations you're lucky if it's only an hour during the summer."

They sat down near the fireplace. In moments they heard their name called.

They accepted their menus and scanned the options. After they placed their order with the waitress, Trent took Shelby's hands in his.

Shelby looked into his eyes. She'd never noticed his chocolate brown eyes had flecks of gold. Her heart beat a bit faster with the mere touch of his hand.

"I asked for a window table so we could enjoy the view, such as it is, in the dark," Trent stated. "However, I like the view across the table even more than the one outside the glass."

Embarrassment caused warmth to spread up her neck. "How sweet of you to say. I must admit I like looking at you as well."

"Now I know you're lying," he joked. "Who wants to see an old army vet with scars on his face?" Trent shrugged, his embarrassment apparent..

"It's something I no longer notice." Shelby hoped he knew how sincere she was. "However, I have wondered why you don't have surgery to correct it." At his look of discomfort she stammered, "I, uh, I don't mean you need to fix it, I'm curious why you haven't." Her face and neck grew warm.

He paused a moment before he replied. "It reminds me every time I look in the mirror how precious life is and how suddenly it can vanish."

"Oh, wow, that takes my breath away." She understood it was how he remembered those who he'd fought with and didn't come home.

"It's not what I meant to do." He gave her a crooked smile. "You're the only person I've ever told. Trust me, I've had lots of people ask."

She nodded. "Thank you for sharing, I think I might understand a fraction of how you feel."

At that moment their food arrived and they dug into their meal. With mutual consent, they changed the subject.

Once finished they drove to Market Common where a movie theater took up a corner of the shopping area. As they looked at the options Trent cocked a brow at her. "Anything in particular you want to see?" He paused a few moments before winking at her. "Please don't pick the chick flick."

She laughed at his comment. "I'd been hoping to see it."

"If you let me off the hook, then I won't ask to see the latest action film."

"Deal. So we're left with Disney, horror, sci-fi, or romantic comedy. My vote is for the romantic comedy." She looked at Trent to gauge his response.

Trent grumbled a bit before agreeing. "All right. The previews looked okay."

They watched the film all the while alternating between groaning at the intentional puns and then laughing hysterically at the funny one-liners. They sat holding hands most of the time. Shelby had to rummage in her purse in the dark to find tissues for both of them. She laughed so hard her jaw hurt.

After the show ended they walked back to Trent's truck.

Shelby said, "How could it be awful and funny at the same time? Overall I did enjoy it. Thanks for a great evening."

"The fact we were together made it great for me." He opened her door and helped her into his vehicle. Trent started the engine. Before he pulled out of the lot his phone buzzed with a message. Checking it, he frowned at the information.

"Something wrong?"

"No. A friend wants to meet up."

"Must not be a great friend if you frowned like that."

"No. I mean, yeah, he's a good friend. The message is a little cryptic."

"Go ahead and call him."

"I'll do it later." He smiled and switched subjects. "For a first date I think it went well."

"I like to think this is more than our first date."

"You're right. It is." Trent drove the vehicle out of the parking lot. "But I want us to have more like this one. Are you still willing to put up with me?"

She laughed at him. "Of course I am. I can't think of anyone else I'd rather be with right now or any other time."

Shelby saw how her comment pleased him. They chatted about unimportant things on the way back to the resort. Trent walked her to her suite.

She smiled up at him. "Care for a gin and tonic?"

"I would love one." They entered and Trent hung their coats on the hall tree while Shelby prepared their drinks. In moments, they both sat on the couch sipping their cocktails.

"Since I shared a piece of myself with you earlier ... the reason I haven't had my scar removed. I have a question for you."

Trent looked so intense Shelby shuddered inside as Trent continued.

"It might make you uncomfortable, but I hope you can share it with me." He paused a few seconds when she frowned. "Mr. Harper and later your brother both mentioned you'd had some difficult times a few years ago."

Shelby drew in her breath as she put her glass on the table and then placed her hands in her lap to keep them from shaking. The fact other people talked about her made her cringe. She'd already decided to tell him, and now the moment had arrived. She closed her eyes to gather courage.

She opened her eyes, but before she could say anything, Trent continued as if he saw her distress.

"Did you have a boyfriend who was, well, abusive? I want you to know I'm not like that. I've never hurt a woman. And never will."

"Thank you, Trent. However, that's not what happened." Shelby wrung her hands and looked at the floor.

"If it's this hard to tell me you don't have to." Trent put his arm around her.

"I need to tell you. I want to tell you." She knew her comment sounded like she tried convincing herself more than Trent. She glanced at him and saw his concern.

With a deep breath, she started. "My sophomore year at college someone hit me on the back of the head." She paused to look at him before continuing.

"You were mugged?" Trent wore a puzzled expression.

She shook her head before taking another deep breath. "Not exactly. While unconscious, I was raped. I woke up in the hospital."

Trent's expression changed quickly to one of concern. "Oh, Shelby, honey." He gathered her in his arms. "My God. I never dreamed." He rubbed her back, which felt comforting. "Did they find the guy?" His voice changed to a growl.

Shelby shook at the recalled pain and distress. "No. His DNA is on file. There were other victims. If he's ever arrested, they'll have evidence for a trial." Something she hoped for and dreaded.

"I had no idea. I'm so sorry."

She laughed without humor. "No need to be sorry. You didn't do anything."

"No, but a man did this to you. And I'm a man. I'm sorry some piece of shit did it."

"Now we have that out of the way, can we talk about something else?"

"Of course. How about I fix you a fresh cup of coffee. I think yours is cold."

"Thanks. I could use one."

As Trent stood up she watched him. Would he turn away from her now that he knew? She had told one other boyfriend. He'd been appalled, and then never called her again. Like it had been her fault. A common enough reaction. She'd blamed herself for months until Amy helped her understand.

"So, how about those Clemson Tigers?" Trent asked.

"What? Oh, yeah, the football team. They are doing great this year. It's about time. Didn't your brother, Jason, go to school there?" She appreciated the change in subject.

"No. He went to USC. He graduated with honors."

"How about you? Do you plan to work on a degree?"

"Maybe. I don't know what I'd study."

They talked about football and college for a while longer. The mundane discussion calmed Shelby's nerves. Before long they laughed, and she relaxed.

Trent took the glass out of her hand and set it down on the table next to his. He gathered her close and pressed his lips against hers. He tasted of gin and something else. Something like gentleness, power, and desire all rolled into one. How could you taste that? His muscles flexed under her fingertips. She sensed his power, but it didn't cause her to fear him. His control made her want to feel him when he let go. Moving her hands from his arms to his back, she slid one to the back of his neck as she changed from being the recipient to the aggressor. She pressed against him until he shifted and lay down on the couch.

His hands moved to cover her breasts. He continued their kiss, but his hands stilled. He pulled away about an inch. "I don't want to pressure you into anything you don't want. Tell me if you want to stop. Anytime." His voice had lowered an octave.

She could tell from his voice and the bulge in his pants he wanted more. And so did she. When she pressed her hand on his, indicating her agreement, he no longer hesitated. Alternating between massaging her breasts and flicking his thumbs across her nipples excited her.

There had only been one boy before the rape. Her first. At least her rapist hadn't had that satisfaction. It had been a couple of years after the rape before she'd managed to become intimate again. She had gone about it with a kind of clinical detachment. Wanting to eliminate the doubt she could perform. It hadn't been particularly satisfying to her or her partner.

Then she relaxed enough to allow a more natural process to take over. There had been very few men in her life and she'd begun to wonder if there would be anyone special. Now she knew. He lay beneath her. The someone she'd waited for.

Their clothes stood in the way of what she wanted to feel. Naked. With that image in mind, she rose up and started unbuttoning his shirt.

"It would go a lot quicker if you helped," Shelby said, a bit breathless. "Start by taking off your tie."

"You're sure?" Trent's voice had a quiver she hoped meant he wanted her as much as she wanted him.

Her heart swelled with appreciation that he asked her permission. "Don't I look like I know what I want?" She looked him in the eye and cocked an eyebrow.

"Yes, ma'am." He grinned. "I believe you do." After he shucked his tie, he started removing her clothing while she finished his buttons, and then spread open his shirt.

After he'd pulled her sweater over her head, her breath caught as she surveyed his gorgeous chest and stomach which were marred with small scars. Trent didn't notice because he'd unclasped her bra, tossed it aside, and then held her breasts in his hands. Surprised she didn't feel shy or embarrassed at his perusal and touch, she delighted in touching him. She grinned when he let out a slow hiss as she tweaked his nipples.

Trent picked her up and took the few steps to her bed, placing her on it with great care. He set about removing his boots, socks, and jeans. Shelby watched in fascination as he released his staff which had strained against the zipper of his pants. He took a wallet out of his pants and removed a couple of foil packets. Condoms. She was glad he'd been prepared. He placed them on the night stand then returned to the end of the bed, allowing her to look her fill. He grabbed one of her ankles to remove a boot. How could something so simple feel so erotic? He placed her foot on his leg within an inch of his erect member. Grinning, his look dared her to move it closer. Taking her other ankle this time, he slipped the zipper down in slow motion. The feeling of total control allowed her to move her bare foot toward his crotch and nudged his staff. Mesmerized, she watched as it twitched and jump.

With such little experience she didn't know sex could be so interesting and fun. Of course she probably felt that way because of Trent. No other man had ever made her feel so excited. Her desire to be one with him must have become apparent.

Trent stopped, closed his eyes. "In a moment I'll let you have better access."

Removing the boot he slid between her legs and reached under her skirt. To give and receive better access she propped up on her elbows. She smiled when she noted he watched her swaying breasts. He found the elastic of her tights and slowly slid them down along with her panties. Stopping every couple of inches he caressed the recently bared flesh. Would she be able to hold on? Her nerve endings became so sensitive each caress drove her wild. She didn't know if she wanted him to go on like this forever or hurry to the next step. Once the tights exposed her opening, he used his thumbs to run up and down her mound, eliciting a groan of pleasure from her.

"Oh, yes!" The sensations filled her with wonder and expectations. If he could cause her to feel like this with his hands, what else could she expect?

To her surprise he grabbed the edge of her tights and pulled them down with quick efficiency, taking them off before reaching for the zipper of her skirt. Shelby couldn't believe her shyness and nervousness had disappeared so completely. She lay flat then tilted her hips up to allow him to remove her last piece of clothing. Free of all barriers she kept her hips up in an unconscious offering. Whatever he planned next she wanted to experience it all. She'd never felt so sensual.

Trent kneeled between her legs, running his hands up and down her thighs. Each time he reached the top of her legs he rubbed his thumbs across her opening causing her to strain toward him, asking for more.

"Before we go further I think it's time for one of these." He took a packet from the night stand and handed it to her. "Why don't you put it on me?"

She fumbled with the packet as she opened it and slipped it on his shaft. Another first. For some reason the fact he allowed her to do this seemed special. Like giving her power. She enjoyed the feel of him and took the opportunity to grasp his balls in her hand.

He gently lowered her to the bed and took her buttocks in both hands, nestling his member on top of her mound. He didn't enter her as she expected, but started kissing her body and moved up to her breasts. When he took one in his mouth, she sucked in a quick breath as the pleasure poured through her.

"My God, Trent, I don't know if I can take any more." She grabbed his head and kept it pressed to her breast. Her heart pounded. Her physical sensations were only exceeded by the feeling of affection.

"I know you can." Trent switched to the other breast, causing her to twitch and tremble.

Shelby alternately ran her hands up and down his arms, feeling the muscles beneath the flesh, and then ran them through his hair, encouraging him to suckle her breasts. She gyrated her hips in an effort to have his shaft enter her. After a few moments he let go of her breast and moved his mouth to hers. Sucking on his tongue, mimicking what she wanted him to do with his member, she could now reach down and take his staff in her hand. Gently but firmly she grasped him and stroked him repeatedly. Aroused by the groan of desire she elicited, she flicked her thumb across the tip.

Before she had time to take more than a breath, Trent growled, grabbed her buttocks with both hands, and then pushed into her wet and throbbing womanhood. A burst of delight raced through her. Trent paused an instant as if to enjoy the moment then he started thrusting slowly. He pulled almost all the way out before plunging back into the depths of her womb. Then he leaned in closer, but kept the pace slow and ran one hand across her breast, teasing her nipple into a tight bud. She didn't understand how each sensation could continue to become more powerful and ecstatic. Would she burst into flames?

"I hope you don't plan to finish any time soon. This feels too good to stop." Shelby played with his nipple, causing it to pucker. Delighting in her ability to please him made her euphoric feelings soar higher.

"The plan is to finish together, rest, then do it again. Any objections?" Trent looked down with a smile, lighting up the night.

"I can't think of a one." In reality, she couldn't think of anything once he smiled. Although desire coursed through her, something else touched her. A feeling of being home. With Trent. Like she belonged here with him. Not simply the incredible sex. It was as if he made her whole again.

Moments later Trent let go of her breast, shifted his position, and increased the speed of his thrusts. She reached around with her arms, encouraging his efforts, and then raised her knees to give him fuller access. With thrusts of her own, the cravings soared and finished with a burst of passion.

She'd never experienced this type of loving. The gentleness of his strength, the time he spent to elicit every drop of pleasure for them both. She realized the other encounters she'd had were mere ruttings. True, the physical experience had been more than wonderful. However, this time her heart felt like it would burst with joy and fulfillment. She searched for the right word to describe her sensations. Love? The idea came as a jolt. She'd fallen for Trent. The Trent with her now, not the boy she'd once known.

They both lay motionless, sucking in gulps of air. Shelby placed her hand on Trent's hip as he slid his arm beneath her head, his other hand grasped her shoulder and pulled her closer. She grinned at the gesture, all the while delighting in the warmth and closeness. Eventually Trent rolled out of bed and padded to the bathroom. No doubt he disposed of the used condom. Moments later he returned. "How about we snuggle under the covers?"

"Good idea. As soon as I take a turn in the bathroom."

When Shelby saw her face in the mirror, she almost didn't recognize the wanton who stared back at her. Puffy lips, her hair with a sexy disheveled appearance. She looked as if she had a secret. A secret so wonderful it would astound the world. Finishing up she returned to the bedroom where Trent had picked up their clothing and draped it across the chairs. He'd turned out all the lights except the bedside lamp. He lay on his side on the bed facing her. The blankets were pushed down and the sheet pulled across his legs, but not covering his impressive erection. He grinned as he saw her eyes widen and a smile spread across her face.

"I thought we'd rest a bit before the next time." Shelby slid in next to him.

"Plans can be altered when the need *arises*. Don't you agree?" Trent chuckled at his own pun. She joined him in the laughter.

He started playing with one of her breasts and buried his face in her hair. "Mmmm, you smell good." He nipped at her ear.

The erotic sensation surprised her. "And you feel good." Taking his shaft in her hand, she stroked him. Eager to feel him inside her again, she pushed him on his back and straddled him. She didn't take him inside immediately. She had something to do first.

Trent took advantage of his position and took a breast in each hand, a sensuous smile on his lips. "I like the access from here."

"So do I." Shelby grinned as she plucked another condom from the night stand.

This time she didn't fumble with the packet. After rolling it down his thick rod, she placed her hands on his chest, lifted up, and impaled herself on him with a satisfied moan. In moments they rushed headlong to another orgasm. Fast and furious she rode him until he flipped her on her back without separation. He growled her name as he pumped the final time into her, bringing them both the release they craved.

Exhausted he slumped onto her. She wrapped her arms and legs around him, reveling in his heavy weight. They lay there once again gasping for air. Feeling his heart racing with hers gave her a surge of joy. Joy knowing they were one. At least for now. After a few seconds, as if recognizing his weight would be too much for her, Trent slid off, resting by her side, breaking their connection. Shelby was surprised how bereft she felt when he slipped out of her womb.

This time Trent fell asleep while Shelby watched. She stroked his face, tracing the scar that meant more to him than a disfigurement. Her realization that she loved him caused a moment of panic. How had this happened? She'd been so careful around men for so long she hadn't noticed when he slipped through her defenses. The recognition made her want to protect them from reality. Did he need protecting? From Beau? From himself? Would he love her?

CHAPTER TWENTY-ONE

The next morning Trent eased out of bed trying not to wake Shelby. He had no idea what time she had to be at work. His internal clock woke him. Gathering his clothes he crept into the bathroom. While taking a shower he reflected on their night together. He couldn't wipe the smile off his face until he considered her story of the rape. What kind of man raped a woman? When serving in the army in Iraq he'd known a few women who'd been raped. It had been his job to arrest the men and put them on trial. He never understood how some men thought raping a woman was somehow their right. He wanted to castrate them.

Since he didn't have a razor or toothbrush it didn't take long to finish getting ready. Easing open the door, he strode to the couch to put his boots on. Hearing the rustling of bedcovers, he looked up as Shelby pushed up to a sitting position. The sheet fell to her waist, baring her breasts. She rubbed her eyes and yawned. God, she was gorgeous. Her hair looked like a lion's mane, wild and untamed.

"Hey, why didn't you wake me?"

Between her pretty little pout and perky breasts they almost had him tearing off his clothes. "I wanted to let you sleep. After last night you needed it." He couldn't help but smile at the memory.

"Hmm." Her pout turned into a sexy grin. "I figured we could, um, you know, one more time before you left."

The fact she couldn't say *have sex* caused him to chuckle. "You can't imagine how much it hurts me to say no." He meant that literally and figuratively. "I have to go to work. Thanksgiving made a mess of the regular schedule. We both have tomorrow off. How about I bring you some breakfast in the morning and we spend the day together?"

He almost swallowed his tongue when she stepped out of bed and walked toward him. "It would be better if you came back tonight so we could spend tonight *and* tomorrow together." A naked Shelby sat down straddling his lap, legs spread, chest to chest.

He didn't know where he found the strength to say, "God, you can't imagine how much I want to." Sweat popped out on his forehead. "But I have previous plans for tonight." He couldn't help but put his hands on her breasts. Caressing them, his mouth watered thinking about sucking them like he had last night.

"That cryptic message from your friend last night? You can't change it to another time?" She played with his nipples through his shirt.

"Baby, I wish I could."

"Please? For me?"

"Sorry, I can't."

The pout returned. Did he see suspicion in her eyes?

"How about you come by when you're finished with those other plans?" Shelby nipped at his lower lip.

That idea sounded great. "It might be close to midnight. You sure it'd be okay?"

Nodding, Shelby grabbed his head with both hands and kissed him like no other woman. A few moments later he managed to take her shoulders and gently push her far enough away to break the kiss. His breathing came in jagged spurts while he gathered his strength. "I have to go, Shelby. You're torturing me. Please." He placed his hands around her waist and set her on her feet. Bad idea. He groaned as he inhaled the smell of her feminine essence mere inches from his face. Of their own accord, his hands moved to caress her cute ass.

Shelby stepped back and he looked up at her. The light in her eyes almost made him combust. "I'll let you go for now." It came out in an almost purr. "Call me when you arrive at the parking garage."

She turned and strutted to the closet, grabbed a short robe, and then slipped it on. Trent got his breathing under control. He looked at his boots in an effort to distract his wayward notions. Hearing the coffee maker, he managed to shove his feet in the boots and tie them. Rising, he had to adjust his shaft inside his jeans. There would probably be zipper imprints on it the way it strained against the metal.

"Take this with you." Shelby handed him a coffee mug with lid. "Remember to bring it back for a refill." He bet she had no idea how sexy she looked and sounded.

"There's no place else I'll go for refills." Trent liked the way she grinned in understanding.

He turned and strode to the door, then grabbed his jacket from the coat rack. Shelby matched his steps. "Until later?"

"Yes, until later." Trent leaned down and kissed her one last time, keeping his hands at his side. Her lips posed enough of a temptation.

When Trent walked out of the resort and into the parking garage the cold air smacked him in the face. Exactly what he needed to help him concentrate on something other than Shelby. The miles sped by as he tried to think of that night's meeting. The one with the head of the DEA task force. Nothing less important would draw him away from Shelby. Her sexy pleas had tortured him. He almost told her the truth. Now he understood the warning not to become involved when undercover.

The message he'd received indicated the task force would not be watching the Friday night event. Trent would scope out the setup. He'd determine if this was the regular method of shipment or if it varied each time. Did they always have it on a Friday night, the same time? If not, who decided, and how?

He'd learn more tonight about what would be expected of him, and he would collect some new electronics to help.

He felt in control of his libido by the time he arrived home. He shaved, brushed his teeth, and changed clothes in record time. Arriving at the plant at the stroke of seven the guys ribbed him since he normally arrived at least fifteen minutes early. Old army habits lasted a lifetime. If you were on time you were late, at least that's what his old drill sergeant always told them.

When his shift ended, he headed back home to gather up his notes for the meeting and pack an overnight bag. They planned to rendezvous at a restaurant in Murrells Inlet a few miles north of Georgetown, but not as far as Myrtle Beach. This time of year not a lot of people crowded the restaurants, so they could sit in a corner table and not be overheard.

"Jim, hey buddy, good to see you. How's the army treating you?" Trent ambled up to his DEA boss and shook hands. The ruse continued until they'd been seated and given the waitress their order.

"I want you to know what a great job you've done so far," Jim stated, signaling the change in topic. "You've managed to gain Beau Jackson's trust. We never expected it to happen this quick."

"He's too confident. I'm sure he believes since we were friends in high school I'll be loyal to him, no matter what. Did your tech guys figure out how far they checked me out?"

"They did. Good thing we had the army's cooperation in altering your records. Mr. Jackson's men managed to hack into the army personnel database and verify your dishonorable discharge. They downloaded all the details." Jim noticed Trent's shocked expression. "Well, I should say the fake database the army set up for this type of situation. They've had a number of attempted attacks and set up a decoy to capture the hacker's information while allowing them to think they succeeded."

Trent relaxed once he heard about the smokescreen. "Good. I needed to make sure my cover hasn't been blown before I go forward." Trent said moments before the waitress brought their food. They grew silent until once again alone.

Jim frowned. "We'd pull you out if that happened." He shook his fork at Trent.

Nodding his understanding, Trent still felt the need to come up with several scenarios in case the real database had been hacked. There were no certainties when it came to technology.

Trent still didn't understand. "Are you allowed to explain why the DEA is not arresting everyone during the upcoming shipment? Sounds like it's all hands on deck."

"It could be a test for you, the new guy. We want to make sure they are confident in your loyalty. Also, we want to find out exactly how the big shipments go out. They only do this about once a month. At least that's what we think. We aren't really sure." Jim's frown deepened at this admission.

"You've confirmed the smaller shipments?" Trent hoped his intel had helped.

"Yeah, all those deliveries you've told us about to the supposed research building. The ones where you've given us license tag numbers and container numbers. Half the time the trucks arrive empty and leave with product. The deliveries to the building where you work are legit."

"It makes sense." Trent was relieved his intuition had been on track. "So why these other shipments?" He couldn't understand Beau's greediness.

"We believe these are the big ones that travel via ship to northern ports. If we can find out the ship they use, it could break this wide open."

"You haven't stopped the truck shipments?" Trent's eyebrows rose to his hairline.

"Not yet. Thanks to you we have the route and who is involved. If we close them first it might change the schedule for the ship," Jim explained. "We also want to catch Mr. Jackson red-handed. Otherwise he'll open up shop somewhere else."

Shaking his head Trent admitted, "It's still hard for me to believe he's behind all this. His family's always had money. What motivated him to do this?"

"You mean his family had money. The key word is *had*." Jim sat back and pushed his empty plate to the side. "It's taken us a while to put all this together, but it looks like the housing bust put his parents into bankruptcy. By the end of his sophomore year their money had disappeared. That summer he started cooking meth. Once he graduated from MIT he set up shop in Georgetown. We figure he'd made a deal with at least one of the big kingpins in Boston. We're pretty sure his monthly shipment goes there. Too many boats and ships travel up and down the coast to determine which one has his product on board. We've heard about these loads but don't have details. This is where you come in." Jim signaled the waitress. They ordered coffee and dessert.

When the waitress left, Trent explained, "Ah, I see. Now it makes sense. Neither he nor his parents could handle the scandal of losing all their money. So they allowed him to set up shop on their family land." Trent nodded absently as he continued to ponder how devastating near poverty would be for the proud Jackson family. They'd been in Georgetown since before the American

Revolution. Bringing down a Jackson would be difficult on the community and now he understood the extent Beau would go before he'd give it up. That made him a very dangerous man. This meant more than money to the proud man. It meant saving his family name.

"I have some electronic devices for you in the car. There are a number of tracking devices. Once the ship docks behind the plant, hide one on it if you can. Slip some in various containers so we can determine where this stuff ends up." Jim gave his instructions in a no-nonsense voice. "I also have a small microphone you can wear. It records on your secure cell phone. You'll need to sync them up before you leave home."

Trent frowned at the instructions. "The damn secure phone is a lot bigger than a regular cell phone with the extra battery pack." Shaking his head, he protested. "If they catch me with it I won't be able to explain. What about using a regular cell phone?"

"More power on this one. It will pick up sound better than a normal phone since you'll be outside. However, we understand if you don't use it. If we record some admissions from Beau it would be great, but keeping your cover is more important. Only use the device if it's safe." The expression on Jim's face telegraphed the danger underlying the whole undercover operation and the potential for things to go wrong.

"All right. No promises." Trent couldn't imagine how he'd know ahead of time if it would be safe, but he'd hang on to the secure phone in case.

"If you turn it on, we'll be able to capture the recording back at headquarters. Use the code words

Frances Marion if things go south." Jim stood up, indicating the meeting had ended.

Trent grinned at the American Revolutionary name he'd use if a problem arose. Frances Marion had led spy ring in the area and hit the British on several occasions.

Trent accompanied Jim to his car, pretending to have a last word with his army pal. Jim grabbed the electronic equipment from his car. Trent accepted it, surprised at the small size of the package. Slipping it into his inside jacket pocket, he then shook hands with Jim.

Deciding he needed to keep the package out of sight, he took some duct tape from the tool box mounted to the bed of his truck and secured the electronics to the underside of the passenger seat. Satisfied it would do for the time being, he jumped into the driver's seat and set off for Myrtle Beach.

Checking his watch he noticed it was only ten o'clock, well before the time he told Shelby to expect him. He took a detour to pick up a bottle of wine and some flowers. Arriving at the parking garage, he phoned her as she'd requested.

"Hello." Shelby's husky voice indicated she'd been asleep.

"Hello to you sleepy head," Trent teased.

"Oh, Trent." Shelby sounded totally awake now. "Fabulous. You're early."

"I hoped you'd be pleased." He couldn't help but smile at her enthusiastic response.

"Of course I am. Come on up." Shelby's eagerness spurred him on.

Trent knocked on her door while holding the flowers and wine, his overnight bag at his feet.

"Trent?" Came the question from the other side of the door.

"Who else?" He wondered at her extra caution.

The door opened a couple of inches. Pausing a moment when it didn't open completely, he nudged it open and stood gaping at the wondrous site before him. Shelby stood a few feet inside the room, her magnificent curly locks framing her face, eyes wide with anticipation. She wore some fluffy, transparent scrap of fabric the same shade of turquoise as her eyes. It barely covered her breasts and stopped several inches above her knees. The transparent material left all her womanly assets on display yet covered.

Gathering his wits, he kicked his overnight bag inside, closed the door, and set the wine and flowers on the nearest flat surface. He gathered Shelby close. "Oh, sweetheart, you look magnificent."

He captured her lips with his and drank in her essence. His phallus strained against his zipper trying to break the barrier to reach what it wanted most. After several minutes Shelby struggled to break their embrace. He released her lips and backed up a few inches, still holding her in his arms. They both breathed deeply.

"I'm glad to see you, too." Shelby's anticipation showed in the heightened color of her cheeks and the puckering of her nipples.

"I guess I forgot to say hello."

"That's okay. I like the way you showed it. Why don't you take off your coat? Or are you cold?" She opened his jacket and slipped her arms around him.

"Definitely not cold." Trent shrugged out of his coat, letting it drop to the floor. He picked Shelby up and walked the few steps to the couch. Sitting down he placed her on his lap. "Now, where were we?" He leaned in for a kiss when she put a finger to his lips, stopping him.

"Aren't you going to give me a minute to put the flowers you brought in some water?" she said with a teasing smirk.

"Right. Sorry, guess I wasn't thinking." Not with his brain. "I also brought some wine. Would you like me to open it now?" He hoped like hell she didn't.

Shelby stood up and glided over to the flowers and wine. "Not right now. Maybe later." She put the wine in the refrigerator. Reaching up to the top shelf of a cabinet, she took down a vase. Trent stopped breathing for a moment when the motion raised her garment enough to fully expose the right side of her delicate ass. God, he would need CPR if she kept up the torture.

After filling the vase with water, she dropped the flowers in and walked over to the coffee table in front of Trent. She smiled mischievously and set the vase down. He knew she leaned over on purpose to expose more of her breasts to him.

Trent groaned. "Are you done or do you plan to prance around in front of me a while longer?"

"Aren't you enjoying the sights?" Shelby cocked her head to the side and smiled.

"I am enjoying everything you have to show me. I'd like to give you a little hands-on demonstration of exactly how much." Trent stood up and swept her into his arms, carrying her to the bed where he gently placed her on the sheets that had already been turned down. Lit candles on each nightstand glowed and he saw one flickering in the adjacent bathroom. They smelled like pumpkin pie. His mouth watered for more than dessert.

A sigh escaped Shelby. She wrapped her arms around his neck and didn't let go when he released her. He kissed her and drew in her scent.

"I think you have too many clothes on. Take them off." Shelby started unbuttoning his shirt.

"Great idea. Don't move. I want to continue what I started." In no time his boots, jeans, shorts, and shirt lay on the floor. He grabbed some condoms from his overnight bag and placed them on the nightstand. Before climbing into bed beside her, he looked her over head to toe. Paying special attention to her breasts and the V between her legs. He loved the way she turned pink at his perusal.

"I like this thing you're wearing." Trent still stood next to her and fingered the material barely covering her womanly mound.

"It's called a negligee." Shelby giggled. "Are you going to join me or simply stare?" She ran her hand up his leg and cupped his balls.

He flinched with pleasure. "You obviously wanted me to stare or you wouldn't have worn it." He let his fingers wander closer to her mound. He noticed her nostrils flare in anticipation.

She grinned and said nothing for a moment. With one finger, she skimmed up his shaft, circled the tip, and went back down. "I can't deny it." Her voice sounded husky with desire.

Trent slipped between her legs, opening them wide as he rested his elbows on either side of her. "I like the way this stuff feels." He ran his fingers across the top of the material. He lifted her breasts free of the fabric, exposing them to his touch. "Hmm, I like this even better." He nuzzled each breast then selected one to suckle.

He loved her slow and easy in case the previous night's activities had made her sore. Marveling that each time he entered her the sensation felt better and better. After they both reached the pinnacle of desire Trent lay exhausted next to Shelby. She continued to enthrall him. He'd had lovers before. Not many since he'd spent a lot of time in the Middle East and women were scarce. At least women available to him. He'd enjoyed the women who shared his bed and they'd enjoyed him. Nothing compared to what he experienced with Shelby.

Is that because he loved her? What? Wait a minute. He needed to think this through. Love and great sex were not the same. No, make it mind blowing sex. It didn't mean he loved her. How would he know? Thinking back about his parents, he recollected how much they touched and looked at each other. Being a child he didn't recognize their behavior as desire, He only knew the feeling of love that encompassed their whole family. When his Dad died, he knew his mother had cried. She tried not to let them see, but in the morning her eyes had been red. She shed her tears at night so they wouldn't notice.

How would he feel if something happened to Shelby? He'd want to kill the person responsible, that's how he'd feel. The surge of anger surprised him. Even without a real threat, he felt a need to pound someone into the ground.

He needed to think about this. What it meant to the two of them. What it meant to his undercover operation. Until it ended he wouldn't be able to tell her the truth. The last thing he wanted was to start a relationship with lies between them. So what should he do?

CHAPTER TWENTY-TWO

Shelby woke to the smell of coffee. Still groggy from sleep, she sat up in bed. A steaming cup sat on the nightstand next to her. She heard the shower running. A smile spread across her face in recognition. Trent. They had the whole day to spend with each other.

Trent stepped out of the bathroom in a cloud of steam. He dried his hair with one towel and another wrapped around his waist. Shelby's mouth watered at the sight of his washboard abs, his masculine arms and legs, and the dark hair smattered across his chest. The tattoo of an eagle on his left arm looked like it would take flight as his arm moved. She knew he'd said something, but she'd been so intent on his body she didn't understand. "What?"

"I said the bathroom is all yours." Trent lowered the towel from his head. His eyes went directly to her chest and his breath caught. Slowly his gaze wandered to her face. "You really have to stop sitting in bed like that or we'll never leave the room."

She couldn't help but grin at his comment. "I don't think you'll hear a major argument from me if we don't." She eyed the bulge under his towel with interest.

Trent turned his back to her. "Stop it. I promised myself we'd go out for breakfast and a walk on the beach." He looked over his shoulder at her. "We might need a nap after that." His wicked grin caused her nipples to pucker. He glanced down at her breasts again, then swiftly turned his head. "Go on, go to the bathroom."

"Yes, sir. Right away, sir." Shelby bounded out of the bed. Intentionally, she took her time gathering a clean pair of panties and bra, and then walked past him, being sure to brush her breasts against him. At his groan she chuckled, entered the bathroom, and closed the door.

Humming while she showered and washed her hair, she considered her current state of happiness. Not wanting to waste the precious time with Trent, she pulled her wet hair into a pony tail to let it dry naturally. After applying a light layer of makeup, she walked out of the bathroom. To her surprise, the room now stood in perfect order. Her negligee placed precisely on the bed.

Standing proud in her bikini briefs and demi bra, she put her hands on her hips. "Thanks for making the bed. If you need a job as a maid we're always hiring."

Trent sipped his cup of coffee and watched her with interest. "Habit. The army teaches you to make up your bed the minute you get out of it, but no thanks on the job offer."

Shelby smiled then turned and rummaged through her small closet, picking out a pair of jeans and a turtle neck sweater. Slipping them on, she knew Trent watched her every move.

"I know those can't be all your clothes. I don't see a sundress or pair of shorts in there."

"You're right. It's too small to keep all my clothes. Fortunately, Mom and Dad have plenty of closet space. I rotate my clothes every few weeks." Shelby put on her socks and boots.

"Okay, I'm ready." She stood looking at him for approval.

"You were quick. I figured I had time for at least one more cup of coffee."

"If I dried my hair and put on full makeup, we'd be here for another thirty minutes. Be thankful."

"I am, I am."

Trent stood up, gathered her in his arms, and gave her a kiss powerful enough to make her knees weak. "I wanted to thank you for last night." He pulled back a couple of inches.

"Thank me?"

"Yes. Walking into the room with you wearing that, um, negligee had to be the best present I've ever had."

"I'm glad you enjoyed opening the present."

"Oh, yeah. Now I'm going to stop talking so we can be on our way. Any further talk about the negligee and we may end up back in bed."

Shelby chuckled as she walked to the door, snagging her coat on the way out. "Promises, promises. Feed me now. I'm hungry."

Trent followed her out of the room and down the hall. He showed her to where he parked his truck. "Good lord, it's cold out here. Guess I've spent too much time in the Middle East. I don't remember the winters being this cold."

"Last year was brutal. The high daytime temperatures stayed under forty-five degrees for several days and we even had about a half inch of snow one day."

They both realized what they'd said and laughed at themselves. "Guess it's a good thing we don't live in the north, we'd never survive." Trent laughed again as he drove to a local pancake house.

Shelby's stomach growled as he parked his truck. "I think we arrived in the nick of time. I'm about to starve."

"Sounds like it." Trent chuckled as he climbed out of the truck.

They enjoyed their breakfast with about half a dozen other local patrons. Shelby knew the waitress from her frequent visits. She chatted with them and Shelby could tell she couldn't wait to ask her about Trent. The next time she came here, she'd have to spill all.

"How about the walk on the beach I mentioned earlier?" Trent asked as they exited the restaurant.

"I'd love to. I never tire of it." Shelby grinned at him. The awesomeness of this moment almost overwhelmed her. Her feelings only grew stronger the more time she spent with Trent. "This time of year it's a bit chilly especially when the wind is blowing, but it's so peaceful. Not many people will be out there."

"Exactly." Trent drove to one of the piers and parked. "Smart idea to bring the scarf."

"Always. And gloves too." Shelby stuck her hand in the pocket of her coat. "Oh, I forgot I have some hand warmers. Do you want a couple?" She held out a handful to Trent.

"Hand warmers?" Trent snagged a couple, activated them, and stuck them in his coat pocket. "Why in the world do you have those? I know the temperatures don't go down that low."

"Uh, well, I think Mike gave them to me." Shelby faltered as she tried to think of a plausible lie. Did he know? How could he? No time to be paranoid.

Trent locked the truck and took Shelby's hand. "Your brother? Why would he give you hand warmers?"

Lord, now she had to continue the lie. "He'd gone hunting and had some left over. Guess he didn't think they'd be any good by next year." She could do this. His curiosity was normal. Right?

"Probably not. They'll feel good on a day like today." Trent squeezed her hand. "Hey, how come you're so quiet? And what's with the frown. Is it too cold out here for you?" He took her hand in his and put them both in his pocket.

Shaking off the disturbing notions, she replied, "No, not at all. Sorry. Thinking about something, that's all."
"Not pleasant things, it would appear." Trent frowned. "Anything you want to share?"

She determined to not let her future plans spoil the day. "A situation at work I need to figure out. Employee issues. You know how difficult those can be." Not a complete lie, she did have some problems with the staff.

"Not really, when you're in the army you have two kinds of people. The ones who give orders and the ones who take orders." Trent chuckled. "Not much discussion there."

"I suppose you don't. Trust me, orders would make it easier." She warmed up to the subject. "Misinterpretations of events and conversations happen all the time. Being the referee has its down side."

Shelby changed the subject. "How is Mr. Harper? Have you seen him lately?"

Trent went along with the change in topic. "We have dinner together about once a week."

"You do? That sounds nice. For both of you. Who does the cooking?" Once again, she marveled at the consideration Trent showed to other people.

He shrugged as if everyone had dinner with a man old enough to be their grandfather. "We trade out. I have to admit it's nice not to do it all the time."

Perhaps she could surprise him sometime with a special dinner. "So what is something you never fix that you'd like to have?"

"My mom's lasagna. I've made lasagna a couple of times, but it never turns out the way she made it." As he shook his head, he gave a big sigh. "I have no idea what special something she added to make it so good."

"Hmm. I know my mom and several of the church ladies used to swap recipes. Your mom could have shared it with them. I'll ask her if she knows."

"That'd be great." The smile he turned on her took her breath away.

Trent seemed to think the fact she'd stopped walking meant she wanted to leave. "I'm ready to turn back. Are you?"

It had gotten cooler so she agreed, "Yes, the wind has picked up."

Walking in a comfortable silence back to the truck, Shelby considered a future with Trent. Could they have one? If he became involved with Beau's drug operation would she be able to accept it? No. She'd have to make sure he didn't become involved.

"Do you mind if we go to the hardware store?"

"Of course not. Do you have a DIY project?" she teased.

"All the time," he acknowledged. "I almost forgot. I promised Mr. Harper I'd help him put in a new faucet in his kitchen if he'd help me with an electrical issue."

"Electrical?" She should not have been surprised, the old trailer probably had more than electrical problems.

Trent nodded. "I have a light flickering on and off. Mr. Harper is a licensed electrician so I asked his advice on how to fix it. He told me a couple of things I needed to pick up. There are a few possibilities and he didn't have all the supplies."

As they made their way to the local big box store, Shelby reveled in the feel of a couple doing routine chores. Is this how it would be if they married? It sounded silly, but she couldn't wipe the smile off her face.

As they made their way to the electrical section of the store, they ran into one of their high school chums.

"Hey, man, what are you doing up here?" Chuck directed his question to Trent although he nodded to Shelby in recognition.

"This is a bigger store than the one in Georgetown. Thought I'd see if they have a better selection of lights."

"I didn't know you two were together," the curious man stated.

"Uh, no, I ran into Shelby in the parking lot." Trent denied their involvement. "She asked me to help her locate something."

Shocked, Shelby said nothing. Did he not want people to think of them as a couple? It felt like a knife stabbed her in the heart.

The man narrowed his eyes and gave a slow nod. "See you at work." He continued down the aisle.

"What was that all about? Ashamed to be seen with me?" She clenched her teeth as she spoke and looked at Trent. She felt hurt and mad at the same time.

"Of course not. Any man would be proud to be seen with you." Trent ruined it by saying, "I, uh, didn't want the guys back at work to rib me about us. You know how guys can be."

"No, I guess I don't. What would they say?" Shelby crossed her arms and glared at him.

"They can be crude. Like asking about our sex life." Trent waved his hand in what looked like annoyance and turned to look at the electrical supplies. "Not something I plan to discuss with anyone."

"Oh." She wouldn't want to discuss their sex life either with a group of coworkers. But guys did that all the time, didn't they?

"Guess you haven't hung out in too many locker rooms." Trent turned back to her and smiled, which usually made her stop thinking.

"No, guess not." Something still didn't sound right to Shelby. First, the mysterious friend who sent a cryptic message. Then, the meeting he couldn't change. Followed by his denial about their relationship. She didn't like the way things added up.

Trent gathered up the supplies and they checked out. As they made their way to his truck, she thought she spotted the guy they'd spoken to earlier, but she didn't mention it. Shaking off the uncomfortable feeling, she sat back and enjoyed Trent's company.

"I forgot something. Stay here with the truck and I'll be right back."

Trent left before she could say anything. She noticed he stopped to chat with the man they'd seen earlier. Why? Then he went back inside. She watched the man drive away then Trent came back out of the building. It looked like Trent didn't want the man to see them drive away together. Why not? She had a bad feeling.

"You hungry?" Trent asked when he returned empty-handed.

"Not after our big breakfast, but if you are I have some lunchmeat and bread at my place. I can make you a sandwich. Didn't you find what you went back for?"

"They were out. A sandwich sounds great, I am a bit hungry. What do you want to do for dinner later?"

She needed to make a list of some pointed questions to clear up this situation. She'd think it over and confront him when they returned to her place.

"I hadn't thought that far ahead. Want to pick up some take-out Chinese? After dinner we can make some popcorn and watch a movie."

"You sure you don't want to go out?"

His question confused her more. So, he didn't want that man to see them together, but he wanted to take her out. What was going on?

"No, Trent, I don't need to have you take me to a nice restaurant every night. If I'd planned better I could have fixed something." She preferred to have him all alone. There were too many questions she needed to ask without being overheard.

"I think you did a fantastic job planning." Trent grinned as he pulled into her resort, parked, and leaned over to give her a kiss before she managed to step out of the truck. Both of them grinned and held hands as they walked to her room. It occurred to her the only time he held her hand or kissed her happened when they were alone or somewhere so remote, like the employee parking area, no one they knew would see them. Now she knew she was becoming paranoid.

Entering her room, they hung up their coats. Shelby started taking things out of the refrigerator to make Trent a sandwich. "Do you like mayo, mustard, or both?"

"Actually I prefer mayo on one side and butter on the other."

"Butter?" Shelby paused and looked at him. "Okay. I can do that. I've never known anyone who put butter on a sandwich." She turned around and took the butter out of the fridge.

Trent sat down at the small table. "I've gotten ribbed about it more than once. Something my mom always did. I have no idea where she picked it up." He shrugged. "It's all I knew so I didn't realize other people didn't do it until I joined the army. That became one of many things to make me stand out." Shaking his head, he put his elbow on the table and propped his chin on his palm.

Shelby placed a plate with his sandwich in front of him. "You say that like it was a bad thing." She sat down on the other chair.

"Remember as a kid you wanted to be like everyone else. So you'd fit in?" Trent took a bite of the sandwich.

"Yeah, but you said you were teased in the army."

"I wouldn't call it teasing." Trent paused a moment. "I said ribbed, but that's not accurate, either. Harassment is more like it." Nodding at his own correction, he took another mouthful.

Shelby frowned. "Why would anyone care about how you ate your sandwich?"

He swallowed. "It's not so much about caring, but something to pick on."

"I still don't understand." Shelby frowned with uncertainty. "What else would they harass you?"

"My accent, of course."

"You've lost most of it."

"That's intentional. It took time. I tried to mimic guys from the Midwest. They didn't receive as much harassment."

"What's the point in all the harassment, or bullying, or whatever?"

Trent finished his sandwich and wiped his mouth. "It's how some of the drill sergeants get you in line. They try to break you down."

Shelby raised her eyebrows and felt her jaw drop. "Again, why?"

"To wash out the guys who can't take it. They figure if you can't handle it, then you won't be a good soldier. I can't say I agree, but there you have it."

"I had no idea." She shook her head. Then she tried to lift the mood. "Well, I for one love a southern accent."

"Well, ma'am, I'll do my best to pick it back up." Trent replied with the deepest accent she'd heard in a while.

Shelby grinned and gave him a peck on the cheek. "You do that."

Grabbing her around the waist, he pulled her to his lap. "You make the best sandwiches ever. Now what do you want to do?" Trent wiggled his eyebrows.

Her phone rang.

"You don't need to answer that, do you?" Trent frowned.

"I probably should. Sorry." Shelby released a huff of impatience. She grabbed her phone and looked at the display before swiping it. "Yes, Mom, what can I do for you?"

CHAPTER TWENTY-THREE

After listening for a while, her frown growing, she said, "I'm glad he's okay. What about you? Yes, of course, I'll be there. I did have plans, but they can be postponed." She listened more. "Don't be silly. Of course they'll understand. It'll take a few minutes to wrap up, but I'll be there as soon as I can."

Closing her phone, she looked at Trent. "I'm sure you realize the call was important." Her sigh expressed her own regret.

"It sounded like it. It's okay. This won't be our last day together." Trent sat on the couch and pulled her to him. "I won't tell you I'm not disappointed, but life happens."

"It's my brother, Mike." Shelby wrapped her arms around Trent and gave him a kiss.

"What's up with him?" Trent looked puzzled.

"He had a car accident and is in the hospital." She waved her hand when Trent looked concerned. "He's okay and so is the person in the other car. They are discharging him right now. However, they think he has a concussion. They don't want him to sleep too deeply. The doctors told us we need to wake him up every two hours to make sure he's okay."

"So it means you're spending the night." He nodded his acceptance.

Shelby pouted as she agreed. "I'm afraid so. I have to see for myself he's all right. Thanks for understanding."

A few minutes later, Shelby walked hand in hand with Trent toward the parking garage. "How about Friday night? Do you have plans? I can come to your place if it's easier. You have to be at work earlier than I do."

Trent frowned. "Friday won't work for me."

When he didn't expand on the reason, she said, "Do you have a date with Mr. Harper? I think he'd be okay with me joining the two of you."

"No, sorry, that's not it. Beau has something planned and the guys who work for him are being called in to help." Trent shrugged. "He's probably having a party. I'll be part of a security detail."

"Oh? A party?"

"It's a guess. You know how it is. When your boss tells you to be somewhere at a certain date and time you show up and do whatever."

"The bosses I've had are more forthcoming. If I'm asked to work extra I'm told what I'll be doing."

"As a security person you don't always know until you arrive. It cuts down on problems."

Shelby paused at the door of her car. "Give me a call when you know your schedule and we'll set something up."

"I will. Say hello to your family. I hope Mike feels better. Good thing he has a hard head." Trent's crooked grin showed his attempt to make her laugh.

She returned his grin. "I'll tell him you said so."

Giving her a kiss goodbye, Trent waited for her to slip into the car before shutting her door, and then walked to his pickup. Shelby couldn't help sighing. *He's always such a gentleman.*

Reversing out of the parking slot, she headed toward Georgetown. With the call from her mother she never did ask Trent about his mysterious behavior. Adding those questions and his comment about the Friday night work she frowned as she considered the implications. Could this be the big shipment? The more she thought about it the more certain she became. Calling Amy to discuss a rendezvous felt wise.

She dialed her phone. What would happen if Trent worked with Beau on the shipment? "Amy, it's Shelby." She quickly relayed the information Trent had given her.

"I've heard comments from some of my clients that made me think something might be going down. I didn't know for sure until now. You're right. This could be our chance to verify and gather info for the DEA."

She turned onto her parents' street. "I'm pulling up to my folk's house right now. When I can talk again, I'll give you a call."

She heard the pause on the other end of the line. "You're in Georgetown?"

"Oh, sorry, I forgot to tell you about Mike." She hadn't realized until now how rattled she'd been at the idea of the shipment.

"Your brother Mike? What about him?"

Shelby gave Amy the short version of what happened to her brother.

"I'm sure your mother is beside herself with worry. I'll be over in a couple of hours. When you have time we can talk."

"Good idea." Shelby knew Amy would ground her and felt better already.

She made her way into the house. "Mom, Dad, I'm here." Shelby put her purse and overnight bag on the kitchen table and hurried to Mike's old bedroom.

"I'm so glad you could come." Tina gave her a hug so hard Shelby had difficulty taking a breath.

"Of course, I'm here. Where else would I be in a family emergency?' Shelby hugged her mother back.

From the bed, she heard a grumble. "I can't believe it. Mom, you told Shelby to come? It's only a bump on the head. The doctors aren't even sure if it's a concussion."

"Hush. I'm here to help Mom and Dad." Shelby patted Mike's arm then shook her finger at him. "You lay there and do what Mom tells you to do."

"The doctors told me to take it easy. I don't have to be in bed. I can sit up."

"No, you don't, young man," their mother admonished. "You'll stay right there until tomorrow."

With a big sigh, Mike gave Shelby a pleading look. "See. She won't even let me go to the bathroom alone. She makes Dad go with me."

Shelby stifled a laugh. "I'm sure it's for your own good. At least Dad's here and she's not the one going with you." At Mike's look of horror, a little giggle escaped.

"Mom." Shelby turned and took her mother by the arm. "I'm sure it's okay if he is alone for a couple of hours. We'll check on him again then. That's what the doctors said, right?" Ushering her mother out the bedroom door, she glanced at Mike. He mouthed *thank you.*

She made her mother sit at the kitchen table next to her father. "Have either of you had anything to eat?"

"What? Oh, I don't remember." Her mother shook her head and put her face in her hands. "I can't believe this happened."

Her father laid his hands on the table. "Breakfast. We were eating breakfast when we received the phone call."

"There are a lot worse things, so be grateful it's only a bump." Shelby's mind drifted back to her own days in the hospital. No, stop, she couldn't go there. "I'll make you both a cup of hot tea with sugar. How about a sandwich?" Shelby didn't care how they answered, she'd insist her mother and father both eat something.

She struggled to keep the conversation flowing. "I spoke to Amy earlier. She's going to stop by." The water came to a boil, and she fixed them each a mug of tea. "There, drink this, you'll feel better."

"Amy's coming? How nice. She's always so helpful and kind."

"Yes, she is. And she's a friend. We have some things to discuss so I decided it would be a good time to see her."

"Yes, of course dear, that's fine." Her mother switched back to the topic of her brother's possible concussion and what the doctors told them to watch for.

Prior to Shelby finishing lunch preparations, her mother said, "Let me check on Mike." She left the room before Shelby could stop her.

Shelby set their sandwiches on the table and waited a few minutes then went back to Mike's room. Leading her mother by the hand, she made her sit at the kitchen table.

"Now eat, both of you." Shelby glared at her mother. "Did the doctor say it would be okay for Mike to have something to drink or maybe some broth?"

Her dad checked his watch. "The doc said after six hours he could have a small amount of liquid if he didn't have any nausea."

Shelby went to her brother's room with a tray containing a mug of clear broth and a cup of hot tea. She found him sitting in a chair, scrolling through his phone.

He looked up and sighed. "Thank God it's you. Mother would have made me lay back down." He eyed the tray in her hand. "Is that for me? I'm starving."

"Only liquids for now." She gave him the mug of broth first as she sat on his bed. "So, what happened?"

"A simple case of wrong time wrong place." Mike gave her a detailed account of what happened.

"So no one received a ticket? That's crazy." Shelby shook her head at the recount of the freak accident. She suspected Mike held something back. She could tell when he lied. He wasn't lying but she didn't think he told the whole truth. Why not?

"Crazy is right." Mike grabbed his cell when it indicated a text message arrived. "It's a text from my insurance company. Dad sent them the details along with photos. Now they want the police report."

Distracted by the new issue, Shelby didn't question Mike further. "I'll ask Dad to take care of it for you. You know it's best if he has some task to perform."

"Right. And it will be a big help." Mike grimaced.

"Do you have a headache?" Shelby asked, concerned.

"Yeah, I didn't want to say anything to Mom. She'll freak out."

"I'll grab one of the pills the doctor prescribed. I'll make sure Mom doesn't see me."

"Thanks, Sis. You can be all right sometimes." Mike repeated a phrase they'd used with each other for years and made her smile.

Shelby managed to refill Mike's iced tea and snag the pills while her mom talked on the phone.

"Here you go, little brother. I'm only giving you two. We need to know if your headache continues. Let me look at your eyes." Grabbing her brother's chin, she examined him. "The doctor said to make sure the pupils were equal." Satisfied, she let him go. "So far, so good."

"You're planning to stay the night?"

"I think Mom and Dad will worry less if I'm here. I'll do my best to run interference, but you know someone has to check on you every two hours. If I do the late night hours, you'll manage a little sleep. Besides, I need to go to work in the morning."

"You'll be dead on your feet. I'm sorry I'm making this tough for you." A frown appeared on Mike's face.

"I know you'd do the same." It occurred to Shelby he'd done exactly that a few years ago after she'd been raped. "Did the same. When I needed you." She patted his hand and gave him a look of gratitude.

Mike's face turned crimson at the reminder of her rape. "That was different."

"Different, but the same." She needed to change the subject before she became misty-eyed. "Go on to the bathroom before Mom comes in here. At least, I won't make Dad go with you."

Mike stood up and tiptoed to the bathroom, peeking around the corner to make sure his mother didn't look his way.

Shelby had to laugh. She'd probably be the same way when she became a mother. That idea took hold and she smiled. A mother to Trent's children, she hoped. The notion made her conjure up the image of two children, a girl looking like her and a boy looking like Trent. A happy family. Could it happen some day?

Mike returned from his covert bathroom mission. "Why the big grin? Did you remember a good joke?"

"No, thinking what Mom would do if she found you."

"Don't remind me." Mike grumbled as he sat down in his chair, moving slow and deliberate. "It's only a concussion. Why the big deal?"

"You know how Mother is. Ever since my sophomore year, anything that happens to either of us is monumental. I'll go back in and tell Mom you're fine for now. I'll try to keep her in the kitchen for a while to give you some alone time. I know she'll check on you before she goes to bed. I'll bring some more ibuprofen with me when I come back, in case you need it."

Shelby strolled back to the living room, noticing Amy had arrived while she'd been with her brother. "He's fine for now. I told him I'd be the one waking him up every two hours tonight. The both of you need to sleep. You look like you need it more than Mike." In spite of the early hour, she wanted her parents to rest. They looked exhausted. It would also give her time alone with Amy.

"Oh, sweetie, we don't expect you to stay up all night with him. We'll share the responsibility," Tina protested.

"No, no, I insist. You won't have any quality sleep, and he'll need you tomorrow. I'll take the couch and set my phone alarm to wake up."

Her parents looked at each other and her dad shrugged. "Maybe she's right. We'll need to keep an eye on him tomorrow, too." He patted her mother on the back. "If you feel as bad as I look, then we do need some sleep." Greg looked at Tina with a crooked grin.

Shelby could see her mother's hesitation, but she finally relented. "All right. You promise to wake us if he becomes worse, right?"

"Of course. Now go on to bed." Shelby made shooing motions toward her parents.

Tina looked at Amy. "Thank you, dear, for coming by. I know Shelby will enjoy a nice chat." Slump-shouldered, Tina wandered to the bottom of the stairs where Greg stood waiting for her. As they climbed the stairs to the master bedroom, their weariness showed in their slow methodical steps.

After her parents left the living room, Shelby whispered to Amy all the information she'd gathered from Trent and her conjecture of what would happen Friday night.

"Yes, I can see why you think that is the night. It explains some of the other information I've heard over the last few days."

"Shall we meet at your place and drive out around eight or nine o'clock?"

"I've been thinking about that. The only reason no one caught us was because nothing happened. We should drive out to old Rupert's boat landing and go in my canoe down the river and watch from there."

"What?" Surprised, her question emerged too loud for the quiet house. She immediately lowered her voice to a harsh whisper. "Are you crazy? The river is full of gators and snakes and other creepy stuff." A shudder erupted. "No way."

"It's winter," Amy insisted. "Gators don't swim around much in this weather."

"What about snakes? Water moccasins and copperheads are nasty and mean. Nope. Not doin' it." Shelby crossed her arms for emphasis.

"Shelby, it's the best way not to get caught." Amy grabbed her arm and squeezed.

Shelby frowned and considered the plan. "Maybe. If they have a lookout at the main road they'll spot us immediately if we go by car."

"Exactly. So you've been thinking about it, too?"

"I have." Shelby gave a single nod. "But I didn't come up with the canoe idea. I thought we'd walk in." She opened her hands palm up and shrugged.

"Good lord. We'd have to park so far away it would take us all night to hike through the brush and trees with only pen lights." Amy's eyes grew wide.

"Yeah, I came to the same conclusion." Shelby drew in a deep breath. "All right, we'll use your canoe. I'm taking Dad's gun in case of gators."

"Agreed. I'd rather be found out than eaten by a gator. I'll bring mine, too. You do know how to shoot, right?" She tilted her head sideways at Shelby with a suspicious look.

"Of course, I know how." Shelby couldn't help but show her indignation. "It might be a good idea even without the gator problem."

"Hmm, maybe so." Amy stood up. "I need to head back. See you Friday." She gathered her belongings and shrugged into her coat.

Shelby accompanied her to the door. "Thanks for stopping by. I think we have a good plan this time."

"I hope so." Amy hurried to her car in the cold weather, leaving Shelby standing at the door feeling more than a bit forlorn.

Shelby closed the door and wandered into the kitchen where she poured a glass of milk and grabbed a couple of cookies. She sat at the kitchen table, brooding about what would happen on Friday. Would Trent refuse to go along with the drug operation once he found out what transpired in the other building? If he did, would Beau hurt him or, worse, kill him? For some reason, Beau figured Trent wouldn't object. So what did he know about Trent that she didn't? Ideas swirled around in her mind until her phone buzzed, indicating the time had arrived to check on Mike.

After she made sure his pupils were not dilated, he didn't admit to any nausea, and he could read a sentence from a magazine, she let him go back to sleep. She lay down on the couch, determined to catch a few winks, but her mind turned to Trent and how he would react to the drug operation. Before she knew it, her alarm once again vibrated. She spent the rest of the night tossing restlessly on the couch and looking in on Mike. When she went to his room at seven in the morning, she heard her parents moving around. After putting on a fresh pot of coffee, she cooked a light breakfast for them all.

"Oh, sweetie, this is so nice of you." Her mother patted her on the back and gave her a peck on the cheek, but looked dismayed at the food. "I don't know if I can eat."

"Sit down and try." Shelby placed a full plate on the table and then poured a mug of coffee. "I bet you're more hungry than you realize." Setting the mug next to the food, she turned to fix the same for her father.

Greg came down the stairs. "Smells great. How's the patient this morning?"

She knew he tried to make things seem normal by giving her a smile.

"I went up a few minutes ago and there is no change. Still good. I bet the doc gives him the all clear this afternoon."

Relief flooded her mother's face. "I hope you're right, dear." Then she took a sip of coffee. "Maybe I will try some breakfast."

"Good." Shelby smiled as she watched her mother do more than pick at the food in front of her.

Chatting together, they finished the light fare, and then Shelby started clearing the table.

"Let me do that. You cooked. I can clean up." Her father picked up his plate and headed to the sink.

Shelby gave in to her father's wishes. "Thanks, Dad. I need to head back to work."

After he set his plate near the sink, he gave her a hug. "I hope you slept a little last night." He looked her in the eye as if searching for an answer to a different question.

She pecked him on the cheek. "I'll be fine. By the way, I took your gun. Amy and I plan to go to the shooting range in a few days."

"Is your carry permit still valid?"

"Yes, I checked."

"Then that's fine. Be sure to clean it before bringing it back."

"Always."

"Give me a call this afternoon when Mike receives the okay from the doctor." Breaking the embrace, she shrugged into her coat, and then picked up her purse and her father's gun case.

"Will do." Her father went back to clearing the table. Her mother waved and sipped her coffee.

As Shelby drove back to her place, she wondered what would happen on Friday. Would Trent be there? If he was, what would they do?

CHAPTER TWENTY-FOUR

Friday night arrived all too soon. Shelby wore the same outfit as last time—dark jeans, black sweater, knit cap, gloves, and coat. This time she tripled the socks since she recalled how cold her feet got. Once again, she stopped at Walmart to pick up hand warmers. Meeting Amy at her house, they barely spoke as she climbed into Amy's car. The canoe had already been tied down on top.

Shelby tucked her jeans into her socks to make sure nothing creepy-crawly could climb up her legs. She double-checked the safety before putting her dad's 9mm in her coat pocket. To make sure she could shoot if needed, she had also nabbed his hunting gloves. The fingers of the gloves could be removed. It meant her right hand would be cold, but better cold than snapped off by a gator.

Shelby finally broke the silence. "You're sure gators don't swim much in the winter? I know they are nocturnal by nature."

Amy nodded. "I looked it up on the Internet to make sure. They are dormant in the winter." She looked over at Shelby. "That's different than hibernating. They burrow in mud holes on the bottom of lakes or on the sides of rivers."

Shelby blew out her breath. "Oh lord, we'll be traveling along the river banks."

"I know, but they should stay put. If they come out it's during the day when the sun is out. I also checked on snakes. They won't be out either in this cold weather."

"Good. I feel a little better. I didn't think about them last time, but we didn't see any then, either."

"Exactly. Now if we can keep out of sight of Beau's crew, we'll be fine."

They parked in a boat launch area a couple of miles short of Beau's plant. That way they wouldn't drive by the entrance and alert anyone to their presence. After they unloaded the canoe, Amy backed the car into the trees so as not to be seen by passersby.

Shelby whispered, "Good thing you camouflaged the canoe. The shiny aluminum would have been seen for miles."

Nodding, Amy replied, "My nephews had a blast painting it last summer. I had no idea at the time how important it would be. Okay, time to be silent."

They slipped the boat into the water with little noise, though even the whisper it made sounded loud to Shelby. They dipped their paddles into the water without splashing. Silently, they made their way to the back of the plant. The night vision goggles Amy had procured sure came in handy. Before they left, they'd agreed to moor the boat across from the river entrance to the plant. They'd chosen a spot where the branches of a large tree hung over the water. Easing under the branch should provide more than enough cover.

After using some rope to secure their tiny craft to some trees, they took out all the items they would need during their watch. That's when Shelby noticed a problem.

She hadn't realized how much their faces shone in the dark until Amy turned toward her. They'd have been spotted in seconds had someone been looking. Shelby motioned to Amy, who shrugged her shoulders and shook her head, indicating she didn't understand.

With great reluctance Shelby took off her left glove and reached over to grab a handful of mud. She proceeded to cover her face with the icky goo. *Oh. My. God. This stuff stinks to high heaven.* Amy nodded and did the same thing. Washing the mud from her hand in the river turned out to be difficult. It stuck like glue. She did the best she could, tucked her freezing hand back in the glove, and then put another hand warmer inside.

Now the waiting game started. Would they find out about a drug shipment? Would Trent be there? If he was, would she have the courage to tell the DEA?

CHAPTER TWENTY-FIVE

The importance of the mission required Trent to use the secure phone with the extra microphone. Catching everything on tape would mean the difference in developing a sting operation immediately or not. Making sure no one came near enough to notice, he retrieved the package from his truck, went in the house, and taped the device under his armpit.

After Trent drove to the plant, he jumped out of his truck and ambled over to Beau in the parking lot of the Research and Development building. "I'm here and it looks like a lot of other guys are too." He looked around at the other men. "What's up?"

"I heard you and the luscious Shelby were an item," Beau said, ignoring Trent's question.

Trent tried not to show his surprise. "You know how it is." He gave a shrug. "We see each other now and again. Nothing serious."

Beau eyed him. "Maybe not to you, but I bet Shelby would have a different take on it."

Again he shrugged. "Can't control what she thinks." He knew if he protested too much it would sound desperate. Considering his desire to keep Shelby out of this, he didn't want Beau to use his feeling toward Shelby against him … or her.

"I hear the two of you have been seen together a lot lately."

Continuing his nonplused demeanor, he replied, "So? I've also been seen with Mr. Harper. Nothing going on there either." Being irritated would serve his purpose better so he demanded, "You going to stand around and ask about my love life or are you going to tell me what you want me to do? I can always leave."

Beau didn't appear to be satisfied with his response, but dropped it. Trent figured the upcoming events were more important to him than who Trent spent time with.

"We're getting ready for a special shipment." Beau watched him, probably waiting for a reaction.

Trent frowned as if he didn't understand. "Shipment? At this time of night? Who does business like this?"

Beau continued in a low tone. "It's best if this type of shipment is under the radar so we do it after the regular employees leave for the day."

"This type of shipment? Regular employees?" Pretending to be confused, he asked, "What the hell is going on?"

"Drugs. That's what. It's how I make my real money. You have a problem with it?" Beau growled and fisted his hand, the one without a gun. The rest of his body tensed.

Trent didn't think it wise to sound too eager, but he did think it best to show some surprise. "Drugs? Well, I've been wondering about this other building." Nodding in understanding, he continued. "It makes sense now. So this gig is going to pay better than usual. Right?" He grinned as if he'd won the lottery.

Beau relaxed and smiled. "Exactly. You in?"

"Hell yeah." Trent punched Beau on the arm.

"Then we need to set the rules. You don't talk to anyone about this except the people you see here tonight. And I mean anyone. Especially the luscious Shelby."

Trent quelled his desire to punch Beau in the mouth for saying Shelby's name like she was a slut.

"That's why you've been nosy about who I'm seein'?" He frowned.

"Her family is known to be unsympathetic about this operation so keep your mouth shut around her," Beau insisted. "I don't want them to have any details."

Trent gave him the best stupid grin he could muster. "No problem. We don't do much talking when we're together." He wiggled his eyebrows. "You know what I mean?" It took a monumental effort to drag his relationship with Shelby down to the level Beau imagined it.

Beau appeared to relax a bit at the suggestive comment. "I hear ya. That'll work out for her brother. I'd hate for him or some other family member to have another accident. One with a worse outcome."

Trent clenched his teeth at the idea. He knew the comment to be a test and did his best to keep his face expressionless. He shrugged as if he didn't care.

"Mike doesn't like me much. The feeling's mutual."

Beau studied his face and must have liked what he saw. "I'll remember that if we need to remind him again to keep his mouth shut."

"Again?"

"Let's just say the accident he had wasn't exactly unintentional."

Trent kept his face impassive. "I see. It wouldn't hurt my feelings if I did the reminding for you."

Beau stared at him for several seconds. "Good to know. You take the river area. Keep watch and make sure the only thing out there is the boat picking up the shipment. Take this two-way radio and report when you hear propellers."

Trent needed to talk to Mike to warn him. No, he couldn't do that. It might compromise the mission. He couldn't let Shelby's family be hurt. He'd talk to Jim and see what he suggested. For now he needed to focus on the mission. "No problem. Can I pick up some extra gear?"

"Good idea. Night vision binoculars would be a smart choice." Beau waved toward the building with all the weapons, then turned and walked toward the other men.

"Yeah, I had the same plan." Trent strode over to the small building holding the arsenal of weapons where he'd initially picked out an MP5 and Uzi. He'd brought them along, added more ammo, the binoculars, and a flak vest. He hoped he wouldn't need the extra ammo, but it would be less for Beau's men to use in a possible shoot out.

Taking up his post at the water's edge, he put the binoculars to his eyes and scanned the area. He saw some branches floating down the river and nothing more. He listened for any noise out of the ordinary, but only heard night birds, like the hoot of owls and squawks of night-herons, along with frogs and the whirr of mosquitoes. Insects weren't much trouble in the winter. Being this close to the river the damn mosquitoes always buzzed around.

Recalling Beau's remark about Shelby and her family caused him unease. He understood Mike knew of the drug operation, had even threatened him at Thanksgiving. At that time he assumed Mike had some connection to the operation. Now he realized he didn't. Since Beau made sure he had an accident he must have interfered in some way. There would be a confrontation if Mike found out about Trent's role in tonight's events. Would Beau harm Shelby if he suspected Trent betrayed him? Hell yes, he would. A chill shot down his back that had nothing to do with the frigid air. He'd need to rethink his relationship with Shelby. He'd never endanger her or her family.

Shaking off theories that would distract him, Trent set about considering his mission. His post set him up perfectly to plant the tracking devices the DEA provided him. All during his musings he looked through the binoculars. Watching and waiting. It reminded him of the patrols he'd gone on in the Middle East. Of course, when he'd been there the temperatures had climbed so high he felt as if he'd combust. In South Carolina, the extra warmth of the flak vest felt welcome on this cold wintry night. He grinned at the idea of cold weather. Being Southern born and raised, temperatures in the low forties felt glacial to him. His old first sergeant had been from New Jersey and enjoyed regaling them of the real winters where snow was plowed higher than the mailboxes and the ground remained hidden until April. No way would he live in such a climate if he had a choice.

As he scanned the opposite bank again he noticed a slight movement. He stared harder and noticed a ripple in the water as if something had entered the river. Something big. A gator? Unlikely during this cold weather. He focused on the spot and strained to hear what had caused the ripple. Sound always carried over water so he tried to hear anything not attributable to nature. What if he spotted someone? He knew they weren't DEA. They'd assured him he would be on his own this time. They wanted information more than an arrest. He knew if he alerted Beau he'd send men over to investigate in a flash. Could it be the local cops? It wouldn't be unheard of for an operation like this to be surveilled if they suspected something illegal. Or could it be a rival? Now that would be worth reporting.

This type of shipment had been done many, many times without interference. He pulled the radio out of his pocket to report when he heard the low growl of a motor coming up the river. He whispered into the radio about the approach. All activity stopped and lights went out. They'd make sure the boat matched their expectations before approaching with the cargo.

Beau and a couple of other men joined him as they waited for the vessel's appearance. In moments it arrived, and Beau confirmed its identity. Even motoring at a slow speed it did cause a wake. Trent watched the spot where he'd seen movement earlier. Sure enough he spotted a small craft, probably a canoe. He even thought he heard a muffled yelp. So who waited out there? It couldn't be more than two people, so the possibility of a rival gang didn't add up. Deciding to continue his silence since it might be some local police, he made no mention of the event.

"All hands on deck for loading. It should take no more than five minutes," Beau said and Trent shouldered his weapons and pitched in. It couldn't have worked out better for him to place the transmitters. Once on board the boat he found the perfect spot for the last transmitter. It should avoid detection even when they did routine maintenance. Satisfied with the successful mission, he smiled and hopped back on land.

"Trent, you stay at your post. They'll continue upstream a ways to turn around and then back down. Watch to make sure it returns in a reasonable time. When it's out of sight join us in the building." Beau trotted off with the rest of the crew.

As instructed, Trent watched, concentrating on the place where the small canoe hid in the trees. Other than the problem during the wake, whoever occupied it kept quiet and remained motionless. They were disciplined. Must be local cops. Although there had been the screech. A female cop? He frowned as he puzzled over the possibilities. Before long the other boat motored back down the river again, no doubt sloshing water into the small craft across from him. No screech this time.

He turned and found his way to Beau and the rest of the crew. A party ensued, with lots of liquor and drugs passed around. He managed to smile and accept a glass of something. Being careful not to consume anything, he took every opportunity to spill some of his drink so as to have an empty glass to refill.

Beau wandered over to him. "That was an easy payday, right, Trent?"

"Yeah, boss, I won't mind more of those." Trent agreed with as much enthusiasm as he could muster.

"We do this about once a month. Some times more often, some times less. Depends on the demand."

"So where does this stuff go?" Trent took the opportunity to quiz Beau.

Shaking a finger at him Beau replied, "A secret for me to keep. We make more for local distribution so if you're interested, Jamie can hook you up."

"I'm good with just booze. However, I might know some guys who would be interested."

"Off the wagon?" Beau jeered. "Fine, fine. More money in my pocket. Jamie will set you up with whatever."

"So what kind of drugs?"

"Meth and ecstasy, sometimes special K. But only for the shipments out."

"Hey, didn't you earn a degree in chemical engineering?" Trent acted like the thought occurred to him that moment. "Is that where you came up with this plan and learned to make it?"

"Cook it. The term is, cook it." His exaggerated nodding emphasized the fact he was drunk or stoned. "That's where I learned to cook. The plan came later. Glad you're with us." Beau motioned him over to a table with a metal box on top. He flipped open the box and pulled out a stack of money. He shoved it into Trent's hands. "Here ya go. Your share of tonight's profit."

"Hey, this is great. I know exactly what I'm going to do with it." Trent took the dirty money, assuming it would become evidence.

Beau swallowed a big gulp of whatever liquor filled his glass. "Good, good. Be sure to take the luscious Shelby someplace nice. Maybe a fancy hotel." He laughed as if he'd said the funniest joke ever.

Trent shook his head. "Nah, I don't want her asking questions about where the money came from. I'll find a couple of willing ladies and show them a great time and then they can show me their appreciation. If you know what I mean." Trent grinned and winked.

Beau slapped him on the back. "Great idea. I know some women who will make you happy. Twins. Blonde hair and big tits." Beau used both hands to indicate the size of their breasts.

Trent waved his hand in a negative way. "No thanks. I've been eyeing a couple. Until now I didn't have the bread to make their dreams come true." He laughed at the crude comment, knowing it would satisfy Beau.

"Well then, I guess you have things all lined up. Good luck." The lascivious smile Beau gave repulsed him, but he kept the information to himself.

Trent continued to spill his drink and talk with the rest of the crew, trying to find out more information about the boat and where it was headed. No one knew except Beau. At least they wouldn't tell him. He didn't worry about it. The transmitter would provide information soon enough.

Finally, some of the men left and Trent felt relieved to join them. He'd only hung around because he didn't want to look suspicious departing early.

"Don't forget, be at work at noon. No excuses." Beau shouted at the men leaving.

Although Trent wasn't the first to leave the building, he managed to be the first out of the parking lot. The others had trouble opening their car doors and finding the ignition. He had no intention of having a wreck with all these crazy drunks and stoners.

Arriving back at his house, he double-checked to make sure no one followed him, and confirmed all the blinds were down and curtains drawn. He tore off the tape holding the secure phone.

"Ouch. That hurt like a bitch." He muttered to himself when it took some hair with it. It had been uncomfortable as hell, but he thought it the best place to record anything and keep it out of sight.

He dialed the number for his contact. "I'm back. Everything went well. Did you hear anything?"

"Good. Not much. Service went in and out. Do you usually have cell service out there?" Trent heard the frustration in his contact's voice.

"Like you said, it's in and out. I didn't convince Beau or anyone else to tell me where the shipment would land. Or who planned to receive it." Trent paced the floor while he spoke.

"That's okay, the transmitters are doing their job. We'll find out before too long." Trent heard the sigh at the end of the statement and knew he wasn't alone with his anxiety.

One important tidbit came to mind. "Did you hear him say they do this about once a month?"

"No, we didn't. You must have been inside. There was a lot of interference." The information perked up his contact. "Write up everything now before you forget since we weren't able to record the whole conversation."

Trent huffed at the comment. "Man, I'm wiped out. Can't it wait until morning?"

"No. Do it now," came the firm reply. "You'll forget half of it if you sleep on it."

"All right. All right. Once I've written it down, do you want me to take it to the dead drop at the cemetery?" He plopped down on the couch, suddenly exhausted.

"That'll be good. We haven't used that one in a while. Can you do it before you head to work tomorrow?"

"Yeah." It occurred to Trent he should find out about the people who'd watched the operation. "By the way, do you know if any local cops or some other agency staked out the area tonight?"

"No, why? Did you see someone?" The disembodied voice expressed more curiosity than alarm.

"I did. I have no idea how many or who they were. Someone watched from the river bank across from the dock. In a small canoe so I doubt there were more than two people."

"Shit. I hope they don't blow this." Now his contact sounded worried. "I'll see what I can find out. You didn't say anything to Beau, did you?"

Trent couldn't believe he'd asked. "Hell no. Whoever they were would be dead if I'd done that. At first I suspected it might be a rival gang, but since it looked like only two people and they stuck to watching, I discounted it as a possibility.

After Trent cut the connection, he stood up from the couch and went to his makeshift desk, the dining room table. He pulled out his laptop and set about detailing the events of the evening. Choosing to leave off the part stating Beau's snide comments about Shelby, he stopped typing for a moment. Beau had mentioned their relationship on other occasions. Trent had decided previously to continue seeing Shelby, thinking he could keep her safe. However, they'd been seen together at least once too often. Mike already had one accident. He couldn't let another one happen to either of them. He would need to end things with her. The idea cut deep. Their relationship had moved on to such intimacy he knew she'd be devastated. And so was he. The idea of her or someone else in her family being hurt physically by Beau and his men solidified his resolve. No matter what, he needed to end it.

CHAPTER TWENTY-SIX

Shivering in their wet clothes, Amy and Shelby paddled back to the boat landing. After they'd pulled the canoe out of the water, they slipped into the car.

"I've never been this cold in my life. Can you make the heater work harder?" Shelby asked.

"I wish I could. At least mine is working." Amy peeled her coat off.

Shelby had already removed her hat—about the only thing not soaked. She struggled out of her coat and tossed it in the back seat next to Amy's. "I'd love to take off my jeans, but I know I'd never get them back on."

"I have some old beach towels in the trunk." Amy hopped out of the car and snatched the towels and returned in a flash. "Maybe we can soak up some of the water from our pants using these. Here." She handed one to Shelby.

"Ah, that feels better." Shelby wrapped it around her legs and tried to soak up the water from her jeans.

"Doesn't it? You know we're going to have to go back out there and put the canoe on top of the car."

"Yeah, I know. I need to warm up first. Then we'll tackle it." Shelby pulled up her pant legs and dried off her legs from the knees down.

"At least our top half didn't end up wet as well." Amy followed Shelby's lead.

"Thank goodness."

They both luxuriated in the warmth of the car heater. Finally, Shelby said, "It's time. We can't sit here all night."

They struggled back into their wet coats and stepped out of the car. The cold hit them like a brick wall. "Damn, this is worse than before," Shelby admitted.

"Don't think, just do it," Amy advised.

They managed to maneuver the canoe back on top of the car and tied it down. Amy floored the accelerator, pushing her car to arrive home as quickly as possible.

"Get out of your clothes and I'll wash and dry them. You can have a pair of my sweats." Amy headed toward her bedroom.

"Thanks. Do you mind if I take a hot shower?" Shelby yelled as she stripped off her clothes in the laundry room.

"Go ahead, but don't take long. I'll be right behind you." Amy emerged wearing a warm looking bathrobe and handed Shelby a towel and warm garments.

After Shelby had showered and put on the outfit Amy provided, she made her way to the kitchen and fixed them both some hot tea. She chose the decaffeinated variety so it wouldn't keep them up too late. However, she didn't think mere caffeine would keep her awake at this point. She could fall asleep at the kitchen table.

The tea was ready about the time Amy walked into the kitchen. "Ah, thanks, Shelby. Exactly what I needed. Between the shower and this, I might feel human soon."

Shelby replied, "I know what you mean. Aside from the canoe being swamped, I think we had a successful night."

"I agree. We have the name of the boat and the date of this shipment. This should catch the attention of the DEA."

Shelby frowned and pursed her lips. "The only problem is the lack of evidence that the shipment contained drugs." She stood up and started pacing around the small room.

Amy looked startled by her comment. "But surely the fact it occurred in the middle of the night and men with guns stood guard should indicate something illegal."

"You don't have to convince me. It's the DEA we need to satisfy." She knew her anger showed on her face.

Nodding her agreement, Amy switched subjects. "I'm sorry about Trent."

Shelby's eyes filled with tears. She refused to let them fall. "Me, too. I couldn't believe it when I saw him standing there with an Uzi. He might not have known about the drugs before tonight, but I have to admit he's in with them now."

Amy reached over and patted Shelby's hand. "Maybe now he knows, he'll quit."

"Maybe." Shaking off the unpleasant thought, she felt grateful Amy went back to their earlier discussion.

"We'll have to state our case to the DEA and see what happens."

"Let's each make a list of points to make sure we cover everything."

"Good idea." They each took a few moments to write down their thoughts.

After they both put down their pens Shelby picked up her phone. . "The division office is in Atlanta and the address is listed online. I know we don't want to drive all the way there, so we'll have to settle for a phone call. There's a number for Florence."

"I'd hoped we could speak to someone face-to-face."

"Me, too. The other option entailed submitting a statement on their website." Shelby wrinkled her nose. "The whole thing might sound like a hoax on paper. Once we make this report, I'm hoping they send someone out here."

Amy shrugged her shoulders. "Not much choice. Go ahead."

"Let's compare notes before we make the call."

They reviewed each other's notes and marked a few things on both sets before dialing. Shelby enabled the speaker phone so they could both hear and talk.

After going through an operator they were finally connected. "Drug Enforcement Agency, Senior Agent Callahan speaking."

Shelby and Amy provided all the details they had.

"Thank you, ladies, for your information. The DEA has something we call a Post of Duty in Myrtle Beach, so we'll have someone contact you soon. They'll want to set up an interview."

Shelby felt a sense of relief. "Good. It will be easier to give them a map for the location of the plant and some other details." The tightness in her chest lessened.

After they said goodbye and disconnected the call, they both looked at each other.

"That went well. Didn't it?" Shelby felt a bit disheartened.

Amy reached over and patted her on the arm. "I think we'll have the answer to that question once we receive the call back."

Shelby gave her a crooked smile. "At least they didn't call us crazy or tell us we had no proof."

Amy returned her smile. "Yeah, I suppose."

Shelby drew the map.

Amy stood up and started walking toward the bedroom. "Let's try to get some sleep. Maybe they'll call before you leave in the morning."

"Agreed." Shelby had stayed at Amy's on other occasions so she knew where the blankets were kept. She made up the couch and fell asleep as soon as she was prone.

Shelby's cell phone rang a few hours later. In spite of her deep sleep she woke immediately and snatched it up. "Yes? Shelby Cornwell."

The person on the other end explained who he was and why he called. Shelby went to Amy's room and shook her awake. "Let me put you on speaker phone. My friend, Amy, is with me and she'll want to listen." Her smile said it all. The DEA had returned their call.

"Ladies, I want to thank you for the information you've provided. I'd like to set up a time when we can go over your statement. I also understand you have a map..."

"Yes, we do. We can meet today if you're available." Anxious to finish, Shelby started talking before he finished his sentence.

"We have an opening at four o'clock this afternoon. Let me give you directions to our facility."

After she disconnected the call, Shelby let out a big sigh. "Thank God. It's almost over."

"Our part in this, at least. What I haven't asked you before now is, what about Trent? Are you going to tell the agents about him?"

Shelby frowned. "I've been trying to decide." After hesitating several seconds she took a deep breath. "No, I'm not. Not right now. I'm going to confront Trent. I want to hear his side of the story. If I can convince him to give it up, I doubt any of the guys who are really involved will mention his name. What would be the point?" Shelby looked at Amy, hoping she agreed.

Amy remained quiet for several minutes. "All right. I won't give them his name either. However, if Trent continues his work with the drugs, we know it's only a matter of time before he'll be caught." Amy leaned forward and stared directly into Shelby's eyes. "You *cannot* tell him about this meeting. Understood?"

The idea of not telling Trent the whole truth didn't feel right. However, Amy had a point. If she did tell him and he continued his work with Beau and the drugs, he'd share the information. Then all their work would be for nothing.

Slow to respond, Shelby said, "Okay. I promise I won't say anything to him."

Amy smiled a sad smile. "I know it's difficult, but it's for the best."

Shelby threw on some clothes and sped back to the resort. She dressed for work and stepped into her Boss's office.

"Excuse me, sir. I need to take about three hours personal time this afternoon. I'm ready to work now and I'll come back after my appointment."

His frown told her he wasn't happy before he spoke. "What time do you need to leave?"

"About three-thirty."

"If you have all the preparations for the Talbot party ready by that time then fine. You need to return to make sure nothing's gone amiss. Understood?"

"Of course, sir."

Shelby planned to start looking for a position at another resort after New Year's. Dealing with this man became more unbearable each week.

The staff and she made quick work of setting up for the party.

Shelby met Amy in front of the Post of Duty location. Ushered into a small conference room an agent joined them.

"Let's go over the story again." The agent said immediately after their introductions.

"Didn't the other people give you a transcript of what we said?" Amy asked, her eyebrows raised.

"They did. We want to start from the beginning and hear it all again. Sometimes people make inflections when they talk and it can be important."

So they told their story again the same way, with Shelby starting the conversation and Amy taking over when Shelby stopped. Each of them looked at their notes.

"So why do you have notes?" The agent had recorded the conversation and made notes on a pad.

"We wanted to make sure we didn't forget anything."

The agent turned to a fresh page in his notebook. "All right. Now let's go back again and take this one step at a time."

They sat in the office about three hours going over every detail of their statement. The agent asked them all sorts of questions. It started with their suspicions and ended with the night they took the canoe out.

"Again, I want to thank you ladies for providing this information to our office. I commend you for your interest in your community and your desire to rid it of this problem." The agent's friendly expression morphed into a stern one. "However, now that you've given us the information, please do *not* continue any type of surveillance or attempt to find out more details. It is too dangerous. You've already risked your lives doing what you've done. Please don't speak of this with anyone else."

"We wanted to give you the best possible evidence," Shelby said.

"I understand. However, you could have been killed. People involved in making and selling drugs will eliminate anyone who interferes. Now leave this to us." The agent stood up as if to leave.

"Will you tell us after you've made an arrest?" Amy asked before he left the room.

He turned and gave them a stern look. "It doesn't work that way. You'll know when you read it in the paper."

Shelby asked, "Will it be soon?"

As the agent turned back to the door, he said over his shoulder, "I have no idea how long it will take. We'll need to verify all this information. You've given us a lot to look at."

He left the room. Amy and Shelby looked at each other, then the door opened again. The receptionist returned to escort them out of the building.

"I don't know what I thought would happen, but not that." Shelby huffed and waved her hand in irritation.

"I figured they'd rush out to Beau's plant and arrest everyone. Of course, we should have realized they need to confirm our information. Plus we both know we didn't give them any evidence of the actual drugs."

Shelby opened the car door. "At least they know where to look. And they will. They also have the name of the boat. That has to be worth a lot."

Amy peered at her. "We have to keep this to ourselves. You can't even tell your parents."

"I know, I know. That's going to be the hardest part of all."

CHAPTER TWENTY-SEVEN

"I suspect a couple of local ladies were the two people across the river from you, watching the other night." Jim made the announcement during a secure phone conversation about a week after the night shipment. Jim normally let a lesser agent handle these reports.

"What? They weren't cops?" Trent sat up straight in the recliner where he'd been lounging. All the blinds and curtains in the house remained firmly closed to make sure no one saw him.

"Nope. Ordinary concerned citizens," Jim replied.

"My God, they could have been killed." His statement came out in a whisper.

"If it had been anyone except you on watch that night, they probably would have been." Trent could hear the concern in Jim's voice.

"I hope you told them to stay out of this mess." Trent's voice sounded harsh even to his own ears.

"I didn't speak to them, but yes, they received a stern warning to stop investigating and leave it up to us. I knew right away they must be the two you'd seen because they had the name of the boat."

"They better listen to you. It could have ruined our investigation." Trent's comment came out more like a growl.

"The point is they didn't know about an investigation. It is good to know there are people in the community who want this to stop."

Trent's breath came out in a whoosh. "You're right. But it makes my head explode thinking about what could have happened."

"Yeah, it does."

"Speaking of people in the community not liking the drug operation. Beau told me about an accident he engineered. To remind someone to keep their mouth shut. Is there anything we can do about it?"

"Not if we want to keep our advantage of surprise." Jim paused a moment and then continued. "If you hear about a specific threat I'll contact the local police anonymously. That's the best I can offer right now. So let's move on. You said you are in Beau's confidence and in on the local distribution."

Trent set aside any opinions about the people and switched to the real reason for their conversation. "Exactly. Jamie's in charge, but he takes his orders from Beau. I can tell."

"Why do you say that?" Trent heard Jim tapping his pencil on the desk. "I understand he's the head man, but you don't think Beau trusts him enough to handle it without instructions?"

Trent knew his opponent well. "Beau's always been a control freak. No way would he allow anyone to do anything he didn't plan ahead of time."

"So if we take out Beau the operation dies?"

Trent stood up and paced while talking. "I feel confident it would."

"That's good to know." Jim's voice sounded skeptical. "It might make this easier."

"Did you find out where the shipment ended up?"

"We did, thanks to the transmitters. They must not have found them because we've been tracking the boat since you inserted them. Eventually the battery will wear out. We've gained a lot of information in the meantime."

Trent suspected the boat's destination, but he wanted to confirm. "Did it go back to Boston?"

"Yeah, exactly like we thought. He must have made contact with one of the big distributors back when he attended MIT. They made an agreement of some kind for Beau to start his own plant, but continue cooking for the Boston kingpin."

"Sounds right to me. So what's the next step?" Trent was anxious for the undercover operation to end.

"Try to find out as much detail about the local distribution. Do you think Jamie has anything written down? Or is it all in his head?"

It felt good that Jim had confidence in his intuition.

Trent frowned because he'd wondered the same thing. "A very good question and I've been thinking about it for a while. He might have information on his phone. Can you gain access to it?"

"That's a sticky situation. I'm not sure we can, even with probably cause. So far all we've done is track a ship and the cargo. No proof of drugs. We don't have enough evidence right now. Plus we don't want to spook him. See what you can do."

"All right. I think his wife might be the way in." Trent felt sorry for Missy, but she might be the key.

"She mad at him?" Trent heard the surprise in Jim's voice.

"I have no idea, but I know she's also Beau's mistress." That one issue could mean success or failure for Trent.

"What?" Jim paused. "That could get ugly."

"I think it already has. For her at least." Every time he'd seen her lately she'd been so drunk or stoned she could barely walk. "I think she might be getting tired of Beau using her for a booty call. She'd divorce Jamie in a second if she suspected Beau would make her his wife." Trent shook his head at her misfortune to fall in love with the wrong man.

"But you don't think he will."

"Nah. He's using her. Always has. She's not good enough to marry." Saying it out loud made it sound even uglier.

"Not good enough for a drug manufacturer and distributor?" Jim sounded surprised.

"Not good enough for the Jacksons of Georgetown, South Carolina."

Jim guffawed at the distinction. "Oh, sorry. I forgot about all the family history."

"Believe me, it's an integral part of this whole thing."

"I'll take your word. I'm only interested in what you can find out about the local distribution. We want to round up as many of those people as we can." Jim circled back around to the primary mission.

"I'll see what I can come up with. Will there be a task force at the next big shipment?"

"If you can find out when it is and have names of the local distributors, it would be a great time to round everyone up. Let me know if you hear about a date."

After ending his call with Jim, comments about Missy and her relationships made Trent think of his romance with Shelby. He'd been plagued with the knowledge he needed to end it. Perhaps they could reunite once this mess came to a conclusion. If she didn't hate him for arresting all her friends in Georgetown. Or if he failed to protect Mike. There were a lot of ifs.

Dreading to do it, he took a deep breath and picked up his phone to dial her number. "Shelby, how are you?"

"Trent. I'm glad you called."

Did he hear hesitation in her voice? Or was it his own nerves? "If you're free I'll stop by Tuesday evening. Maybe have some dinner and see a movie?" Trent didn't think they'd make the movie. He planned to break things off after dinner.

"Yes, I'd like to. What time can I expect you?" Shelby's voice held a note of frost.

It must be his guilty conscience, but he could swear she didn't sound pleased about the date. "How about seven o'clock?"

"Great. I'll be ready. I'm sorry to cut you off, but I have something important going on right now. A Christmas party set up."

Well, that explained it. She probably had people standing close enough to hear their conversation. "See you Tuesday." Trent had barely said goodbye before she disconnected.

The next day dragged by since he kept trying to think of a way to let Shelby down easily and yet leave an opening for future reconciliation. Would she be interested in him if she found out he worked as a cop? A lot of women didn't want to be involved with cops due to the danger. Then again, other women thought men with guns were sexy. He had no idea which category Shelby fell in. Round and round he considered several scenarios and discarded them all.

Tuesday arrived. He dawdled on his way home from work, dreading the upcoming confrontation. After arriving home he took a quick shower, and then drove to Shelby's resort. When he knocked on her door, it took forever for her to answer.

She gave him a peck on the cheek. "Trent. Come on in. I need to put my coat on and I'll be ready." Grabbing her coat, she shrugged into it. The smile on her face didn't match the look in her eye.

"Great. How about Travinia Italian Kitchen over in Market Common?" Trent asked as they walked toward the parking garage.

"Perfect. I'm starved." She didn't sound enthusiastic in spite of her words.

It might be his nerves, but their conversation on the way to the restaurant seemed stilted to his ears. Being a Tuesday night and off-season the restaurant didn't have many patrons, so they were seated right away.

While perusing the menu he tried to lighten the conversation. "You seem quieter than usual tonight. Having to deal with all the Christmas cheer a bit too much?"

Shelby didn't pick up on the humor. "It is a busy time of year for me. All the local businesses are having their Christmas parties. Once New Year's is over it will quiet down again for a few months."

After they ordered, the conversation lagged, and they both drank more wine than usual. When their food arrived Shelby picked at hers. For someone who said she was starved, she didn't eat much. Trent had to admit he didn't have much of an appetite either.

He paid the bill and they walked to the car. "Shelby, I have something to say to you."

At the same time, Shelby said, "Trent, we need to talk."

Trent laughed humorlessly. "Should we head back to your place?"

"I think it would be easiest." Shelby didn't look at him.

A few minutes later they arrived at her suite. Trent took her key and opened the door. They both took off their coats and Shelby fixed a drink for each of them. It looked like a delaying tactic to him. Whatever she planned to say wouldn't be good.

"I hope you don't mind if I go first." Shelby settled onto the chair across from Trent.

"Go ahead." He knew what she planned to say. She didn't want to see him again. Resigned, he sat in silence.

Shelby fiddled with her glass, then looked at Trent and blurted out, "I know you're involved in the drug operation at Beau's plant."

He tried to not let her see how freaked out he was. He felt the blood rush to his brain and took a deep breath to calm his nerves before he answered with as little emotion as possible. "I work for Beau as a security guard."

"Yes, during drug shipments."

Trent eyebrows shot up. "What?" How did she find out? She couldn't know for sure.

"Don't bother to deny it. I know." Shelby put her glass on the coffee table and stood up. She paced around the room for a minute. "I can't be involved with someone who does that sort of thing."

"So you're breaking up with me?" Making the statement in a composed voice took a lot of willpower.

"Maybe." Shelby made it sound like a plea. "If you plan to continue working with Beau, then I guess I am. What I'd prefer is for you to stop working for him. Then we can still be together." Shelby sat down again and looked Trent in the eye. Her eyes implored him.

Trent took a moment to digest the information. How did she know? He'd think about that later. She'd handed him the perfect reason to break up with her.

"Shelby, you don't understand. This is an opportunity for me to make some real money. Money that can give me, us, a better life." Trent set down his glass, working hard to explain reasoning for something he didn't even want.

Shelby made slashing motions with her hand. "I don't want to have anything to do with money from drugs."

"It's money." Trent threw up his hands. "If I don't take it someone else will."

"No, I don't want you working there."

Trent huffed out a deep breath. "A lot of people do."

"I know that, but I don't want you to be one of them."

"So what do you want me to do?" Sarcasm dripped from his words. "Work at the paper mill?"

"You don't have to work in Georgetown." The entreaty in her voice was unmistakable. "You can find work here in Myrtle Beach or Charleston."

"Doing what?" Trent stood up and paced around the room, throwing his hands up in the air. "Being a night guard at a hotel? Or maybe a waiter at a restaurant?" He put his face directly in front of Shelby. "Yeah, like I have a lot of experience. Not something I want to do. No. I'm going to stay right where I am, doing exactly what I want." Trent stood with his arms crossed and a frown on his face.

"But you could end up dead." Her statement came out in a tiny voice and her lower lip trembled.

He considered her statement. The same would be true if she knew about his real job as a cop. So they probably wouldn't have a future together even if she knew the truth.

It took everything Trent had not to cave to her demand. "That's unlikely. I've asked around. Beau doesn't have any competition nearby. He took care of that a few years ago." He started pacing again and waved his arms.

"There haven't been any gun fights in a long time. The cops leave him alone. It's a piece of cake."

Shelby looked at him for several seconds. "It might not always be that way."

"Why? Do you know something?" He stared hard at her. "Have you talked to the cops?"

"No. No, of course not." Shelby looked down at her glass. "I want you to be safe. I don't want you arrested. Please." She looked back up at him with tears ready to fall. "Won't you do this for me?"

"I'm doing this for me." *God, I sound like a selfish bastard.* "I thought I was doing it for *us*, but I must have been wrong."

"Then you won't quit?" A tear rolled down Shelby's cheek. Her face turned to stone.

"I can't." That said it all. The truth sounded ugly.

"Then I'll have to ask you to leave." Shelby stood up and walked to the door. "Don't call. Not unless you change your mind." She opened the door and waited for him to leave.

"So we're done?" Trent walked over and picked up his coat.

"Yes. I guess we are."

"Fine." Trent stormed out of the room. After he made it to the parking garage he leaned on his truck. God, that was the hardest thing he'd ever done. Even more difficult than when he joined the army at eighteen, leaving his sixteen-year-old brother alone with their dying mother.

He pounded his fist on his truck. He didn't care that he dented it in the process. Swearing a blue streak, he opened the door, climbed in, and shot out of the garage, speeding all the way to Georgetown.

It took a couple of hours to calm down enough to think rationally. So how had Shelby found out about his being a guard during the drug shipment? Her brother, Mike? He had something to do with the drug operation. Trent still didn't know what. Mike made it clear at Thanksgiving he didn't want anyone associated with the drug operation to be involved with his sister. So he didn't think Mike tipped her off.

What about an informant? No, that couldn't be right either. Jim would know about one, wouldn't he? Jim had assured him the local cops had no ongoing investigation. Even if an informant existed, how would Shelby hear about it?

He'd pushed the next idea to the back of his mind. It couldn't be true. Shelby had been one of the women in the canoe. If he asked Jim he could confirm it. All this time he tried to keep Shelby unnoticed by the DEA and the men associated with drug manufacturing. He'd failed in preventing Beau's awareness from the beginning. He had too many eyes and ears in the area who would report back. As far as he knew the DEA had been kept in the dark until she walked into their office.

No matter. He'd distanced himself from Shelby to keep her safe. Maybe he could explain after Beau went down. Of course, her brother might go down at the same time. Family meant everything to Shelby. Would she forgive him? His job as a cop meant he'd still be in danger. Would Shelby want him? He hoped so. It was important.

Why? Why this gut-wrenching desire to be with Shelby? He'd been wrestling with the answer for some time now.

He hadn't realized until that moment that he loved her.

CHAPTER TWENTY-EIGHT

Shelby cried after Trent left. Why didn't he listen to her? He'd be arrested with the rest of Beau's crew when the DEA verified her information. Images of the raid rolled around in her head. Trying to stem the tears, she made her way to the bathroom and prepared a cold cloth for her eyes. Now she had a headache. Great.

She made a cup of chamomile tea. Perhaps it would soothe her enough to allow some sleep. Her phone rang. Trent? Her hopes soared for a moment until she recalled her warning not to call. Looking at the caller ID, she smiled when she saw Amy's name.

"Hello, Amy."

"Shelby. You sound awful. Do you have a cold?"

"No. I've been crying."

"Crying? What happened? Is Mike okay?"

"Yes, yes, he's fine. No lingering problems with his concussion. It's Trent." Her voice cracked when she said his name. Not able to continue, she sat waiting for Amy to say something.

"Trent? Did you break things off with him?" Amy's voice held sympathy.

"Yes. I told him he had to quit working there. He won't. I begged him, Amy. Begged him and he still won't do it." She felt more tears starting to fall.

"Oh, Shelby, sweetheart. I'm so sorry. You knew it might happen." Hearing Amy say it out loud didn't help. However, she knew Amy was right.

"I thought he cared enough for me." Shelby realized her voice had turned into a wail. "He actually said he did it for us. So we could have money." Sniffling, Shelby stopped talking. With an effort she controlled her tears. "Money isn't important to me."

"I know it isn't. Maybe it is to Trent. Perhaps he needs the stability money can buy."

"But he'll be arrested." Shelby sobbed.

"I know. I know. All you can do is be there for him when it happens. If it happens."

"What do you mean, if it happens?" Amy's comment stopped Shelby's bout of crying. "Of course it will. The whole crew will be arrested."

"I know it's what the DEA wants to do, but what if they do it on Trent's day off? Or he calls in sick that day? A lot of things could happen and he won't be there during the bust."

Shelby smiled. "Thanks, Amy, you've given me some hope. But you know your suggestions are unlikely."

"Do you want me to come over?" Amy asked, the sympathy apparent in her voice.

"No, thanks. I'll be okay." She'd forget Trent and move on. In different circumstances earlier in her life she had to move past something even more devastating and she managed. She'd do it again.

"Are you sure?"

"Yes, I am. I'll be fine." This time Shelby said it with more confidence.

The Christmas holiday approached and Shelby's resort held many of the Christmas parties for locals and tourists alike. This year, thanks to the new ideas Shelby had, their resort hosted family reunions. To locals the weather felt icy cold, but people from the north thought it delightful. They booked suites where families would celebrate Christmas with relatives unable or unwilling to head farther north. During the daytime, her busy life kept her happy and satisfied. At night, not so much. When she finally managed to go to bed, Trent appeared in her dreams. Erotic dreams. She dreamt of Trent's hands on her breasts and his tongue in her mouth. She could almost feel his body weighing on hers. She'd wake unsatisfied and cranky.

On her day off she made plans to have dinner with her parents and brother. She hadn't seen Mike since his concussion.

She brought deviled eggs and an ambrosia salad, easy things to make in her cramped kitchenette.

"Hey, Mom." Shelby walked through the back door and gave her mom a peck on the cheek.

"It's so good to see you, dear. Let me have one of those and we'll put them in the fridge for now." Tina took the ambrosia and then the eggs and placed them in the refrigerator.

"So how's Mike?" Shelby settled into a chair at the kitchen table.

"I'm fine, Sis." Mike strode into the kitchen from the living room, a beer in his hand.

"No headaches?" Shelby looked him over as if she could see some outward sign if he told the truth or not.

"Sheesh, how many times do I have to tell everyone?" Mike shook his head and took another swig of beer. "I'm fine. No headaches. No nausea. No sensitivity to light. No balance issues. Nothing. Nada. I'm fine." Setting his beer on the table, he sat in the chair next to Shelby and glared at her.

"Okay, okay. I had no idea you were so sensitive." Shelby grinned and raised her hands in defeat.

"I'm not." Mike grumbled, but looked a bit ashamed of his outburst. "Everyone asks me that same question every day and twice on Sundays."

"Now dear, no need to be defensive." Tina brought over some stuffed celery, carrots, and olives as an appetizer. Setting the plate on the table, she patted Mike on the back.

"Sorry, Mom." Mike took a deep breath and then slowly exhaled.

"I'm so glad the two of you could join us for dinner. Shelby, it sounds like you've been super busy at work," Greg said.

"Yes, I have. Which is nice for December. We don't normally have this much activity. My idea for reunions seems to be working well."

"You're having high school reunions at this time of year?" Her father's eyebrows rose almost to his hair line.

"No, not high school reunions. Family reunions. Mostly retired people who've moved here and don't want to go back north for Christmas, so they've convinced their families to come here for a reunion and celebrate Christmas a bit early."

"Great idea." Tina passed out plates and silverware. "I know if I lived where it snowed so much I'd come down here."

"Exactly," Shelby continued, "especially after the last couple of years when the winters have been so brutal. And Mrs. Jackson is having a family reunion on Christmas Eve. She originally specified the day after Christmas but she switched to the day before. I don't think I'll have another day off until Christmas."

"Your boss should be happy."

"He's floating on cloud nine one minute and barking at me to make sure nothing goes wrong the next."

"All right, everyone." Tina placed a platter of fried chicken in front of them. "Dinner is ready. Shelby, give me a hand putting things on the table."

They sat eating and chatting, each bringing the others up to date on the events of their lives over the past couple of weeks.

"So, dear, will Trent be joining us for Christmas dinner?" Tina's smile indicated she'd be happy if he did.

Shelby hadn't mentioned her breakup with Trent. It still hurt too much. "No, he won't be joining us." She looked down at her plate, not wanting to make eye contact. She didn't elaborate.

"Oh, is he visiting his brother?" Tina asked.

"I have no idea what he'll be doing for Christmas." Shelby took a deep breath. "We aren't seeing each other anymore. Pass the potatoes, please, Mike."

"Good for you." Mike gave her the bowl.

"Now, Mike, don't be like that," Tina admonished.

"I can't help it. He's not right for Shelby," Mike grumbled.

"That's not for you to decide." Greg patted Shelby's hand in sympathy. "Whatever the reason, I'm sure Shelby knows best."

"Thanks, Dad." Shelby gave her father a smile that felt more like a grimace.

"How about you, Mike?" Tina switched the focus to her brother. "Will you be bringing Joyce?"

"I know she has plans with her family Christmas morning. What time is dinner?"

"We're flexible. We can have it around one o'clock, but if she can't make it, then perhaps we can have it at six o'clock." Tina looked at Shelby, concern showing in her eyes.

Mike stuffed more ambrosia salad into his mouth. "I'll check with her and let you know in a day or two."

"That'll be fine, dear."

Shelby picked at her food. She managed to keep thoughts of Trent at bay most of the time. When she did think of him—the future they might have had—either tears welled in her eyes or she had a massive headache. Forcing herself to be happy, she pushed his memory away again and switched the subject to Christmas decorating.

"Are we ready?" Tina asked.

"Of course." Shelby closed the dishwasher. "Mike and Dad should have the tree up by now." They walked into the living room together.

"Oh, Mom, what a great tree." Shelby admired the blue spruce in the corner of the room.

"I'll have you know I'm the one who picked out the tree." Her father puffed out his chest.

"Oh, excuse me, Dad. Then I commend you instead." Shelby bowed to her father.

"Let's light this thing up." Greg handed Mike the last string of multi-colored bulbs. Mike stood on the ladder and placed them with care.

"Hit it, Mom." Mike perched on the ladder.

Tina clicked the floor switch attached to the lights. The room came alive with the twinkle of hundreds of colorful bulbs. "Oh, it is so pretty. I think it's the best one ever." Tina clapped her hands.

Mike and Shelby laughed. "You say the same thing every year, Mom."

"I know, I know. And I mean it every year. They are more beautiful." Tina smiled while Greg stood next to her and gave her a hug as they admired the tree.

"Okay, let's get this party started." Shelby turned on some Christmas music and took out the first box of ornaments.

The family enjoyed their tradition of dressing the tree together. At the end of the evening, all four of them crowded onto the couch facing the tree, sipped hot chocolate, and reminisced of previous Christmas mornings.

Shelby said goodbye and headed home. After such a wonderful family tradition how could she be sad?

Christmas music played on the radio in her car. As she approached the bridge connecting Georgetown to the Myrtle Beach area traffic slowed. Puzzled, Shelby craned her neck trying to see the problem. Hmm, must be something on the other side of the bridge. Traffic moved, but it only crawled.

As she reached the top of the bridge she spotted a tow truck just past the end on the right. Someone must have had an accident. No police car in sight, so there must not be an injury. Good. That would be awful.

The traffic inched along due to onlookers. Everyone tried to figure out what happened before moving on. She, for one, did not care as long as people weren't hurt. However, as she approached the vehicles, the blue truck caught her eye. It sat next to a silver jag being hooked up to the tow truck. Looking back at the truck, she spotted a woman with long blonde hair in the passenger seat. Missy? Was that Missy Strong's Jaguar being towed? And Trent talking to the tow truck driver? What on earth had happened? She didn't see any damage to the car, but in the dark she could have missed it.

Having passed the distraction the cars zoomed past her. Realizing people were honking their horns at her, she sped up. If not an accident, then what? Why was Trent there? If Missy's husband, Jamie, found out there would be hell to pay. His jealousy was well known in town.

CHAPTER TWENTY-NINE

Trent cursed his luck. Heading to Myrtle Beach for a solitary dinner he'd spotted a silver Jaguar behind him as he approached the bridge. As the car zoomed past, he realized Missy Strong sat behind the wheel. She swerved and almost hit him. Slowing down to allow her plenty of room, he watched as she ran off the road and the car stopped with a jerk. He pulled in behind her.

Trent jumped out of his truck and ran to the driver's window. "Missy, Missy. Are you all right?"

"What? What happened?" Missy slurred her words. She looked at Trent bleary-eyed, her mascara running down her face. "I know you."

"Yes, Missy, you know me. I'm Trent Meyers. What happened?" He almost yelled the question.

"I don't know." She started crying. "He doesn't love me." She hiccupped and kept repeating it over and over.

Trent threw up his hands. "You can't drive like this even if your car is okay. I'll call Jamie and have him come pick you up." He reached for his phone, but stopped at her distraught expression.

"No! No! Don't do that. He thinks I'm at my mother's. You'll ruin everything." Again she sobbed and hid her face in her hands.

He put the phone away. "I won't let you drive, and we can't leave your car here."

Her head jerked up, eyes wide and her hands shaking. "Don't call Jamie. He'll find out. No, I can't see him like this."

Trent had no idea why she said that. Someone must have called the police because a car pulled up behind them.

"What kind of problem is there?" The policeman pulled out a notebook as he approached.

"Sorry, officer. I'm not sure. I was driving behind her when her car veered off the road. It doesn't look like she hit anything." Trent pointed to the car.

The officer peered closely at him. "Trent, is that you?"

"Yes. I'm sorry, who are you?" Trent was startled at the question.

The officer stuck out his hand. "Kevin, Kevin James. I'm a friend of Jason's."

Trent automatically took his hand and shook it. "Oh, yeah. I didn't recognize you. It's been a while."

The officer looked at the woman in the car. "That's Missy Strong, isn't it?"

"Yeah, it is. I work for Jamie. I recognized her car." He waved a hand in her direction. "She's been crying. I think that's why she drove off the road." It was a sorry excuse, but it's what he suspected.

"Oh, man. This is not good. He'll be pissed."

"Don't I know it? Unless you need to write something up, can you call a tow truck? I'll drive her to her mother's."

The officer paused a few minutes before replying. "Sure. I don't see any damage. She's upset, but that's it. I'll call a truck. Where do you want it towed?"

Trent shrugged. "She doesn't want Jamie to know so let's have it sent to her mother's house. I don't remember where she lives. Do you?"

"Yeah, it's right down the street from my folks. I'll set it up." Kevin called for the tow. "Can you stay with her until it arrives? It's less than a mile so it'll be here in a jiffy."

"Sure. We'll be fine." Trent agreed reluctantly.

"The longer I'm here the more people see me. That won't be a good idea for her." Kevin seemed concerned for Missy as he continued. "Someone's bound to report back to Jamie. You need to take her away."

"I will. Look, here comes the tow truck." Trent pointed toward bridge.

"I'll leave now. Good luck." He scribbled on his pad of paper. "This is her mom's address. Give it to the driver."

"Thanks. We'll be out of here in a minute." Trent spoke to the back of the officer as he hurried toward his car and left in a flash.

Trent noticed the traffic slowed down as people craned their necks to view the destruction. Kevin had it right. Jamie would find out in short order. He better get Missy out of here. Helping her from the car to his truck took more effort than he expected. She wobbled as if drunk or stoned. Great, he thought in annoyance. Good thing Kevin hadn't noticed. She hung on him as he maneuvered her inside. Finally getting her settled, he returned to the car and grabbed her coat and purse. He checked the trunk and found a small suitcase. He took it as well. Since he knew she didn't want to go home, she'd at least have whatever it contained.

Retrieving a credit card from her purse, he tossed the other items behind Missy's seat and then headed back to the tow truck. Giving the slip of paper with her mother's address and the credit card to the driver, he waited impatiently. It only took a few minutes before the driver handed him a receipt to sign. He took it to Missy, who could barely write her own name. Handing it all back to the driver, Trent grabbed the receipt and hopped in the truck.

"Missy. Missy, wake up. Do you want me to take you to your mother's?" Trent gently shook her. She'd fallen asleep. She must be stoned.

Blinking furiously, Missy looked around the truck. "Where am I? Who are you?"

Trent felt his frustration level rise. "Trent. Trent Meyers. Do you want me to take you to your mother's house?"

"No. Not there. She can't see me like this." Shaking her head, she grasped his arm.

"Then where?" He ran his hand through his hair.

"I don't have any place to go." Her eyes pleaded with him.

"How about Beau's?"

She wailed. "No, no. He doesn't love me. I hate him. I won't go. You can't make me." She tried to open the door.

Trent attempted to calm her down. "Okay, okay. I won't take you there. Never mind. I'll figure it out."

Trent put the truck in gear and merged into the traffic. He kept heading toward Myrtle Beach with no idea where he'd take her. Not to Jamie's, not to Beau's, and not to her mother's. What a mess. He should have left her on the side of the road. No, he couldn't do that.

He drove about twenty minutes then took her to a coffee shop to see if he could wake her up. Again.

After parking the vehicle, he gently shook her. "Wake up. We're here."

Sitting up straight she looked around. "Where? Where are we?"

"At a coffee shop. Are you hungry?" Trent opened his door.

"Yes, I think I am." Missy looked surprised at the realization.

Trent went around to her side of the truck. "Missy, come on. Let's go in." He pulled her out of the truck.

"Trent. What are you doing here?" She acted as if she were seeing him for the first time.

"You ran off the road. I had your car towed." Trent explained as they walked into the diner. Her gait indicated she'd sobered up a bit.

She gasped. "You didn't have it sent to my house, did you?"

"No. I had it sent to your mother's. Is that all right?"

"Yeah. I guess. That should be okay. Jamie thinks I'm there." Nodding, Missy slipped into a booth. "Why are you doing this for me?"

"Your car ran off the road, I thought you might be hurt." When the waitress came by Trent ordered two coffees. "We'll need a minute to look over the menu."

Nodding, the waitress walked away with a backward glance at Missy. He couldn't blame her, Missy looked a fright. Her hair stood out as if she'd been yanking on it, her eyes red, and mascara tracks ran down her cheeks.

"You said that. So why did you stop?" Her brow knitted and she tilted her head as she looked at him.

"It seemed like the right thing to do." He hadn't considered doing anything else at the time.

"Thanks. I guess." Missy looked into her cup as if it held some answers.

"You've been crying. How come?" He didn't really want to know, but he needed to figure out what to do with her. He'd also told Jim he planned to talk to her.

She grimaced. "Beau."

"What about Beau?" Had he hurt her?

"He tossed me out. Said he didn't want a drug addict for a girlfriend."

"What?" That comment took him by surprise.

She snorted. "I know. Considering he's the one who got me started."

"I'm sorry, Missy. You said you loved him."

"I did?" She scrunched up her face. "Well, I suppose that's true. Doesn't mean he loves me." Her sigh indicated her resignation.

"No, I suppose it doesn't." Trent had no idea what to do. "Let's order something to eat. You might feel better."

Nodding, she picked out something, then excused herself and headed to the bathroom. Maybe he could convince her to check into rehab. He searched on his iPhone to find a nearby place. There were three close by.

Missy returned to the table. Her hair looked a little better and she'd removed dark smudges of mascara.

"Good lord, Trent, you could have said something," she whispered, her uneasiness apparent.

"About what?" He didn't understand her comment.

"About what, you ask," she mimicked. "My face, that's what. I looked a fright."

"Missy, I was too worried about you to say anything about your appearance." He knew better than to say she looked okay.

"Humph. You'd be the first man."

"Look, I know you're feeling low right now. If you don't want to go back to Jamie or Beau or your mom, then where do you want to go?"

She looked like she would start crying again. "I don't have anywhere."

Trent patted her hand. "What about rehab. Would you consider it?"

Missy took a long time before she answered. Their food arrived and she picked at the omelet she'd ordered. "Why do you care?"

"You're a human being. We grew up together. You need some help. Taking you to rehab would be good for you." All those things were true. How could she not know?

"You've been nicer to me than anyone in a long time." She gave him a sad grin.

Floored at her answer, he replied, "I think I'm doing what anyone else would do."

"No. They wouldn't. No one has. I think you're right. Maybe rehab will help. My mom's been after me for months to check in. She gave me a brochure, but I threw it back at her. I've done some stupid things."

"She's your mom. I know she loves you no matter what." He knew that much about moms. Most moms. He hoped Missy's did.

"I think you're right. At this point, she may be the only one."

"Do you remember the name of the place?"

Missy rattled off the name of one of the places Trent had looked up. "Finish your food, and I'll take you there."

Trent polished off his meal and pulled up the information about the rehab location on his phone. It had an after-hours number. He dialed and handed the phone to Missy. He heard her explain her addiction and desire to accept help. Nodding and agreeing to something he didn't hear, she disconnected.

Missy took a deep breath. "They have space available. I can check in right now. They'll have someone waiting at the door."

"Good. I'm glad you decided." Trent patted her hands, picked up the check, and scooted out of the booth. Missy shuffled behind him.

Once they climbed back in the truck, she said, "Thanks, Trent. I was lucky you came along when you did. Do you have any idea what I planned to do?"

Trent pulled out of the parking lot. "I have no idea."

"I planned to drive my car into the ocean."

Her simple statement shocked him. "What? You planned to kill yourself?"

"I didn't think anyone would care. Even my mother yelled at me and told me I was a lost cause."

He didn't know what to say. "Maybe you should call your mom so she knows where you are."

"I'll do that. After I check in. I want her to know she was right. Not about the lost cause part, but the part about me needing to go to rehab."

"Of course. She'll be glad."

"Yeah, I think she will." Her tone indicated it came as a surprise to her.

Trent drove Missy to the facility and assisted her with the check-in process. While returning home he thought about the collateral damage Beau's drug operation had created. It bolstered his commitment to complete his mission as soon as possible.

The next day Jamie confronted Trent in the plant parking lot the minute he stepped out of his car. Livid that Trent had done something with Missy, he screamed, shook his fists, and threatened all kinds of bodily harm. Trent stood his ground in silence waiting to see if Jamie took a swing at him or would be satisfied with ranting. When Trent didn't respond, Jamie wound down and finally demanded to know where he'd taken Missy. When Trent told him he'd taken her to rehab, Jamie appeared stunned. Trent didn't tell him which rehab center and knew none of the centers would give out patient names unless the patient signed a release.

Trent explained Missy's car running off the road and how he'd been right behind her. He didn't mention the entire conversation they'd had, but said she asked him to take her to rehab.

Jamie's face went from purple with rage to a simple frown. He thought about it a long time. "I guess it might be the right place for her. Hell, maybe I should join her."

To Trent's surprise he said no more, turned, and stormed to his office. The totally unexpected outcome might indicate hope for the two of them. According to Missy, Beau didn't want anything to do with her which gave Jamie and Missy a   better   chance.

CHAPTER THIRTY

"That's what I heard," Amy explained as she spoke to Shelby on the phone.

"Wow. If that's true, then he might have saved her life," Shelby whispered in awe.

Amy had related the story going around Georgetown about how Trent kept Missy from driving into the ocean. Then he took her to rehab. Small-town gossip took on a life of its own, so no telling how much was true.

"He probably did. She's been unhappy for a long time. The man must be a miracle worker."

"Wait a minute. You told me to stay away from him."

"I know. It doesn't add up, does it? First he tells you he wants to make money with the drug operation, and then he takes Missy to rehab. Those things don't go together. Not in my mind."

Shelby was puzzled by her friend's comment. "So what do you think is going on?"

"I have no idea. All I'm saying is that his behavior is not logical."

Shelby tried to stand firm. "Until he tells me he isn't involved with drugs, I don't want to see or hear from him."

"Agreed, but it sounds like there may be some hope. Maybe he'll figure it out for himself that shipping drugs around the country is bad for everyone."

"It would be good if he did. I appreciate you telling me. Waiting for the DEA to do something is killing me. If I couldn't talk to you about it I might go mad."

"Speaking of the DEA I might have some information."

Shelby sat up straight and blinked her eyes. "What? You're just now telling me?"

"The other news seemed more important."

"Hmm. I suppose it was. So, tell me about the DEA."

"It's not exactly about them." Amy hedged. "I've been hearing some rumors again about another shipment. It's from the same person who told me about the other time. The one where we didn't see anything."

"So they might be wrong again."

"Exactly. Do you think I should alert the DEA?"

Shelby heard the uncertainty in Amy's voice.

She pondered the situation for a couple moments. "Yes, I do. They told us not to do any more investigating. All you can do is provide them with what you've heard. They may have found some other sources since we first talked to them, so maybe they can verify it. Be sure to say it could be wrong. Let them decide what to do." In spite of not wanting to do the initial investigation, having been told not to, it annoyed her. How crazy was that?

"You're right." Amy sighed. "So maybe this will be all over soon."

"What date did you hear?"

"December twenty-third."

"Two days before Christmas? If you're right, there could be a whole lot of people having a horrible holiday."

"The story I heard said winter break for the college kids is a big pay day for the drug dealers. They want to capitalize on the demand."

"That's sick. Then I don't feel sorry for them if they end up in jail." The knowledge that Trent could be one of them sat heavy on Shelby's heart.

"My thoughts exactly."

After Shelby disconnected the call with Amy, she considered Trent's behavior. It sounded like he'd really saved Missy's life. The night she spotted him on the side of the road she'd wondered why he'd been there. How noble. Yes, noble described Trent. So how could he work with drugs? It didn't make sense. She paced the floor thinking about how she'd rejected him. Should she call him and tell him she wanted to try again?

No, she couldn't. Not while he still worked with Beau and his drug operation. She had to be true to her own values. Would he be at the upcoming shipment? Would the DEA try a sting operation? What would she do if they arrested him? She'd seen Trent and the other men with guns. The DEA would go in well-armed. He could be shot. Or killed.

CHAPTER THIRTY-ONE

"Trent, I've got a job for you." Beau had tracked down Trent doing his rounds at the plant.

"Sure, boss, what do you need?"

"Remember our talk about Mike Cornwell?" Beau looked at him closely.

Trent didn't like the way his gut clenched at the mention of Shelby's brother. "Of course. What do you have in mind?"

"The last lesson didn't seem to work. He needs a more serious reminder. I think a trip to the hospital before Christmas might be appropriate. If he doesn't make it, I won't be unhappy. Understand?"

Trent noticed how Beau watched for his reaction. Another test.

He answered in spite of the lump in his throat. "Lesson? Before Christmas?" Did this mean Mike didn't work for Beau? What the hell?

"Exactly. Something to keep the rest of the family out of my business."

"Consider it done." Trent knew better than to argue. He wanted to know more about what Mike said or did to cause Beau's anger.

The next delivery was scheduled for December twenty-third. He'd have to stall Beau to have Mike's *accident* until after it. If the raid happened there would be no need to follow-through or contact the local police. Any interference at this stage could jeopardize the whole mission.

In order to have the DEA stake out the place, he needed to find the information about the local distributors. Otherwise, they wouldn't agree. They wanted to tie up all the loose ends at once. No half measures. The sting needed to happen. Mike's welfare depended on it.

When he'd told Jim he had a plan to obtain the information from Missy, Jim had been skeptical. He'd soon find out if he could convince Missy to talk. Frantic to talk with Missy, he drove to the rehab center the moment he left work. Maybe she would know about Mike and what he'd done.

He strode into the building and to the reception desk. "I'm Trent Meyers to see Missy Strong."

"One moment, sir, I'll see if she is allowed to have visitors."

Cooling his heels at a rehab center increased his frustration. He paced around the small area until someone called his name. "Mr. Meyers, the doctor will see you."

"Doctor? I'm here to see Missy Strong." She had him mixed up with someone else.

"Yes, sir. First you must speak to her doctor." She motioned him to come through the door.

"Very well." Anxious to see Missy, he passed the receptionist as he went into another small room. No one occupied the room, but in a few moments a woman in a lab coat entered.

"Mr. Meyers?" At his nod, she continued. "I'm Missy's doctor. She had you listed as someone she would agree to see if you visited. You aren't a relative, are you?"

"No, I'm not. I'm a friend." What would he do if she wasn't allowed to see people other than family?

"If what she's said is accurate, you are the one who saved her life." The doctor studied him.

Trent felt his face flush. "I wouldn't go so far as to say that."

"She did. I won't allow anyone to see her who is any way connected with drugs. I wanted to see you for myself before I agreed to the meeting."

Trent told her the truth. "I would never bring her or anyone else illegal drugs. Is she doing better?" He hoped the doctor didn't know where he worked. She probably knew about the plant.

"She has made a lot of progress," the doctor admitted. "Very well. I'll have her sent in. The mirror on the wall is two-way. We won't listen, but we will be watching."

Since Trent didn't plan to give Missy anything, her comment didn't upset him. Should he mention his run-in with Jamie after he'd brought Missy to the center? Not unless she asked. When Missy arrived, he saw more of the girl she'd been in high school than the woman he'd brought here. She'd made a significant transformation in the days she'd been here.

She walked up to him and gave him a hug. A common gesture in the South, but somehow this time it didn't seem artificial or automatic. He returned her hug and patted her back.

Missy said in calm voice, "Trent, I'm so glad you stopped by to see me. I'm not sure if I told you how much I appreciate all the help you gave me. You saved my life."

Her assertions made him feel uncomfortable. "I wish you'd quit saying that. I didn't do anything anyone else in my shoes wouldn't do."

Missy looked at him for a few moments before she replied. "You believe that, don't you? I'm sorry I don't. You are the best human being I know." She grinned when she saw him squirm. "What did you want to see me about?"

"Am I so obvious?" Now he felt like a heel. "Don't you think I came by to check on you?"

"I already said you are the best human being I know. However, I've done nothing but think since I arrived here. One of the things I thought about is you. Why are you working at that plant? Know what I came up with?"

"That I needed the money?" he joked.

"No." She watched his reaction closely. "Although I'm sure you wouldn't turn it down. I think you're undercover."

"What?" Stunned she'd seen through him. How well had he kept the secret from others?

She grinned knowing she'd hit on the truth. "Don't worry. I won't say anything to Beau or Jamie. Or anyone else."

"But I didn't admit anything."

"Forget it. I know what I know." She waved a hand as if it didn't matter what he said. "What do you want from me? I'll be glad to tell you all about the operation, if that's what you need."

"You will?" It took a moment before Trent admitted his status. "Okay, I'll level with you. Yes, I'm undercover. Now I've confessed, you have my life in your hands."

"Ah, turnabout is fair play." He could see she approved his tactic. "All right then. What can I tell you?"

"I need the names of the local distributors. Do you know who they are?" He didn't waste any time.

"Uh, that's funny." Missy gave him a knowing smile.

"What's funny about it?" He didn't see the humor.

"A couple of months ago I decided if I had some information on Jamie or Beau I could use it somehow. So I searched Jamie's phone and found exactly the information you requested and a bit more. I never did figure out what to do with it to make things better for me. You can have it. I figure I owe you."

"I didn't ask because you owe me." Trent felt bad he had put her in this position.

"No, you wouldn't, would you? Like I said earlier, you are the best human being I know. You want me to do the right thing. Yes?"

Trent hoped to play to her morals. "It occurred to me it could help you feel better about yourself."

"You may be right. Give me a pen and paper." He handed her the tools, she jotted down a file name, and then handed it to Trent. "I don't have access to my phone. It's not allowed in here. However, I'll tell the doctor I want you to have it. There's a file on it. This is my password to unlock the phone and the name of the file. It also has a password which is listed below. It should provide you with everything you need."

"All the names of the local distributors?"

"All of Jamie's contacts. If there are more, then I don't know about them." She shrugged as if the information meant nothing.

"This will crack our case wide open." He walked over and gave her a hug, which she returned. "I don't know how to thank you."

"It's my way of thanking you. Like you said, maybe I'll feel better about myself now that I've helped the right people for a change."

"I have one more question."

"I'll try to give you an answer."

"What do you know about Mike Cornwell's involvement with the operation?"

Missy gave him a knowing look. "Shelby's brother?"

"Yes." He felt heat flood his face.

"Unless his name is on that list I have no idea. Neither Jamie nor Beau have mentioned him."

"Thanks." Trent planned to review the list before turning it over to Jim.

Missy hugged him again and left with a wave of her hand.

Trent couldn't believe his luck. He took a big chance telling her about his undercover status. What if it was a ploy and she planned to tell Beau? No, he had to go with his gut. She meant everything she'd said. He hoped her time in the center would turn things around for her.

In a matter of minutes the receptionist came back for him and presented him with Missy's phone. He sent the information to his secure phone and returned Missy's to the receptionist.

Jim would go crazy with happiness about this. He'd go a different kind of crazy if Trent told him Missy knew he was undercover.

Trent left the center and climbed in his truck. The moment he arrived home he scanned the list. Mike's name wasn't on it. He wasn't sure what he planned to do if it had been. Delete it? Glad he didn't have to make the decision he called Jim without going through the normal contact.

"This better be important since you've broken protocol."

"It is. The biggest break we've gotten in this case after the transmitters giving you the location of the big shipments."

"You have some of the local distributor names?" Jim sounded gleeful.

"My guess is, it's a list of *all* the local distributors." Trent knew his smile could be heard through the phone.

"How the... Never mind, send me the list." Jim's voice emerged gruff with emotion.

"It should be in your inbox right now." Trent heard clicking noises he attributed to Jim pulling up information on his computer.

"What, he's in on this? No way." The sound of Jim's voice was muffled and unclear at times, and then Jim picked up the phone. "You hit the jackpot, boy. I'll call this in and we'll set up a sting for December twenty-three.

We'll haul in the distributors the same time we nail the crew doing the big shipment at the river."

"I hoped you'd say that. Do you think there's enough time to organize it all?" Trent couldn't keep the eagerness out of his voice.

"I don't care if we have to work twenty-four hours a day until December twenty-third, we'll set it up." Trent heard papers rustle and more clicking of computer keys in the background. "This is going to be one hell of a bust. Good work, Meyers. We'll celebrate when it's done."

"You got it, boss. Now all I have to do is stay in character until the bust." Trent snorted at the idea.

"That's right. Don't blow it now. This is the most difficult and dangerous time for an undercover man." Jim became serious with his comments. "You can see the end. Make sure you don't screw it up."

"No way. Not after all this time."

After he calmed down from the excitement of Missy's list, he considered how this news could affect his relationship with Shelby. Her objection to his drug connection would evaporate. He couldn't fault her for wanting to stay away from that environment. Relief flooded through him knowing Mike wouldn't be part of the sting. He had to stop thinking about Shelby for now. Once the bust went down, there would be ample time to think about their relationship. And he wanted one with her. These last few days since they'd broken up confirmed his feelings. He loved her. He wanted her in his life. For always.

Trent went to work as usual on the big day. After the bust the world would turn upside down for the employees at the plant. The ones who had nothing to do with drugs would be in turmoil. He felt bad for them. Beau handled all aspects of the operation, both the drugs and the legal side. He had a manager at the legal portion of the plant, but the man participated in the illegal side as well. Trent had no idea who would take over. The plant might close. This time of year no one wanted to lose his job.

Beau wandered into the locker room where Trent slipped on his protective gear.

"Thought I'd stop by and find out the plans you have for Mike Cornwell."

"Since the last time he had a car accident and it didn't turn out the way you wanted, I thought a mugging would have better results." Trent still hadn't found out what Mike had done. He vowed to discover it after the sting.

"A mugging? That should work fine. When will it happen?"

"Christmas Eve. I'll tail him and pick the right moment."

"Perfect. Then you can console the luscious Miss Shelby."

"Not likely. She dumped me." He shrugged as if it didn't matter.

Beau's eyebrows rose. "Is that so? Trouble in paradise?"

"She found out about my threesome celebration." Trent knew the subject would come up with Beau so he'd worked out an explanation.

Beau made a *tsking* sound. "Uh oh. Who spilled the beans?"

"I'm not sure but someone saw me. I didn't think fast enough to give her a good explanation and the next thing I know, she slapped me and stormed out."

"Too bad." He could see Beau's interest faded. "Give me a call once it's done."

Beau smacked him on the back then left the building.

Trent felt elated he wouldn't have to put up with Beau after tonight.

The end of shift arrived and Trent drove home. He paced around his small living room, ate and watched TV waiting for time to return to the plant. Anxious to start, he arrived a few minutes before the appointment hour.

"Hey champ, you're early," Beau said when he pulled in next to Trent's truck.

The last thing Trent wanted to do at this time was have a conversation with Beau. "Can't wait to do it. I'm looking forward to another big payday."

Beau continued to stand next to the truck. "Planning to spend your bonus the same way as last time?"

Trent said the first thing that came to mind. "I didn't spend all the money from the last time so I'm going to take what's left of it and the money from tonight and charter a fishing boat in the Keys."

"Fishing? Down in the Keys?" Beau sounded surprised at his choice of vacation.

"It's warmer down there this time of year."

"When you goin'?"

Trent shrugged, feeling like this inane conversation would never end. "I'll have to check with Jamie and see how long he'll let me off. Probably a few days, but maybe I can warm up." He pretended to shiver.

Beau shrugged. "Not a bad idea. Well, let's head over to the arsenal."

They walked along together in silence. Trent worried about the arsenal. If any of Beau's men managed to run inside before the DEA shut it down, the results could mean a lot of deaths. Trent had some putty to keep the door from latching. His team knew about it so if they had to break open the door it could be the one thing that gave the DEA an edge. He hoped his team members arrived at the arsenal first to avoid any extra bloodshed. Both Beau's crew and the DEA would be wearing body armor. Still, it could become ugly fast if the element of surprise disappeared.

Taking his position by the river, he waited for the floating transport to arrive. He knew there were agents posted across the river and in the woods in several locations. They'd been there since after dark. Once all Beau's men arrived, the agents would move closer. None of Beau's men noticed anything amiss. It took a lot of effort for Trent not to use his night vision binoculars to look for the agents he knew to be surrounding them.

Finally he heard the rumbling of a motor and radioed Beau. Same as the last time, Beau arrived at the dock to verify the boat was the one he expected. When the first pallet of drugs landed on the craft, all hell broke loose. A Coast Guard cutter screamed down river to block the vessel. They shone spotlights on the area, which made it look more like midday than midnight.

Trent heard Jim on a bullhorn shouting instructions as agents swarmed out of the forest. Most people froze at the unexpected activity. Knowing what would happen next,

Trent shoved earplugs into his ears. The DEA agents threw flash bang grenades to disorient the men further.

Trent pulled a vest out of his coat pocket with DEA stenciled on the back and slipped it over his head. He pointed his weapon at Beau. "Hit the ground."

Beau stared at him then pointed his own gun at Trent.

Against all his training, Trent aimed low and pulled the trigger.

Beau buckled, grabbed his knee, dropped his gun. "You fucking ass. Traitor. You'll pay for this."

Trent ran over and kicked Beau's Uzi out of the way while the cursing continued. "Medic."

Trent charged into the firefight. It didn't last long. Most of Beau's crew attempted to flee to their cars or dropped their weapons in surrender. A few ran into the woods but met more of the agents and were rounded up in short order.

A few moments after things settled down Jim walked up to Trent and slapped him on the back. "It couldn't have played out better. Great job."

"Thanks, boss. A lot of people and coordination went into this bust. I only did a small portion. Any casualties?" There'd been a lot less gun fire than Trent expected.

"That's the even better news. No one got killed. Only two agents wounded and neither of them critical. Three of Beau's men are in bad shape, and of course Beau himself has a bullet in the knee. The medics think it shattered a lot of bone."

Trent felt a rush of relief. Although he sought an end to this operation, he hadn't wanted anyone to die over it. He'd seen more than enough death while in the army. "That is good news. Have you heard anything about the roundup of the distributors?"

"I received a transmission a minute ago saying it had gone well. I don't have any numbers but we should hear some soon."

"Sounds like a successful mission." Trent walked with Jim toward the transports.

"One of the best. Let's get this lot loaded up. We're taking them to the Georgetown County Sheriff's Office Detention Center."

"What about the ones who are injured?"

"There's a medical facility on site. We've called in for additional staff to make sure they're taken care of. The last thing we want to do is send them to the Georgetown Hospital and have one of them escape."

"Especially Beau. No telling who might help him."

"Exactly. Now comes the fun part." Jim grinned.

"What do you mean?" Trent looked at him with eyebrows knitted together.

Jim chuckled. "Paperwork. Mounds of paperwork. I hope you didn't have plans for tomorrow."

Trent huffed a humorless laugh. "No, I don't. I figured it would take a while."

CHAPTER THIRTY-TWO

Shelby turned on the television to listen to the news as she dressed for work. Shocked at the bulletin about a drug bust in Georgetown, she dropped her shoes.

While she listened to the few details provided, she rushed around trying to decide when she could drive to Georgetown. Images of Trent languishing in jail made her crazy. She phoned the lawyer she'd already checked out in the event this happened. He topped the list in Charleston for this type of case. Leaving a voice mail, she hurried to the front desk.

Shelby spent two hours arranging the events at the resort for the early part of the day. She then steeled herself to approach her boss.

"You're going to leave the resort now?" His eyebrows shot up to his hairline.

"It's an emergency. I'll be back before five o'clock to finish arrangements for the Jackson's party although I doubt the Jackson's party will go forward." Wringing her hands, Shelby looked at her watch.

Her boss stood up and paced his office. "Did you reach Mrs. Jackson? She can't back out now. It's too late. We have a contract." His voice rose louder with each word. "You can't leave until you talk to her and settle this. I won't tolerate it." He stomped his foot like a child.

She glanced at the clock behind his desk. "As I said, it is an emergency, otherwise I wouldn't ask. Lucy has all the information and will continue to try to contact the Jacksons."

His face turned so red she suspected he might have a stroke.

"If you leave you'll be out of a job."

His stern announcement shocked her.

Anger pushed her to the edge of her tolerance. "Fine. I'll be back tomorrow and clean out my suite." She turned on her heels and left the office. She heard her boss screaming as she left.

Racing to her car, cell phone and purse in hand, she shook her head at the nerve of her boss. The one time she asked for special consideration, it cost her her job. She wouldn't dwell on it. She had to focus her energy on bailing Trent out of jail.

Trying the lawyer's number again, she reached his voice mail. Since she'd already left a message, she disconnected the call.

Dialing the next number, she sighed in relief. "Amy, thank God you answered. Have you heard?"

"Of course. The whole town is talking. It's wrecking a lot of families. How are you doing?" Shelby appreciated the concern she heard in Amy's voice.

"I'm on my way to the detention center in Georgetown." Shelby hopped in her car and headed toward Highway 17.

"Does he have a lawyer?"

"I have no idea. I called one but had to leave a voicemail message. For all I know he's away for the holidays. What if I can't reach him?"

"Calm down. I'm sure there are others in the same situation. It's important Trent arrange for a lawyer today. You may have to contact someone else."

"Right. Do you have some names?"

"Yes. I'll text them to you. I'll put them in order of how I rate them.

"What would I do without you?"

"You'd Google it, that's what." Amy always knew how to elicit a laugh from Shelby. It broke the tension.

"Thanks." The simple response didn't sound adequate.

"Call me when you know something."

Disconnecting the call, Shelby concentrated on the drive to Georgetown. She arrived in record time at the center. A number of cars sat in the lot. No doubt family members and lawyers clogged the reception area.

Walking into the facility she glanced around at the people. She knew a lot of them. How sad for their town. Approaching a window, she signed in, surprised at how her hand shook, and waited her turn.

"Ms. Cornwell?" The receptionist called her name.

"Yes." She stood up and walked to the window again. "That's me."

"You want to see Trent Meyers?" The receptionist wore a puzzled look.

"Yes. Is there a problem?"

"No. He's down this hall, third door on the left."

Surprised to not see a guard at the door, she opened it and looked at the single table piled high with folders and documents.

She spotted Trent behind the desk. writing furiously. Frantic he might be putting something incriminating on paper, she almost leapt across the room and snatched his pen. "Stop. Don't write anything down until you see a lawyer. Do you have one?"

"What?" Trent looked up. His eyes were bloodshot and more than a day's worth of beard darkened his face.

"Have you spoken to a lawyer?"

"Lawyer. Why do I need to talk to a lawyer?"

Shelby knew Trent's lack of sleep and probably the incessant demands of the police had worn him down.

"Don't let them bully you into saying stuff until you talk to a lawyer. You need to make a deal. Maybe you won't have to spend much time in jail if you hire a good lawyer. I'll help pay for one. I have some money." Everything spilled out in a rush.

"Shelby, what are you doing here?" Trent looked at her, tilting his head and drawing his brows together.

"I'm here to help you. I've called a lawyer. He hasn't called back." Pulling out her phone, she pulled up the text Amy sent her. "There are more lawyers out there. I'll call another one." She dialed a number.

While the phone rang Trent stood up from the table. Trent took her phone and disconnected the call. "Shelby, I don't need a lawyer."

"Of course you need a lawyer. It's the only way to work out a deal." Shelby tried to take her phone back.

Trent kept the phone away from her. "No, I don't need a lawyer because I'm not under arrest."

"Not under arrest." A frown formed on her brow.

"Correct. I'm not under arrest."

"Why not?" She didn't understand.

"Because I'm an undercover cop." Trent looked her in the eyes.

"Undercover?" Shelby felt as if she'd never heard the word before.

Laughing, Trent pulled a chair out for Shelby and made her sit. "Correct. I'm an undercover cop. You have no idea how good it is to be able to tell you." Trent pulled his chair next to hers and sat down.

"But, but, they said…" Shelby shook her head, thinking about the receptionist. "No, they didn't say you were under arrest. They sent me to this room. Why didn't they tell me?" Now she felt indignant someone hadn't told her about Trent when she arrived.

"If I'd been under arrest, you wouldn't have been allowed to see me unless you were my lawyer."

"But all those people out there." Shelby looked back toward the reception area.

"Some are lawyers and the others are family members waiting for the arraignment. No bail posting or seeing the detainee until the arraignment."

"Oh, well, I didn't know." Shelby blinked. What a fool she'd been.

"I can't tell you how wonderful it is to know you came to me. Especially since you thought I was under arrest." Trent's eyes shone as he spoke to her.

"I love you . Of course I'd be here." What else could she say?

"You love me?" Trent looked at her with astonishment.

"Yes. I do. If it makes you uncomfortable, I'll leave. Now that I know you're okay, I don't want to bother you."

"Bother me? First you say you love me, then you want to leave because you don't want to bother me?" Trent stood up and paced around the room a couple of times.

"Oh, hell, woman."

He pulled her into his arms and kissed her until her knees grew weak.

Hearing a light knock on the door followed by a cough, Trent broke their kiss and looked up.

He kept her close but looked menacingly at the door. "What?"

"Sorry to interrupt. You asked me to let you know Beau Jackson's condition. He's out of surgery. They had to amputate, but he'll be okay." His boss grinned as he looked at Shelby. "I'll let you return to your previous activity." He shut the door with a slight click.

"Beau lost a leg?" Shelby was a bit shocked at the news and the intensity of Trent's kiss.

"I had to shoot him before he shot me." Trent released her and ran his hand through his hair. "Wish I could have avoided it." He paced to the back of the room and stared at the wall.

"Oh, Trent, it must be difficult." Shelby walked to him and put her arms around him.

"Yeah, but I had no choice." Trent sounded resigned.

"Don't think about it right now. Kiss me again."

Trent turned, gathered Shelby in his arms, and they stood like that for a minute. He bent his head and captured her mouth with his again. He explored her mouth with his tongue as if there were nothing else in the world. After some time, he pressed his forehead against hers and gave a deep sigh.

Stepping back, he apologized. "I wish I could leave and follow that kiss with more. However, I need to complete this stack of paperwork. Would it be okay if I come by your place later tonight?"

"Yes." Shelby couldn't contain her happiness.

"I'll finish, take a shower, and be there by nine. I'll see you tonight." Trent walked her to the door, then closed it behind her.

Shelby didn't know what would happen between them, but the kiss indicated he wasn't mad at her. After all, she hadn't believed in him. Maybe they could start again. As she walked to her car it occurred to her he hadn't responded to her declaration of love. Was this only a fling for him? No matter. She'd be happy to have whatever he could give. Maybe he'd love her eventually.

Making her way back to the resort, she called Amy with the good news.

"He's an undercover cop? Wow, I should have seen that coming after what he did for Missy. So what does this mean for the two of you?"

"I told him I loved him."

"And what did he say?"

"If you're asking if he returned my declaration, no, he didn't."

"How do you feel about that?" Shelby heard the caution in Amy's voice.

"Hopeful. I hope he'll love me someday. If it doesn't happen, then I'll have some good memories."

"And a broken heart?"

"Maybe. As you always say 'don't borrow trouble.' I'll call you later." Shelby disconnected and pulled into the resort parking garage.

Checking her watch she noticed it was two o'clock. It felt so much later. She spoke with Lucy about the Jackson's party. In spite of being fired she felt obligated to finish the details to cancel everything. At least she assumed that's what would happen.

Entering the office she noticed Lucy on the phone. Lucy set it on the desk without hanging up, jumped out of her chair, and grabbed her. "Thank God, you're back. I can't believe what a tyrant our boss is. I can't do anything right. The Jackson's party is cancelled and I'm trying to stop deliveries. Some tell me it's too late. Help!"

"Calm down, Lucy. Here's what we need to do." Shelby proceeded to tell her the steps and they both started working. Their boss entered the office thirty minutes later.

"Shelby, when you have a minute would you please come to my office?"

"Of course." She schooled her voice to contain little emotion.

She finished her task and made her way to his office.

"Have a seat." He appeared more subdued. "I'd like to apologize for my previous outburst. Since you are back at work I'm assuming you realized I wasn't serious about firing you."

Shelby didn't allow her joy to show on her face. "I did believe you. I came back to help Lucy work out the details. When that's finished, I'll start packing."

The conversation continued with more apologies on her boss's side as well as pleas to continue working. In the end, she agreed to stay with a nice, big raise.

She went back to her room and took a quick shower, then slipped into the dress she'd worn that first night they'd danced. Somehow it seemed appropriate. She poured a glass of wine and waited for Trent.

A light knock at the door came at nine-fifteen. Shelby walked quickly to the door and snatched it open. Trent stood there, wearing the same outfit he'd worn at the reunion. It made her smile. He had the same vision in mind as she.

"You look even more fabulous than usual," His voice sounded gruff with emotion.

"I could say the same about you."

Trent put his jacket on the coatrack then turned back to Shelby. He gathered her in his arms and took her mouth with his. He slipped his tongue between her lips to dance with hers as she poured out her love. The hardness of his manhood pressed against her. She strained to get closer. All too soon he pulled away with a short laugh.

"Wait a minute. I didn't want to jump your bones the minute I walked in here. Sit down. We need to talk." Trent sat on the loveseat and patted the place next to him.

"Would you like something to drink? Wine? A gin and tonic?" Shelby tried to gather her wits. They needed to talk? Did he plan to tell her he didn't love her? She'd told Amy she'd be happy with memories. Would she?

"Nothing right now. Maybe later. Sit down." He sounded impatient.

Sitting down, she placed her hands in her lap and looked at him, waiting to hear what he had to say.

"Earlier you said you love me."

"Yes, I did. And I do. I love you, Trent." Why was he so nervous?

"Today I told you I'm an undercover cop."

"Yes. What a surprise. And a relief." Shelby still didn't understand where he planned to take this conversation.

"How do you feel about me being a cop?" Trent stared at her as if her answer meant everything.

"What? I hadn't thought about it. I'm glad you aren't involved with drugs."

He squirmed in his seat. "So you don't mind if I'm a policeman."

"Mind? Why would I mind? It's an honorable job. What are you trying to tell me, Trent?"

"I want to make sure you'll be okay with it. It can be dangerous work."

Shelby took a moment to consider. She didn't like the idea of him being shot. Could she live with the fear? Could she live without him? "Being a cop is a good thing. I won't lie. I'd be worried about you. So what are you trying to say?"

"I love you. I want to be with you."

She'd been praying to hear those words from him. She didn't want to live with memories, in spite of what she'd told Amy.

"Oh, Trent. I want to be with you as well. The man you've become. Not the boy from high school."

"Even if I'm a cop?"

His whispered question tore at her heart. How could he not know? She rose and went to sit on his lap. She wrapped her arms around him.

"I love you. Being without you would destroy me." She kissed him, pouring out all her passion and love.

In moments their clothes disappeared and they expressed their feelings in the most intimate way. The first coupling was urgent and demanding. The next second they took their time exploring each other as if they wanted to memorize every inch of each other. Night became day.

Shelby rolled over and found Trent awake, watching her. "Merry Christmas."

"Yes, it is." Trent kissed her. "When are you supposed to be at your parent's house?"

"What?" Shelby had difficulty concentrating since Trent held one of her breasts in his hand and skimmed her nipple with his thumb. "Oh, not for hours." Watching his thumb, her desire grew. "Dinner is at six o'clock. We should be there a little earlier." Shelby reached down and found his shaft firm and ready.

"Then there's plenty of time." Around noon, they finally made their way out of bed and into the shower. It was the first time Shelby had ever taken a shower with a man. She knew it wouldn't be the last. They walked hand in hand to the parking garage at two o'clock.

Arriving at her parent's house, she announced Trent's role as an undercover cop who took down Beau's operation.

"That's an exaggeration. I was part of a team." Trent tried to deflect the praise from her family.

Her brother, Mike, said, "Hey, man. Sorry I gave you a bad time at Thanksgiving."

"You wanted the best for Shelby, so it makes it all right with me." He lowered his voice so only Mike could hear. "I know you tried to pull your best friend Benny out of that situation too."

Mike blushed and nodded. "Yeah, I appreciate you giving him an opportunity to turn State's evidence. His sentence will be reduced."

"You took a big risk trying to gather enough evidence against Beau by yourself. You could have been killed."

"Thanks for not saying anything to the family."

Shelby watched the exchange between her brother and Mike. The moment she decided to ask what they were discussing her mother patted her cheek.

"Thank you so much, sweetheart, for recovering our chairs. The shade of blue compliments the couch and the smattering of yellow flowers is festive. We're blessed to have such a thoughtful daughter."

Lively conversation continued with everyone talking over everyone else. The main topic was the drug bust. Overall happiness was sprinkled with sadness for the local families who now had members in jail. Shelby looked up and noticed Trent and her father talking outside. Her father shook Trent's hand. She frowned, wondering what they talked about.

"Shelby, help me with the ham." Her mother motioned to her to join her in the kitchen.

Distracted, she didn't think any more about the men's private conversation.

Dinner couldn't have been more festive or jolly. Everyone settled into the living room after dishes were washed and put away. The family exchanged gifts and Shelby felt guilty Trent didn't have anything to open. She'd be sure to make it up to him later. Tomorrow she'd make him lasagna from his mother's recipe.

As everyone started to gather the remnants of wrapping paper and bows, Trent whispered, "Can we step outside a minute?"

"Sure." What did he want to tell her?

As soon as they reached the edge of the patio Trent reached in his pocket and simultaneously bent down on one knee. "Shelby Cornwell, I love you. Would you do me the honor of becoming my wife?" He presented her with a ring.

Stunned, Shelby stood with her mouth open for a moment. "Trent! Yes, of course, I'd love to become your wife." She threw her arms around him, not waiting for him to put the ring on her finger. She put a hand on each side of his face and pressed her mouth against his.

"I wanted to give it to you earlier, but as a true southerner, I had to ask your dad first. I know it might be old fashioned, but it felt like the right thing to do."

"Oh, Trent, how sweet. I saw you talking to Dad and wondered." Shelby looked at the window and saw her whole family peering at them.

"They're watching right now, aren't they?"

Shelby laughed. "You know they are."

He took her left hand. "Put this on before I drop it." His eyes glowed as he placed the small diamond on her finger. "I hope it's okay. It belonged to my mother." Noticing how loose it fitted her, he grimaced. "I'll have it sized if you'll wear it."

"Oh, Trent. It's wonderful." Shelby glanced at the ring and back into Trent's eyes. "I'll treasure it forever."

"And I'll treasure you."

ABOUT THE AUTHOR

Rebecca Bridges worked for more than thirty years for the Department of the Army as a computer specialist. In addition she served as a Warrant Officer in the U.S. Army Reserves. During her life she's lived in nine different states from California to South Carolina and Texas to Missouri. In addition, she had the opportunity to live in Germany for eight years. You'll notice she's avoided going too far north since she's not fond of cold weather!

Rebecca and her husband decided to retire near the ocean in South Carolina. Having grown up in Oklahoma she could see for miles across the plains where buffalo grass, paint brush flowers and mesquite trees grew. Her view today includes ocean waves, dolphins, pelicans and palmetto trees.

For more information about Rebecca Bridges and her novels please go to her website:

http://www.RebeccaBridgesAuthor.com

Made in the USA
Middletown, DE
10 January 2019